MW01284960

THE VITRUVIAN HEIR

BOOK I: THE UNRAVELING

THE VITRUVIAN HEIR

BOOK I: THE UNRAVELING

A Novel by

L.S. Kilroy

Little Tree Press

Little Tree Press
Massachusetts

First Edition
Copyright © 2015 by L.S. Kilroy
All rights reserved.
ISBN 978-0-9908844-0-8

Second Edition
Copyright © 2023, 2020 by L.S. Kilroy
All rights reserved.
ISBN 978-0-9908844-4-6

Publisher's note: This is a work of fiction, the seed of which formed in your authoress's mind at age fifteen in a history class. Any resemblance to real persons, living or dead, is purely coincidental. So there.

The text of this book is set in Adobe Caslon
Cover silhouette by Rebecca Hope Woods
Character illustrations by lilithsaur
Book design and formatting by Elizabeth Bonadies
Author photography by Kristin Gillis Photography

"An intelligent and futuristic new YA series. Quasi-Orwellian realm riddled with a sinister and suppressive regime – enthralling!"

– CHANTICLEER BOOK REVIEWS

"Kilroy builds a unique world every bit as frightening as Orwell's 1984 *out of the basic building blocks of a classic fantasy."*

– C. WILLIAM PERKINS, STEAMPUNK REVIEWS

"Kilroy has created a fully realized world that blends fantasy, romance, and suspense with astute sociopolitical commentary. More importantly, it's a fun, edge-of-your-seat read that's nearly impossible to put down."

– BRIAN UNDERWOOD, BEAUTY DIRECTOR, WOMEN'S HEALTH

"Readers will revel in The Vitruvian Heir. *Kilroy deftly weaves a magic spell over the reader with her gorgeous prose, bringing Lore's rich and vibrant steampunk world to dazzling life. I can't wait to finally get my hands on the sequels!"*

– E.E. HOLMES, BESTSELLING AUTHOR OF
THE GATEWAY TRILOGY AND THE GATEWAY TRACKERS SERIES

"I highly recommend this book to lovers of steampunk, fierce and strong heroines, and The Delirium Trilogy *by Lauren Oliver."*

– ZACHARY FLYE, ZACH'S YA REVIEWS

"*The Vitruvian Heir* is a deeply political book…It shows humanity up for what it is; an unchanging, scared beast that can only lash out at what it's afraid of."

— STEAMPUNK JOURNAL

"*The Vitruvian Heir* reminds me of The Handmaid's Tale. *Like Margaret Atwood, Kilroy seems to have a knack for creating rich emotional depths and conflicts within characters, while also counterpointing that depth with notably detached descriptions of disturbing events and uneasy encounters.*"

— AMAZON REVIEWER

"Original, dark, witty, action-packed, and fast-paced storytelling artfully done that will leave you dreaming of this uniquely elegant glimpse into a frightening future long after you've read it."

— AMAZON REVIEWER

"Lore really is the best thing about this book — a smart, sassy, and courageous individual who is utterly relatable. The manner in which she deals with horror and the glimpses into her mind show she is very human and vulnerable. The writing quality is flawless and the pacing is relentless…surprises are many, and the book has that 'just one more page' quality that may lead you to sitting up all night."

— AMAZON REVIEWER

"*The Vitruvian Heir* is a fast-paced, captivating adventure written with a dark elegance — a difficult balance to strike, but Kilroy does this artfully and seemingly without effort: the hallmark of a great writer."

— AMAZON REVIEWER

For Mom and Dad,
whose unconditional love has always allowed me to dream freely.

For the memory of my grandmothers, Angela and Bernadette.

And for Steve, because you're my favorite.

"I WANT EVERYONE WHO READS THIS

BOOK TO BECOME A REBEL."

– L.S. KILROY

ACKNOWLEDGMENTS

I released this enhanced edition in late 2020 to celebrate the fifth anniversary of *The Vitruvian Heir*. The feedback I'd received around the original was that people wanted more – more of certain characters and a more drawn out ending. I also included new character illustrations throughout by the brilliant lilithsaur and book club questions for discussion. And I decided to turn it into a trilogy. But several shifts in society have happened since then, serious enough in their impact on women to make this story even more terrifyingly relevant. And so, I revisited the text once more, this time with the assistance of a sensitivity reader, M. (who is so much appreciated but will remain unnamed while she's still finessing her personal brand). This story is now a better mirror of the present. For a taste of *The Vitruvian Heir, Book II: The Awakening*, there's an excerpt in the back. The next two books will both be released in 2023 (I hope!). Finally, I'd like to thank my editor, Jennifer Rees, for painstakingly combing through this manuscript to make it pristine. Now, I'll leave you with the original acknowledgements.

I grew up an asthmatic only child in a neighborhood that skewed very *Golden Girls,* so it was lucky for me that I loved books. After my mother gifted me *Wuthering Heights* at age twelve and I became properly obsessed, I started making up my own stories. I didn't own a computer yet, so my ideas for future novels lived under my bed in a Snoopy and Woodstock suitcase circa 1980. Scores of plot summaries and potential book jackets I'd illustrated all boasted lame titles like *World War III.*

That one is particularly notable because the seed of it grew into the novel you're about to read. During sophomore year, my history teacher had been painting us a picture of the time when Catherine de'Medici ruled the French court. She had a group of beautiful female spies called the Flying Squadron (L'Escadron Volant), whom she recruited to seduce important men in court and then report back to her. I took this fascinating lesson and formed an idea for a new story. What if a future version of the United States somehow comes under the control of an emperor who commands that everything be returned to the Victorian and Edwardian periods – women are stripped of rights, have to wear corsets, etc.? And what if there is a woman who runs an underground circle of female spies trained to extract information from powerful men? What if she is planning a coup? What if she sends her best girl in to charm the emperor himself? But then the girl falls in love with him. My teenage sensibility clearly got the best of me there. This version of the story eventually met its demise along with its bedfellows somewhere between high school and college.

Then, a couple of years ago, when I began noticing a disturbing resurgence against women's reproductive rights among certain states, the germ of this idea resurfaced and became *The Vitruvian Heir*. History repeats itself. And we can never take our freedoms for granted because as long as inequitable patriarchal ideologies exist in the upper echelons of government, they will always be under threat. Women need to realize this at a younger age. The responsibility of protecting those freedoms belongs to each of us. Complicity – whether born of privilege, convenience, or ignorance – has contributed to the oppression of women throughout history, particularly women of color. This is the reason I write: to point out societal flaws through the emotion of human experience in the hope that it makes people think twice about the way things are – or the way they could be. I want everyone who reads this book to become a rebel.

Of course, the artistic process is not a solitary undertaking and there are several people who helped bring this final version to fruition. These are the people I must humbly thank. First and foremost, thank you to my parents, Mary Ann and Vincent, for encouraging my creativity as early as it began and who've always been my biggest fans. My dad devoured the book as soon as I sent him a first draft and, in the interim, has asked me nearly every time he's seen me, "What's going on with the book? When is it coming out?" Dad, I finally have an answer for you: NOW.

Thanks to those who read this work and gave feedback like Rich and Diana Snow, Elizabeth Dixon, Sarah Jane Dixon Klump, and my dear friends Rachel Dixon and Brian Underwood. And an extra special thanks to Christine Braun, partly my inspiration for the feisty Sawyer, who read two drafts and gave notes both times – you're the best. To friend and fellow author, E.E. Holmes, who has been my guide through the Everest of indie publishing – thank you for being so generous with your information and for all of our shop-talk dates, which have evolved from cocktails to a quick 30-minute hello before we both morph back into domestic goddesses.

Much work also went into the physical creation of this book. To the wildly talented Rebecca Hope Woods, the artist behind the silhouetted cover. Thank you for your patience, your vision, and your excellent collaboration. One of my favorite people to work with since 2009 has been the lovely Elizabeth Bonadies, the designer who formatted this text. You are a sheer joy to work with and truly a talent. Finally, a big thanks to Nicholas Santaniello, who helped me build my web and social presence – you are a true friend, and I hope the good things you do for others come back to you tenfold.

Last, but by no means least, to my better half, Steve. Thank you for taking care of me, for sharing your world with me, and for always believing in me. Your love, support, and kindness mean so much more than I can ever write.

And thank you, readers and writers out there. I hope you enjoy my little book, and if you have your own tale inside you, I hope to someday enjoy it as well. Keep writing – the world needs more books worth reading and more original, diverse stories. .

Best,

"I do not ask for any crown
But that which all may win
Nor seek to conquer any world
Except the one within.
Be thou my guide until I find,
Led by a tender hand,
Thy happy kingdom in myself
And dare to take command."

— Louisa May Alcott, "My Kingdom"

"Your pretty empire took so long to build, now,
with a snap of history's fingers, down it goes."

— Alan Moore, *V for Vendetta*

PROLOGUE

He pretended to sleep as she crept up on him from behind. Whenever she decided to pounce, though, he'd unfailingly wake up and seize her. But this was always the best part of their game. Lore clutched her imaginary sword and made her attack. Fallon grabbed her, and they tumbled off his fake throne and onto the floor.

"Fallon, you're dead!" she said, wriggling away from him a little quicker than normal.

At twelve years old, her body had started to change. When it came to spending time with her two best friends, she could no longer roughhouse or take a ball to the chest without the two little lumps that had begun to swell there aching in protest.

"Am not, I woke up and caught you in the act!" He pulled her closer.

He had also been changing, but in a good way. His already husky voice had deepened, and his body grew taller and broader. He looked more like a man every day. Ironically, more like his guardian, Lord Percival Berclay, the current emperor of Vitruvia.

He took a strand of her dark umber tresses and swirled it around on his face. They lay on the floor of his private dorm catching their breaths, their heads close, and everything surrounding them white. The rooms at Chersley Bartlett Academy were as formal as those in her parents' estate, but uniform in the pure, unmarred hue like the innocence they contained. From his elevated and protected quarters high next to the cathedral, they could hear the choir practicing, the voices echoing through the halls like so many seraphim. During languid Saturday mornings when they were allowed to pass the time as they preferred, Lore deactivated her orbis caputs and left them to toddle around on her desk. Her thoughts were free and clear.

On cue, Gideon busted into the room, air guns blazing, his blond hair hanging in his eyes, and a triumphant grin in place. "And now, you're both dead." He joined them on the floor. "I always catch you two like this," he said, no suspicion in his voice.

Lore imagined there should be. After all, she'd been promised to him, hadn't she? She considered them now as they sat beside each other, so drastically opposite in their looks and personalities. Gideon's hair shimmered like spun gold and his elegant features flushed with rosy innocence. His crisp eyes, perpetually full of humor and positivity, seemed to reflect a cloudless canopy of sky. Fallon emanated duskiness and shadow, both in looks and attitude. He had a wry humor, a biting wit, and often appeared moody and brooding. And yet, Lore found herself gravitating towards him. Gideon should have been jealous of her obvious preference for Fallon, but maybe the thought hadn't entered his mind because they'd all been friends for so long. Or maybe, it was simply because she had no choice or say in the matter. She had to marry him. It had been agreed upon by their parents when they were two years old and decreed by the Tree Vale's bishop.

"Anyway," Gideon continued, "don't you think we're getting too old to play Rebellion?"

Rebellion, a game made up six years ago in lower school, had become their favorite weekend morning activity. The mention of this childhood frivolity roused thoughts of her grandmother, Lady Mathilde de Bellereve, and the one St. Lucien's Day only months ago when Mathilde had been allowed to visit – supervised, of course, by someone from the special place where they send batty aristocrats. Some supreme scandal surrounded her grandmother's life, Lore could tell. Her mother, Miranda, who couldn't stop talking under normal circumstances, clammed up like a mollusk when Lore tried to ask questions about why the old woman lived in a nursing home and not with them.

On this holiday, while a sour-faced male servant cut the dime cake, Lore prayed for a moment alone with her grandmother. The latter sat demurely, and her white curls shone like a soft halo of lamb's wool around the creviced plane of her face. It saddened Lore that Mathilde looked so much older than her sixty-two years. Everything about her screamed that she'd been living a life of pain; every part of her seemed stretched and frowning. Yet, Lore saw that her grandmother wasn't insane like her parents and others wanted her to believe. There remained a discerning spark behind those soft, doe eyes – eyes Lore had inherited despite her mother's cheery cornflower blue.

They sat next to each other on a curved, velveteen chaise, as elegant and uncomfortable as the other furnishings in the Fetherston home, full of deep mahogany and heavy ornamentation. She began to notice that while Mathilde hadn't spoken during her visit, she now surreptitiously looked at Lore and then at the lit candlesticks in their brass holders on the coffee table. The girl understood; she was imploring.

"Great Lucien, Lorelei!" Her mother managed to take the holiday's namesake in vain while cursing at her daughter for starting a small house fire.

During the commotion that ensued, Lore ushered her grandmother into a broom closet underneath the stairs, now trampled by servants rushing to help. She reached for the light.

"No, darling. No lights," Mathilde whispered, her voice still carrying that affected lilt of the upper class.

"Grandmother, why won't they ever let me see you?"

Mathilde let out a bitter laugh. "Because they know I'll tell you things – things they'd rather you not know."

"What things?" Lore whispered, leaning in.

The closet door swung open and a plump arm reached in and turned on the light, exposing them. Constance, her mother's young maid, stood with her hands on her wide hips, glowering at them in smug triumph. Before Lore could plead with her to be quiet, she gave a robust, "MADAM! Look who I've found sneaking around!"

In the instant before her parents arrived on the scene, Mathilde slipped something into Lore's hand. Lore closed her fingers tightly around it and watched her grandmother transform back into a dumb mute.

"What the devil do you think you're doing?" Her father removed his monocle so that his brow could furrow without inconvenience. He took her roughly by the arm.

"I only wanted to keep Grandmother safe from the fire." She gave what seemed like a logical defense, but he didn't bite.

"Go upstairs to your room, and there will be no dime cake," he hissed.

"But Father, I–"

"That will be quite enough from you."

His menacing glare implied harsh ramifications if she disobeyed. He may even send her away to the place no one spoke of where they treated young girls who suffered from malcontent. Her best friend, Sawyer, had been sent there a few times, and she always returned quietly submissive, at least for a little while. However, Sawyer had a much higher tolerance for any kind of pain or discipline, especially since she refused to mend her ways. In this moment, Lore decided against headstrong behavior.

Her mother looked on with faux rage peppered with histrionics that could give the most celebrated stage actresses of the age a run for their money. Constance stood behind Miranda, her thick, livery lips with their light fringe of a moustache still in a victorious sneer. The other servants haunted the background, all taking satisfaction in their power over her.

Lore wished for a second that they were porcelain galateans, even though she feared such creatures, but they were no longer allowed within the aristocracy. The lovely, soulless servants, once a programmable race of automata, now remained a coveted privilege of the emperor and his head bishop. Those salvaged after the violence of the Great Rebellion thirty years ago were rumored to be kept locked away in a secret room deep within the Seat. There they stood in the dark like a silent army waiting for someone to reanimate them.

She climbed the stairs to her room, keeping her eyes on Mathilde, certain she would never see her again. The old woman locked eyes with her and, before Lore passed out of sight, winked. Only when she had closed her bedroom door, did Lore open her hand to see what treasure Mathilde had given her. A small key of darkened brass rested in her palm.

As she wondered at the object, she heard her own door being locked from the outside – father's mild form of punishment. She didn't need to guess who was doing it, either, since Constance's heavy breathing permeated walls. But even locked inside her room, she still knew more freedom than her jailer.

Her orbis caputs animated and whizzed around her head. The tiny yocto-creatures – a fat chinchilla riding in a miniature hot air balloon and two flying squirrels – had been gifts from Miranda when Lore first went away to school. They swarmed her with cheer when she returned from classes, hovering around her head, spewing out phrases in her mother's voice that were both reactionary and linked to Miranda's own emotional state.

"HOW COULD YOU BE SO DECEPTIVE, YOU IMPERTINENT, LITTLE TWIT?!" screeched Lord Izzy Holt Hempel from his balloon, his little top hat shaking so much it nearly fell off.

"Oh, shut up already."

She couldn't take solace in them in her punishment. Instead, she sat and stewed about how she had always resisted any kind of closeness with her mother, preferring her father's stoicism above Miranda's erratic moods. She wondered why her father seemed even more distant from her lately. Was it because she'd started becoming a woman, or perhaps he sensed the newfound contempt she held for his shallow position as a merely decorative lord? Instead of dwelling on such negative thoughts, she opened the bottom drawer of her desk and shifted some decorative papers. Underneath them, the tattered edge of her notebook peeked out. As with most everything, documenting this occasion proved to be her only release.

Now, as Gideon spoke of their game, Lore couldn't imagine what it would be like to be a servant, or worse, one of the dregs. Hailing from the Tree Vale, a lush area in the Northeast, she had more rights than others, and she'd been given an education, albeit most of it focused on the domestic arts. But in the Granary and the Turbine, children started working as early as four years old. She knew that from Fallon.

Apparently, that's where Lord Berclay found the handsome little boy and rescued him from a dire situation. No one knew what had happened to him, save for the strange scar that wound its way around his wrist like a snake. And he certainly never spoke about it, if he even remembered. But by his response to Gideon's question, he most certainly did. He looked away from them, his flashing eyes resting on that pale ring of skin.

"We'll never outgrow this game."

Part One:
The Runaways

Chapter I

The bells of the cathedral echoed through the streets of the city's common, ringing for every year of her life, as Lady Mathilde de Bellereve's funeral procession made its way through the public garden. Many visited this historic area as a rite of passage, especially to see its pristine nit – the poor area where the people who worked in the shops and restaurants lived. In other regions, most considered nits dangerous and avoided them, but Boston's nit held the opposite sentiment. Charmingly antithetical to the common perception, tourists often included it on their itinerary as a brief foray into the culture of the place.

Now eighteen, Lore had been right about never seeing her grandmother after that one St. Lucien's Day six years earlier. She followed her parents in the grand procession, appalled at the irony in this ostentatious display of pomp and circumstance when Mathilde had been kept hidden most of her living years. As the undisputed star of this show, her mother certainly treated her role as chief mourner – the eldest daughter of the de Bellereve family and now the reluctant matriarch – as the performance opportunity of a lifetime. Lore watched with suppressed ire as Miranda marched along with intentional determination, her bottom lip quivering while maintaining true chin-up bravado and the flounces of her enormous black hoop skirt ballooning out around her like a dirigible. Two of Lore's uncles, her father, and three cousins carried Lady Mathilde's ivory casket, adorned with peonies and roses, and every member of the distinguished de Bellereve and Fetherston clans were in attendance for this melodrama.

The area surrounding the common normally buzzed with all manner of transport, from Model T's to carriages pulled by gigantic yocto-steam animals; jewel-encrusted peacocks and pert chipmunks had gained popularity among the upper sets. Most of these contraptions carried mistresses who couldn't steer a vehicle of their own volition, as dictated by Vitruvian law. Today though, the perimeter fell silent in reverence as the procession wound uninterrupted through Mathilde's favorite girlhood spot.

Yocto-steam powered nearly everything. It took form as a cloud of microorganisms that, when confined to a small enough space circulated by gears, interacted with each other and produced a measurable amount of energy that traveled through the machine's parts and propelled it around. One could manipulate the amount of energy by adding or decreasing the number of mites within the engine chamber. When the machines weren't operating, the circulating gears stilled and the yoctos simply fell to the bottom of the chamber.

As the procession moved through the flowered paths, Lore saw Gideon's family standing among the mourners. If they'd already been married, he and his parents would be marching behind her instead of her moody cousin, Alastair, the offspring of the fortuitous union of her mother's younger sister, Tildy, to Clarence's younger brother, Holden. Gideon nodded and smiled his sweet smile. Lore's gaze fell beyond him to a lamppost where someone had hung a frayed picture of a dark-haired man with famous mutton chop sideburns. It read: WANTED DEAD OR ALIVE. OLIVER WOODLOCK. FOR CRIMES AGAINST VITRUVIA. REWARD: 100,000 EDISON NOTES.

After a series of natural disasters hundreds of years ago when the country was still the United States of America – the same cataclysms that wiped out digital technology and sent the world into a period of complete chaos – the Tree Vale remained the sole unscathed corner of a drastically shrunken nation. Lore's father, Lord Clarence Fetherston, sat on the Emperor's Council, made up of sixteen lords and four bishops divided among the main regions – the Tree Vale, the Turbine, the Granary, and the Seat – with four lords and one bishop assigned to each region. However, since the lords of the Tree Vale didn't quite have legitimate operational duties like the overseeing of the nation's food, manufacturing, and government, they were looked upon by the other lords as a joke, like dandies or fops.

Cousin Alastair had brought this up the previous evening after a dinner at her parents' estate. He and Lore had ducked away from the adults, stealing into one of the gardens farthest from the house. Two years her senior and ever the rogue, he even swiped a bottle of her favorite effervescent honey wine for the occasion. Over the years, a closeness had blossomed between them, rooted in their serious ways and, though Lore didn't consider herself cynical, she felt herself drawn to that trait in her cousin. They sat in a creaky wooden swing, shoulders touching as it rocked back and forth.

"You know I'm set to take your father's place when he retires. Then I'll be a joke, too." He sighed and leaned his head sideways to rest against hers.

"You could never be a joke."

"That's what everyone thinks, and then suddenly, there you are."

"A role is what you make of it. Maybe my father hasn't made very much of his. Perhaps he's been lazy and complacent."

"No, no. My father told me he felt the same way when he assumed the role from Grandfather – full of optimism and good intentions. He wanted to transform it into a singularly philanthropic function. But, of course, that didn't happen, mostly because of Gerathy's sway. And it'll be the same for me. Good intentions just turn to rot because rot starts at the top. How can anyone else hold themselves to a higher standard when that's the case?"

"You should be careful how you speak." Lore looked around with apprehension. "There could be spies."

Alastair sat back, looked sidelong at her, and smiled to himself. "You really are an innocent, aren't you?"

Lore faltered. "Are you calling me naïve? You should know better than anyone that's not so."

He grinned and raised his eyebrows. "Come now, don't be cross with me. I meant no offense. But sometimes, I feel like your unquestioning belief in the way things are clouds your sight."

She shifted to face him, a crease forming between her brows. "Unquestioning? Me? If anything, I'd say I'm a realist. A pragmatist. There's no reason to question what one knows to be true."

"Well, even pragmatists have their faults now, don't they?" He smirked and tickled her under her chin.

Lore stood her ground. "Don't patronize me, you ratbag."

He laughed. "Good, I love it when you're nice and feisty. You'll need that in life. But truly, I'm not mocking you in the least. There's something you don't realize here, though, and I'm going to point it out to you."

"And what's that? Do enlighten me with your wisdom."

He set down the bottle and took her face in his hands. "My darling, there are spies, but they don't watch us."

Lore thought about this as she looked into his face, all pale and angular with a dramatic widow's peak from which sprung a contrasting shock of sable hair like most everyone on the Fetherston side. He smiled a little, though sadly.

"Do you understand my meaning, dearest?"

"I think so. You mean because we're…" She hated the term 'aristocracy.' "Because of who we are."

"Exactly. We're not the ones who'll rebel, you see, and that's because we have nothing to rebel against." He let go of her face and handed her the bottle.

About seventy years ago, following an attack on Vitruvia by their former ally, Orsia, Emperor Berclay's grandfather, Lord Henley "The Conqueror," established the current regime appropriately known as the Henley Era. Adamant that society abandon its lewd and modern tastes, he demanded a swift return to the gentility and refinement seen in the Victorian and Edwardian periods.

Any history or progress after that time became known as the Malady and had a veil cast over it, dying gradually as the generations who remembered it did. The only group this benefited was the aristocracy. But elite women, though steeped in undeniable privilege, had a more rigid set of rules thrust upon them than even their Victorian predecessors. Married women of the ruling class were not allowed to appear in public without their husbands. Though Lore had accepted this about her marriage, she didn't know if she could live with such a drastic change. The empress made only one appearance each year at the Jupiter Ball, perhaps a punishment for the humiliation of not producing an heir. But the elegant empress seemed like a frightened animal during her annual appearance, suffering from overstimulation. Lore thought about how her house cat, Nibbles, had behaved once when she brought him out on the veranda to play. He nearly went mad at the inundation of his little cat senses. Lore wondered if she would also become like that – or worse, like her mother.

Miranda's life consisted of nothing more than hosting other ladies of privilege for luncheons. They gathered at a long table on the sun porch like so many bored cats and stared at each other over tea. Of course, Miranda tried to liven the mood with gossip and entertainment. If she had her way, they would have functioned more like a gaggle of loud birds than a bunch of sulky felines, but even her alleged charms failed to resurrect their non-existent personalities.

Lore bristled at her future obligations while struggling to breathe through the corset Constance had laced too tightly. She suspected her father reassigned the maid to her during this visit to act as a proper spy and informant. She also knew that Constance took sadistic joy in binding her up in her restrictive garments, while her own paunch hung loose in the skirt of her uniform. The mourning dress itself prohibited movement. Its breathable, black lace tapered downward from the bustle and flared back out at her feet. A high collar buttoned around her neck so tightly that she almost couldn't swallow, fanned up to encircle her face. It itched her chin. Every bit of her felt enclosed, stifled, and trapped.

At least after this, there were two more weeks of freedom in New York until graduation. Lore had no doubt of being subjected to the maid's manhandling during her wedding preparations. With her luck, maybe Miranda even had plans to give Constance to her as a wedding present.

The cathedral came into view in the distance, looming above the trees. Emperor Berclay couldn't attend, much to the chagrin of her mother, whom she overheard this morning lamenting this slight. To have the attendance of the emperor marked a family with honor, but he had been summoned into a social policy meeting with his bishops that ran into its second day. Fallon had to remain at school in New York because he couldn't travel outside the city unaccompanied. He told her instead to meet him later that evening at Bonne Sante, their secret spot.

The bells tolled one last time to celebrate Mathilde's life as they carried her casket up the church steps and into the historic edifice. Simple brownstone on the outside but purely impressive within, the cathedral boasted stained glass windows that overlooked mahogany pews laid with silken fabric the color of sea foam. Hundreds of years ago it must have been another kind of church, but now it held services as the First Church of the True Faith, the national religion of Vitruvia.

Stepping across the threshold, Lore realized she'd be walking down this aisle again in a mere three weeks, not in a funeral procession, but holding the crook of her father's arm and marching towards her own personal death.

Chapter II

To her dismay, her parents insisted that Constance accompany her back to school and remain with her through graduation.

"Lore, you don't keep yourself as well as you could," Miranda said as Lore sat in protest.

Her orbis caputs flew gleefully about her face as Miranda spoke. She batted them away. Miranda pouted like a wounded child.

"Constance can help with that," she continued. "Make sure your eyebrows are tidy for graduation and that your hair looks beautiful when you come back to marry. You'll see, it'll be worth it to look so beautiful."

"Thank you, but I'm not an idiot. I know you're sending her to spy on me because you don't trust me!"

"Now that's just a plain lie," Clarence burst out, "and frankly, how dare you accuse us of something like that. Just because you're privileged that doesn't give you the right to speak out of turn. Don't forget that, especially in your new life with Gideon."

Lore started to come back with a smart reply, but then promptly did as her father said, more out of empathy after what Alastair had revealed than out of deference.

"And if we didn't trust you, we would have sent Constance with you all along from the beginning of your schooling," chimed in her mother again. "This is strictly because you're not so good with your personal grooming, dear."

"Thank you, Mother. That makes me feel so much better."

Though Miranda often played the part of the frivolous socialite, she instantly caught her daughter's sarcasm and turned cold. Lord Izzy floated in front of Lore's face and shook his little head at her. The flying squirrels, Wilfred and Tobias, who acted as his underlings, each perched on one of her shoulders and tsked in her ears.

"Very well," Miranda muttered before standing and leaving the room like a veritable ice queen.

She returned a few moments later holding a small object. "But before you go, this is for you. It belonged to your grandmother and she wanted you to have it." She placed the music box in front of Lore. "We will see you in two weeks at graduation. Goodbye." And without so much as a kiss or even a pat on the shoulder, she left Lore in tears clutching Mathilde's legacy to her.

In the sanctity of the washroom, Lore exhaled, grateful for her first moment alone in the last several days. Just outside the door, Constance packed her trunk, and she needed to be quick lest the maid get nosy.

She surveyed the delicate box. Diminutive and made out of a polished cherry with her grandmother's initials, M.E.B., carved into the lid, a faded, brass lock on its lip beckoned to her. She knew this must be a perfect match for the key she kept on a silk ribbon around her neck. She slid it off. What secrets did this tiny treasure hold? Part of Lore wondered that her parents had even let her have it.

She turned the key in the lock; the clicking sent palpitations through her body. Lifting the lid to the tune of "Greensleeves," she saw only emptiness except for the emerald velveteen lining. Then, the bottom opened, and up rose a clockwork horse holding a fair maiden. The horse galloped along in place to the tune. A rolled piece of paper had been secured on his back. Once the song came to an end, she slipped the piece of paper from its light tether and unfolded the note, written in what she assumed to be her grandmother's final scrawl.

Artemis Craft
Alley 333
Boston, Mass.

She knew this name, Artemis Craft. She had heard it before – where though, she couldn't immediately recall. Stopping off at this location on her way back to school would require some undoubted finagling with Constance in tow.

An hour later, her shiny, black coach drawn by a formidable spider, pulled down the hidden cobblestone alleyway. Fortunately, a new artisanal bakery had opened close by, providing the perfect errand for her maid.

"Miss Lorelei, why are we back in Boston? This ain't the best route back to New York at all."

"That's all right. I know we're a bit out of the way, but I heard about this place and very much wanted to try it. And here we are. Will you please go into Miss Sandrine's Sweet Shoppe there and purchase a few treats for the drive down?" Lore finished, handing over some money to the most affable version of Constance she had yet to see.

"I'm going to do an errand myself. You wait here," she told Macreedy, a name she had given the spider when she received the personal carriage on her tenth birthday.

This alleyway had been difficult to find, tucked down another small street. A passerby may easily miss it if unaware of its existence. Evidently, it had seen more traffic since Miss Sandrine's opened at 336. A telling line spilled outside the door and Constance, at the very end of it, looked impatient on her tiptoes trying to see the rows of treats lining the front counter.

Lore couldn't find a 333 for the life of her. At least not listed on any doors. She guessed it must be the brown door between 331 and 335, blending in with the brick around it and absent of doorbell or knocker. Before she could walk up and twist the knob, she heard a rush of feet and the ground trembled around her. Lore looked over her shoulder to see a mammoth yocto-steam elephant coach rearing up, out of control. Onlookers saw and began to scream. Some started running in her direction, but the hapless driver seemed paralyzed with fear. Lore clamped her eyes shut to brace for the impact. Then, someone pushed her out of the way and lifted her off the ground in one motion. A man with a bowler hat sitting low over his eyes set her on her feet. He ushered her through the very door she intended to try, then moved swiftly ahead of her.

Heart still pounding, she entered quietly into a narrow hallway devoid of windows, the smell of dust and age filling her nostrils until she sneezed.

"Bless you, Lorelei," said a ragged voice from around the corner – a voice still catching its breath.

As she moved into the room, her eyes adjusted to the dim brown of the place. There he sat, the little man called Artemis, hunched over his workbench surrounded by all kinds of gears, clock faces, tools, and illuminated by two lamps directly blaring down on his workbench. A fat orange cat watched with rapt attention while his twisted fingers worked away restoring a miniature grandfather clock. This couldn't be the same person who'd just pushed her out of harm's way. The hat still swinging from a hook on the wall begged to differ.

"You just saved me. Thank you. But how do you know who I am?"

"Well, your grandmother is dead, isn't she?" He said this matter-of-factly without looking up at her. He squinted at his current project from behind massively thick spectacles.

"Yes."

He set down his tools and peered up at her. "My...I didn't get a good look at you before, but you look just like she did as a girl."

"You knew her?"

"Knew her?" He smiled, but his eyes were lost in some other time. "Yes, I knew her. Very well, in fact. And I suppose I didn't expect you to resemble her so closely. I feel as if I'm seeing a ghost."

"I know who you are..." Lore trailed off. "You're the clockmaker."

Yes, she remembered now. It had been all over the news a few years before. Artemis Craft, aristocrat and former weapons engineer and head of the Military Technology Center for the previous emperor, had gone somewhat blind when one of his creations exploded on him and, following his honorable dismissal, had chosen to retire in this tiny, beaten down shop where he spent his days making and repairing clocks. After the five minutes of news coverage, he joined the ranks of quirky, forgotten stories. Why would her grandmother send her to this man?

"At your service."

"I don't have much time. Can you tell me why I'm here?"

"No. I can show you, though." He stood and moved to a shelf. "Now, where did I put it?" He winked at her. "This little hovel I live in is what some might call a mess, a disaster. It has the look of someone who hoards things, yes?"

It did. The stained walls of the cramped apartment sagged with filmy stacks of books and papers, clocks and pieces of clocks, pictures, and notebooks. Lore's organized mind avoided this kind of clutter at all costs, but such a sentiment had been ingrained in her very early on.

"Clutter is the Devil's playground." She spewed out the doctrine as though she were at a school assembly.

Artemis chuckled, a papery laugh almost as thin as his body. "This, my dear, is what you might call 'organized chaos.'" He finished, deftly removing a small journal from the middle of a seemingly arbitrary pile. He smiled again, removing his glasses.

Lore considered him more closely. Underneath his shirt, buttoned to the top and adorned with a tattered bow tie, she could see a leanness about him that might be mistaken for frailty upon first glance, a sinew indicating that he once knew the peak of physical stamina. For all his stooping and hunching while seated at his workbench, he stood at a respectable height. He'd neatly parted a thick shock of silver hair. And, outside of their heavy bifocals, his sharp eyes didn't miss anything.

ARTEMIS

"You're not even a little bit blind, are you?" she asked, taking the journal from his hand.

"No. I'm not really a clockmaker, either."

"What are you, then?"

"Follow me."

She trailed him down another hallway, past a kitchen, bathroom, and a narrow bedroom, to a closet door that opened on a complex vault entrance. He unlocked it now by inserting his face into an inverted mold of his own likeness. The heavy door slowly swung inward, revealing its contents – four walls, every inch covered with elaborate guns and machinery.

"You're an arms dealer?"

"No, no. Just a collector. This is some of my best work, you know." He pointed to two complex contraptions. "Ah, the double-barrel Fairbolt Rogue and the atomic belt blaster – both silent and extremely deadly. No one even saw these beauties. I still dabble in the art of it. I'm working on a few new creations."

"You faked that explosion?"

He simpered. "You're as clever as your grandmother."

"Why?"

"Let's just say I could never fully devote myself to this regime for various reasons – mainly because it kept me from the love of my life. And since then, I've watched it become progressively worse and corrupt."

"You could be killed if anyone heard you speak like that. You know they have yocto-spies everywhere. Even as small as a tick on your cat."

She said this despite what Alastair had implied the other night. Part of her didn't truly believe him or didn't want to believe she really had that much privilege over others. And, after all, it always seemed better to be safe than sorry.

"Humph," Artemis said. "Please, I invented some of those things, don't you think I would immediately sniff one out if it were in my house? No, trust me. I played the part of the nutty old professor so well that they were pleased as punch to let me retreat here, fading away among the ticking hands. Besides, they have a more compatible replacement in there now, working on Lucien knows what – a former apprentice of mine. Hawfinch, he's called. Lafayette Hawfinch. I always thought him a genuine psychopath, especially when he started as a boy. Once," the old man trailed off, "once we were asked to do something quite macabre for Emperor Julian. I had reservations about it, but the boy was all too eager to infuse our science with the sinister side of the occult."

"Occult? How do you mean?"

His face grew grim, creasing at the mouth like a wrinkled envelope. "Well, you may or may not have heard the tale about Emperor Julian's prized galatean."

Lore thought back to her days in lower school. Late one night, Fallon had convinced her, Sawyer, and Gideon to sneak over to his dorm and tell ghost stories. Fallon recited one about his Grandpa Julian that only heightened her fears about the galateans.

"Our cook once told me that when my grandfather ruled as emperor, he had a favorite nephew, Arnold, the son of his beloved younger sister, Sophia Clare, who died in childbirth. Arnold had the delicate features of his mother – her dark curls and her arresting emerald eyes. He served as head of the Vitruvian Guard, acted as my grandfather's trusted advisor, and had just become engaged to one of the Dubonnet women," he'd said in quiet tones, the hand torch under his chin bathing his face in eerie light.

"On the day of his wedding, they found him dead in his room. Grandfather was beside himself. It appeared he loved Arnold even more than my father. He locked himself in a room with the body for days. When Arnold's father finally demanded that he allow the boy to be buried, he conceded, but no one ever saw the body." Here he'd paused, looking at each of them. "And then suddenly, the emperor had a new personal galatean, one with lifelike black curls and emerald eyes. One that looked and spoke just like Arnold. He christened it, Arnaud. All the human staff in the Imperial Chambers were very put off by it. Wild stories circulated that Arnold's real parts had been used to build the galatean – his hair and eyes, he even had a layer of skin over the porcelain on his face. Some said his teeth looked like human teeth. He moved and spoke more like a human than the other galateans. More superstitious servants thought an evil magic had been summoned to create Arnaud, imbuing some of Arnold's spirit into the machine. They said he looked in a discerning way. And apparently, the emperor still had conferences with him during which he received advice from Arnaud.

"During the Great Rebellion, when the people marched on the Seat, they say someone hijacked the Starter, the master generator that gives commands to all the galateans, and reprogrammed them to turn on their owners. But instead of doing violence to my grandfather, Arnaud disappeared and has never been seen again. He hadn't been among the galateans recovered when the final uprising ended. People say this means the Starter didn't even control him in the first place. They say he's been able to meld into society and pass as human. Maybe he's hidden in the nit. Maybe someone stole him. No one knows. But he's still out there..."

"I do know that tale," she answered Artemis now.

"Well, it's not an old wives' tale like it sounds. It's true. The emperor commanded that we make that creature for him with the very parts of that poor, dead boy. At first, my gut told me to refuse. For Lucien's sake, I felt like Doctor Frankenstein. But you can't refuse the emperor. So, I built Arnaud, but I refused the other part, the unnatural part. Hawfinch took care of that. He's much closer to Hell for it than I am. Well, anyway, who knows what he's concocting now. Gerathy thinks he's a genius."

"Unnatural part?"

"Yes, yes. Julian wanted to summon Arnold's spirit and trap it in the machine. And Hawfinch did it – brought the Devil right into our midst."

"Oh dear."

"Oh dear? More like 'Oh dead.'"

"But how were you able to bring all these weapons here without the Seat finding out?"

"A good question, which also relates to the journal I have just handed you. It's a new kind of technology I started developing during my last year there, but I hadn't shared it with anyone yet. It's called innocuous concealment. I take an object that might arouse suspicion, like say, a suitcase full of forbidden books" – he paused and smiled – "and then I manipulate its molecules by coating them with a layer of transformative yocto-particles that I have programmed to look like something else completely. Think of it as a molecular disguise."

Lore considered the journal in her hands. "So, if this were something else disguised as a journal, how would I access the real object?"

"That's easy," said Artemis. "You just have to ask it. You see, the layer of transformative yocto-particles is also responsive."

"Ask it?"

"Yes, you simply say, 'Show your true form.'" As he uttered these words, the book shook in her hands and fell to the floor. Then it unfolded itself and expanded, grew sides and a top, and soon they were both looking down at a suitcase with the familiar initials M.E.B. embossed in the center of the lid. Lore clicked open the gold latches to an inside brimming with books. Lore traced her finger over one dusty cover that brandished the title *The True History of the Former United States of America* by Eloise Leduc.

"A book by a woman?"

"Oh yes, there used to be many of those. Some you've probably even read in class."

"That's doubtful, sir."

"Really? Try me. Give me a title. Your favorite, let's say."

"Why? Are you going to try and tell me that *Wuthering Heights* and *Jane Eyre* weren't written by Ellis and Currer Bell?"

"Just that, in fact. Those were their original pen names. Their real names were Emily and Charlotte Brontë."

"Are you mad?"

He stuck his hand in the suitcase and fished around for a moment, finally pulling out three tattered volumes and laying them out, title up, for her to see.

"You tell me."

"*Wuthering Heights* by Emily Brontë, *Jane Eyre* by Charlotte Brontë, *Pride and Prejudice* by Jane Austen?! Not John Austen? Jane?"

"Illuminating, eh?"

"Well, who else was a woman? Shakespeare?"

"That's never been fully proven, but certainly debated." He winked.

"But how did she even come by these? People hardly mention the Malady, let along possess such artifacts. The risk alone…"

"My dear, there are rebels everywhere."

Lore turned her attention back to her treasure. A folded note perched on top of the tomes. It read:

My dearest Lorelei,

If you are reading this, it means I am gone. These books are my gift to you, and I hope it is not too late by the time you receive them. The titles have long since been outlawed by the Seat as forbidden. Most were destroyed because they were written by women. Within these pages are the truths about the society you live in and how it came to be.

My own grandmother before me, used to tell me of times when men and women were considered equal. But then, shifts began to happen, all leading up to the Great Rebellion thirty years ago. They will lie to you in school. Your parents will lie to you because they have been brainwashed. But not your grandma. Because I still remember.

Lore folded the note and set it back on top, satisfied that this should be her grandmother's parting gift to her. She had always loved reading, writing, and making up stories, but female authors didn't exist in Vitruvian law. Tales she made up in childhood were only known by herself and her closest friends. Sometimes, she'd offer to write their assignments and she never did it because any of them couldn't, but simply because it gave her so much pleasure.

"How do I close it?"

"As you were."

In a snap, she held the blank journal again.

She smiled. "Thank you."

"You know, your grandmother ran away from her wedding," Artemis began.

"I didn't know that. I don't know anything about her."

He sighed. "I bear the responsibility for what happened to her. You should know that. And I've spent my entire life trying to make it up to her. Someday I'll tell you, when we have more time."

"I'm sure you never meant to hurt her."

A tear surfaced and lingered in his right eye without falling. "No, of course not. I loved her very much. I wanted a life with her."

"Oh, I see. Well, I look forward to hearing her story when you're ready. And now, I should really be off. My maid will be back from her errand."

"Yes, of course. Lorelei, I want you to know that whatever happens, you always have an ally in me. And you can always reach me."

"How?"

"While you've been here, I placed a bond on you, a sort of cellular coating that connects us. It's another technology I developed for communication between soldiers during combat. All you have to do is call my name, and I'll hear you. And you'll hear me. Try it from the coach later. A whisper even, will do."

"Okay. Goodbye, then. And thank you for this."

"Goodbye, and good luck with your nuptials." He touched her cheek and then went back to his clock as if she'd never been there.

Back in the coach, Constance preoccupied herself with tulip cakes and barely noticed Lore's return.

"Where'd you run off to?"

"Just wanted to get myself a journal." Lore brandished her prize.

Constance snorted at her and started in on another cake as Macreedy's spindly legs carried them out of the alley and sped towards the cyberway to New York. When the maid finally fell asleep in a sugar coma, Lore tested her new ability.

"Artemis?" she whispered.

"Here whenever you need me, love. Over and out," came the answer.

Chapter III

"I'm going out and you can't stop me. You work for me while you're here. Don't forget that," Lore commanded.

With its fresh white walls and furnishings, Constance resembled a fly in milk in Lore's private dorm. Her black bun, her charcoal uniform, her squat legs in black tights. Her loud breathing countered the whir of the cooling system.

"I don't think so, miss. Your father gave me strict orders not to let you out of my sight for the next two weeks. I reckon they think you'll try to make a run for it."

"Oh really? And why would I do that?"

Constance shrugged.

"And even if I did, why should you care?"

Constance thought for a minute. Lore imagined the inside of her brain as a mess of rusted cogs and wheels like the ones on Artemis' workbench or those that opened the cryptic door to Bonne Sante, where she was trying to go. She needed to ditch the maid if she intended to meet Fallon there later. In her rumination, Constance had come up with an answer.

"Why should you be able to do whatever you want, when none of the rest of us can?"

"So, you're jealous of my freedom and that makes you spiteful. Is that it?"

Constance shrugged again. "I suppose."

"Well, here's what I have to say to you. Remember that time six years ago when you locked me in my room?"

"Miss, I've locked you in your room so many times, you can't expect me to remember just one," Constance replied, crossing her legs with some labor and feigning boredom with a roll of her eyes.

"You know which one I mean. The one during my grandmother's visit and the fire. I remember when you were doing that, I thought, even though she's the one locking me in my room, I will always know more freedom than she. What do you make of that?"

Constance thought again and paused a good minute before she spoke. "It's not my fault I was born into servitude and you wasn't."

"My point exactly."

"How do you mean?"

"I mean, it's not your fault you were born into servitude and I wasn't. But it's not my fault, either. Besides, once I'm married, I may as well be a servant. I'll be a prisoner in my own home."

The maid's face softened. "I see."

"You gain nothing from taking out your anger on me. Just like I gain nothing from firing you if my parents decide to give you to me as a wedding gift, except maybe losing an excellent worker."

Constance smiled. "I am quite good at my job."

Lore felt a pang of guilt for judging Constance, casting her off as ignorant just because she lacked the opportunity. Indeed, the latter had mastered her role to the point where she anticipated Miranda's needs before they even surfaced.

"Constance, what's your surname? You've been with my family for years, and I'm ashamed I don't know it."

"It's Langford, miss."

"Well, that has a nice ring to it."

Constance smiled a little. "I always thought so, miss, even though it's a name none really knows nor does it mean anything to anyone."

"It means something to you, doesn't it? That's all that matters. But look, I'm still going out."

"Just make sure you come back, miss. Or I'll lose my position with your parents, and then I'll really have nothing."

Finally, some give. And maybe there would be some give in her corset now, too, if she and Constance were in a better place.

"What in St. Lucien do you think you're doing?" Constance's mouth hung open in shock. Instead of a fly, she looked as though she should be catching them.

"Changing."

"You can't go out without a corset."

"Yes, I can. This is Manhattan, and I'm headed to an underground club, anyway. No one will see me in my carriage. I draw the curtains and it's nighttime," she said as she shimmied into her shortest dress, a fringed black number with a deep neckline and black feathers capping the shoulders.

New York, being the sophisticated hub of what international business and commerce still existed in their insular nation, had been granted permission by the Seat to be a little freer with its fashions. At some of the trendier locales, one stumbled across women dressing in looser dresses with no defined waists, legs exposed, no corsets, and cropped and waved hair with feathered headbands and beads. The men wore tailored suits with suspenders and bowties, wingtips, pocket squares, derbies, and homburg hats.

Lore wove a shimmered band around and through her coiffed hair and fastened her favorite necklace, a three-strand pearl choker Fallon had given her for her sixteenth birthday.

"If you say so." Constance seemed appalled. "Your mother would die if she saw you."

"Then it's a good thing she isn't here."

Lord Izzy and his minions huffed at this proclamation. "Well, I say!" her mother's voice spewed out of the fat chinchilla.

"Go to sleep, you lot," she said, and at once they settled down and closed their eyes. "Don't wait up," she told Constance and left before the maid decided to prevent her from going.

As Macreedy scuttled to the door of Bonne Sante, Lore felt the anticipation she always did before seeing Fallon. Although, her conscience certainly chastised her about spending so much time with him when more pressing tasks awaited – like discovering the truths in her grandmother's library or talking to Artemis about Mathilde's intriguing past, but she had left the journal at her dorm to be dived into later that evening. Not to mention, the studying she needed to put in for finals next week. All this somehow became less critical when she remembered these secret trysts must end forever in two weeks. Not that they even qualified as trysts; nothing romantic existed between them – nothing physical, anyway. But from the moment she and Gideon became man and wife, there could be no friendship between her and Fallon at all without her husband present.

She knocked five times on the massive portal and the cogs and wheels shifted and formed themselves into the bouncer. "Password," he demanded.

"Half-seas over," she said.

"Nope. It changed, kid."

"Oh right – bee's knees?"

The door opened, revealing a foyer lit by deep purple and bustling with young people. In the center of the room, an enormous cast iron fountain overflowed with champagne. A brass band played, and people romped about to the quick, ragged blues of the sassy horns.

"Good evening, Miss Lorelei," a waiter greeted her with an empty champagne flute. "Master Berclay is waiting for you at the usual table."

Lore filled her glass at the fountain and made her way to their private dining spot, all the way in the back of the club in a curtained alcove where they could see without being seen. At this age, Fallon had shed his army of security guards, and hidden yocto-creatures protected him instead. He had grown to be rebellious. Rather than being stricter, the emperor promised him freedoms if the boy sat in on his discussions with the head bishop whenever he returned home on school breaks.

She drew back the curtain and her stomach somersaulted. He'd removed his suit coat and rolled up his shirtsleeves. His dark hair fell messily across his forehead and there was the slightest bit of scruff on his face. He looked up and saw her, smiling with his eyes as he lit a Lucifer's siphon.

"Took you long enough, but I see why. You look good," he finally said after a deep inhale.

"I wish you wouldn't do that."

"Do what? Smoke or flirt?"

"Both."

He sighed, betraying his humor for just an instant. Their last few outings had been wrought with an almost unbearable tension. First came the bickering. Then, they'd have too much to drink and do everything in their power not to kiss; Lore usually stormed out in tears. The next morning, Fallon would show up bearing her favorite lemon pancakes from the dining hall as an apology, and the cycle began again. Gideon had graduated early to establish himself in his military career before the wedding, and Lore wondered what he might feel if he witnessed this inappropriate dysfunction.

"I don't want this to be another night like we've been having. I definitely don't want you to have to show up with pancakes again tomorrow morning. If we continue on this path, I may not be able to fit into my wedding dress," she said, aiming for some levity.

"Good." He put out his siphon after one last drag and drank deeply.

"Fallon, I mean it. I don't want it to be like this between us. I want these last few times to be fun."

"That's exactly it. These last few times."

"What do you expect me to do?"

He sulked again. "Nothing. You have to do what you're told." He paused. "This isn't just about us being friends, you realize."

"I feel like we have this same conversation over and over, and it's torturous. Don't do this now."

"Why not?"

"Because it's only going to hurt me – and you."

He slid closer. "Why should it hurt you?" he whispered.

"Stop it."

"No, tell me. I need to hear you say it."

She looked into his face now, her favorite face since childhood, but she couldn't find the words.

"Poor little Lorelei. Never able to say what she really feels." He sighed again and grabbed her hand.

"We should stop talking about this now."

She hated showing such weakness. It made her feel desperate and helpless, the same feeling she'd have during their childhood play as he clasped her in his arms. She loved him. With everything in her, she loved him. He watched her now, reading her very thoughts.

"Yes, let's not talk at all."

He leaned in and buried his face in her ear, in the side of her hair. Even Gideon hadn't kissed her save for the chaste peck on the cheek allowed between engaged couples. This gesture felt altogether different – intimate. She felt his hand caress her thigh, and it lit her up from the inside, goosebumps erupting across the warm plane of her skin. His lips burned hot on her neck as he began feverishly kissing the soft flesh there.

"My darling," he whispered so softly that later she'd think she imagined it.

She nearly allowed herself to be lulled into this seduction. He cradled her face, gently turning it to his own, but she pushed him away before any real damage could be done.

"What's the matter?"

"This is wrong." She stood, using all of her willpower to do so.

"I know your heart, Lore," he said, his eyes commanding her back, "and you know mine."

"And we both know the law, so what does it matter?" She turned again to leave.

"Where are you going?"

"Back to my dorm, away from you."

"No, stay – stay with me. We can go back to the way we were." He straightened up.

Lore hesitated.

"I mean it. There's obviously nothing we can do to change this unfortunate situation," he reasoned, speaking like a future emperor again. "This will have to be enough somehow. I'll behave, I promise. In all these years, have you ever known me to break one?"

"No, I suppose not."

"Sit down, then." He patted the seat next to him.

She sighed, feeling her will dissolve just as the moment's passion had. "Well, when you put it like that."

"Believe me, I know how to be convincing when necessity calls," he said. "And I promise, no arguing and no pancakes tomorrow. I may be many things, but a saboteur I'm not."

Hours later, when she unlocked the door to her room, she could hear the unmistakable sounds of voices inside.

"Hey, missy," Sawyer greeted her as she entered.

"What's going on?"

"Nothing. I just stopped in on my way back and have been chatting up your maid here."

Sawyer Hillbury's widower father also happened to be one of the comical lords of the Tree Vale, and he consistently failed to rein in his wild offspring. With her uncontrollable mane of honey curls and her hazel eyes, the boys always favored her. In lower school, she'd been caught kissing on several occasions and once in the bathroom showing her parts to Bastian Withers. Though she took punishment each time, her father's position warranted less severe consequences than others may have received.

Lore loved her unruly friend's ability to get along with everyone. No one escaped her notice. From school custodians and scholarship students – whom some of their elite circle of friends refused to acknowledge – to the women who ran the boutiques, Sawyer loved them all and they loved her. It was no surprise to Lore that she had already won over Constance.

"How long have you been here?"

"'Bout twenty minutes or something. You're up late." Sawyer nudged her. "Out on a date with the future emperor, were we?"

"No." Lore glanced at Constance. "We're just friends, best friends. And we're spending as much time together alone as we can before I'm married. You know how it is."

Sawyer grinned. "Sure, I know."

"Where were you tonight, anyway? Don't you usually go to Bonne Sante?"

"Not anymore. I've been sneaking around with someone."

"I hope it's not who I think it is."

For weeks now, Lore had been forming a theory. Sawyer seemed just a little too interested in the handsome new priest at the boy's upper school. At assemblies, when Lore wasn't preoccupied staring at Fallon, she observed Sawyer, who had become oddly demure at these events. Her friend's eyes would slyly make their way to the faculty box where Father Samuel Hollengarde sought her out with his own gaze.

"You know what will happen to you if anyone finds out."

A moroseness crept into Sawyer's mirthful eyes. She knew better than anyone how they punished disobedient young women.

"What would Sister Martha say?" Lore asked, hoping the thought of disapproval from the one teacher Sawyer respected might be enough to convince her of this poor choice.

On more than one occasion, Sister Martha had saved both girls – Sawyer from her usual brand of trouble, and Lore from a more academic blunder that might have brought serious consequences to both her and her betrothed. Sister Martha taught English and had a passion for introducing them to the classics, even though some had been banned years ago as well. Emperor Berclay still allowed literature that had been popular during or before the 19th century, but he didn't care for anything by the artists of the modern age that followed. The Seat felt that such novels promoted rebellion and mutinous behavior.

"Your story is the best," Fallon had said. They were in their eleventh year and had been given a creative writing assignment in English class, the one major subject that girls were also allowed to take. The boys had the same assignment in their class, and the day before they were due, they'd shared their pieces as they sat around Fallon's dorm.

"Definitely," agreed Gideon. "You should submit it to *The Tapestry*," he said, referencing the school literary journal.

"But girls aren't allowed to submit."

"Who cares? The editor is your fiancé," said Fallon.

"Besides, you can be published anonymously," offered Gideon. "And at least we'll all know it's your piece."

Fortunately, as the advisor for *The Tapestry*, Sister Martha had halted the presses before the edition brandishing Lore's anonymous piece circulated across campus. She sat Lore and Gideon in her office and her already ruddy complexion flushed an even deeper red.

"I don't think either of you quite understand what could have happened if this issue had been released," she said calmly while her knuckles grew white clutching the blotter on her desk. "You couldn't have known this, but we keep a virtual log of assignments that's cross-checked with our journal by the assistant to the dean to ensure that scenarios like this don't occur. Lore, you could have been expelled for that – or worse."

"Really? It's actually in someone's job description to make sure female students aren't published?" Lore couldn't help flouting propriety to ask this. It just seemed too absurd for reality.

Sister Martha's gray eyes darkened as she answered. "My dear girl, you have no idea the lengths to which this monarchy will go to keep women from flourishing. And, in circumstances like this, I can tell you, ignorance is best."

"If anyone should be in trouble, it's me," Gideon said, blushing to the roots of his hair. "I didn't realize something bad could happen to Lore. I just thought her story was wonderful."

Sister Martha snapped out of her dour countenance, smiling her warm, easy smile. "Well, don't let it happen again. And Lore, you are truly an excellent writer, but do be very careful with your talent."

After that, Lore kept her already secret journal even more under wraps, although she did chronicle this event before she tucked it in the depths of the drawer holding her undergarments. She hadn't written anything in it since. She now grew somber at the thought of leaving Sister Martha behind after graduation and being stuck with the fickle affection of Miranda.

"Let's just say, it's worth the risk," Sawyer now said. "Besides, Gunther came to visit my father last week, and I overheard them talking." She spoke of her own betrothed, a bulky second cousin who had recently been inducted into the Vitruvian Guard. "He said that the Seat is going through one of those cycles where security is a bit slim, if not altogether lax. They don't have the capacity to keep tabs on everyone, especially in the nits and around here. They're more concerned with squelching rebellion in the Turbine or the Granary since they depend on those. So, of course, that's where the bulk of them are stationed along with the Vitruvics and the yocto-spies. He said even border patrol is waning."

"Nothing around here is worth the risk – not of that."

"Not of what?" Constance asked.

Lore had forgotten her maid's presence. She hesitated.

"Just tell her," said Sawyer. "She's your maid now, she might as well know these things."

Lore didn't know why she wanted to protect Constance from this knowledge, but she had to know something. There must be some form of punishment like this for maids who strayed from virtue since they weren't allowed to marry or have children.

"If a girl at school is caught with a boy in that way...you know. They operate on her parts."

Constance looked confused.

"They cut off your little nub down there," Sawyer said.

"Oh." Constance seemed to understand Sawyer's crass explanation well enough. "They don't do that to us, but they do take the part that can grow a baby once we start our first bleeding."

Sawyer glanced at Lore. "Did you know that?"

Lore shook her head. "I knew that they weren't allowed to marry or have children, but I didn't know that."

"I would have loved a baby," Constance admitted, automatically cupping her hands where her womb used to be.

They were silent for a moment and Lore regretted bringing up that fact with such nonchalance.

"Well," Sawyer started, haughtiness in her voice, "I'm going to do what I want. Because next year I'll be forced to marry that oaf, Gunther, and I'd rather have my womanhood scraped off so I don't have to feel anything when he's sweating on top of me like a big ginger pig."

"Oh, Sawyer."

"It's true, isn't it? For both of us."

"Please stop. My point is that I'm graduating this year, and I won't be able to keep you out of trouble like I have for the past twelve years. Can you at least, for my sanity, be a little careful?"

Sawyer headed for the door. Whenever things got too real or too emotional, she bailed. Lore grabbed her on her way out and stared into her face. She squirmed and began inspecting the ceiling.

"I'm serious. I know you hate this kind of thing, but you're as close to a sister as I'll ever get. And I know maybe there's no real chance of happiness for either of us, but I still want you to be alive, for Lucien's sake."

Sawyer looked at her, the tears finally making their way down her freckled cheeks. She half-smiled and shrugged her way out of Lore's grip.

"I'll be careful. I promise."

"Artemis?" she whispered as she sat wide awake in bed. Fallon's proclamation of love had made sleep impossible. "Are you awake?"

"For you, I can be," a drowsy voice answered.

"I'm sorry."

"Don't be. It must be important if you're talking to me at – what time is it?"

"It's three o'clock."

"Ah yes, the witching hour. Well, what can I help you with?"

"I don't know. I just wanted to talk. I'm sad, and you know better than anyone what this feels like."

"I do?"

"I'm not in love with my fiancé."

"I see."

"But I *am* in love. You see, it's impossible. What should I do?"

"Well, I can certainly tell you what not to do. Don't do what I convinced your grandmother to do and run away before your wedding. First off, it won't work, especially since you are part of the nobility both in name and in your father's occupation."

"You convinced her to run?"

"It didn't take much convincing. We'd been in love since we were children in lower school, and though we both knew of her betrothal to Francis de Bellereve, we couldn't resign ourselves to living apart. Over the years, we concocted a scheme.

"On the eve of her wedding, she'd escape and meet me in Landraven, the capital city in Hopespoke – a place then only just becoming known as a haven of sorts for those who wanted to escape the repression of the Seat. Before the former United States reestablished itself as Vitruvia and enacted a new constitution, Hopespoke had been a state called Texas. Along with few other states, it seceded and took on a new name. The other areas that survived the natural disasters were divided into the territories we now have, and government remained in Washington, D.C. She succeeded in sneaking across the border, but when your grandmother arrived, she couldn't find me. I wasn't there."

"Where were you?"

"Francis had learned of our plan, and he delayed me. He made me go out with him for his stag night and, before I could slip away, he slid something into my drink – something so strong that it knocked me out completely, and I wasn't even able to communicate my whereabouts to Mathilde. When she arrived in Landraven, she didn't quite make it into one of the underground saloons before an army of yocto-spiders had tracked her down, swarmed her, and immobilized her with bites. Her family brought her back and made her go through with it."

Lore could hear Artemis' heavy sigh.

"I'm sorry to make you relive this."

"No, dear, these are things you must know."

"And after that, you never saw her anymore?"

"No. I didn't want to risk her being hurt again. The spider bites nearly killed her, you see – such flawed and primitive technology. From that day on, everyone suspected the effects of the attack were what drove her mad, but that's not true. My betrayal did. She never understood why I hadn't shown up that night. And, just as I threw myself into my work to deal with my situation, she feigned madness to deal with hers. Eventually, after decades, Francis gave up trying to win her heart, and he and your mother had her committed.

"Six years ago, I had the means to reach out to her again. I visited her in the asylum, and, after that, we spoke every day in the same way you and I are speaking now. Since everyone there believed her to be mad, it didn't matter that they always caught her in conversation with herself. And through this, I can help you as she asked."

"How did she want you to help me?"

"She said that, although she had only seen you very few times, you had spirit and fight within you. 'I could see it in her eyes' she said. 'They were my eyes once, and if someone had been there to help me, you and I could have had a life together. I want her to have a life.' Those were the last words she spoke to me, to anyone."

"What should I do, then? My wedding is in three weeks."

"I think you should start reading. And leave the rest to me."

Chapter IV

Lore scanned the audience on the day of her graduation with eyes that belonged to someone from more than two centuries earlier. In the last two weeks, she had read most of her grandmother's collection. What a strange feeling to look at the world and wonder how her own rights and the rights of others had been stolen out from underneath them. And not just that, but the biting reality that, for centuries prior, privileged white women like her had often knowingly contributed to the systemic oppression of women of color. Being unable to travel freely or cross borders, not being allowed to write or having to remain illiterate, facing forced sterilization and public execution – these were all realities for enslaved women and even in the decades beyond abolition in pre-Vitruvian history. They were all pawns of the Seat – her, Sawyer, her parents and Gideon, even Fallon. Granted, thanks to Sawyer's exploits, Lore hadn't led a completely sheltered life, but even then, she had still been on the verge of complete ignorance. She had been subservient and complacent in the absence of an alternative, and had only the context of her own suffering to draw on. How was it possible for the world to have fallen so backwards?

She glanced over the sea of people – noting the now striking lack of diversity – to the Imperial Seat where Lord Berclay sat between Fallon and the sinister head bishop, Horace Granville Gerathy, with his greasy hair and cruel downturned mouth in a lecherous leer. Students knew not to overstep bounds during Gerathy's visits. The bishops all had their different means of spying. Some used tiny micro machines – insects, birds, and even mites. Bishop Gerathy preferred young boys, particularly dregs from the streets who were swayed by money. Rumors circulated for a while that, in addition to some eerily lifelike galateans, he kept a succession of beautiful boys as his personal valets, all whom he called Ganymede. Whenever one grew too old for his liking, he found another and repurposed the old one somewhere else.

The lower grades and their families sat in attendance in addition to the faculty and staff, which included nuns, priests, and servants. The ceremony took place in the historic district, beginning with a grand procession of graduates marching from their dorms on Central Park West, through the park, and ending at Chersley Bartlett's Fifth Avenue campus.

The amphitheater, carved out of white marble, marked the center of the campus and had been thermally engineered so that even on a sweltering hot day, once inside the emblematic circle, guests felt cool and comfortable. Lore waited for her name to be called and readied herself to be on display, trying to quell the tiny bud of dread turning over on itself in her stomach.

"Lorelei Henriette Fetherston, daughter of Lord Clarence Fetherston and Mrs. Miranda de Bellereve Fetherston of the Tree Vale, graduating with highest honors," the announcer boomed.

She found her parents in the crowd. Her father sported a monocle that he didn't even need and which, when considered with his silken plum top hat, made him seem perfectly flamboyant. Lore had no doubt her mother had bribed his valet to dress him in these foppish ensembles. Yes, Miranda looked proud, indeed – proud and boastful. Lore squinted and could make out her mother mouthing "highest honors" to one of her best friends in the next row. And yet, her parents did look pleased in this moment, but Lore wondered if they were only happy that she'd soon be Gideon's wife and no longer their concern.

In this musing, her eyes met Sawyer's, and her irreverent young friend thought it an appropriate time to make a very inappropriate gesture. Concerned that the bishop had seen it, Lore glanced over to the Imperial Seat, but found, to her disgust, that the bishop's eyes were instead glued to her own face – as were Fallon's. She took her seat and turned her eyes away from them both.

Once the last graduate accepted his diploma, the bishop made his way to the center of the platform. "Good day, ladies and gentlemen, students, parents, and the happy graduates," he began. "Now that our celebration is over, there is a grave matter to which we must attend before we allow you to continue your good cheer."

A pit formed in Lore's stomach. She continued to watch and listen in horror, certain the victim of this most heinous punishment had to be Sawyer. She and Father Hollengarde had been found out and now would be put to death for all to see. A line of galateans formed in the open space in front of the center platform. They wore Imperial Guard uniforms and carried corkers. Lore could barely make out the vacant stares of their artfully chiseled faces.

"Sisters Willomena Fingerton and Martha Rhine, please approach the platform," Bishop Gerathy continued.

Sister Fingerton, a young nun and a favorite among the girls, taught Vitruvian history, which contained everything preceding and including the Victorian and Edwardian periods. Any period of time during the Malady wasn't to be acknowledged whatsoever.

Lore's insides began to freeze as she watched Sister Martha stand, her earthy grace shaken and her customary good-natured smile a sharp line underneath her nose. She and Sister Fingerton, short and girlish with her bob peeking out of her habit, made their way through the throng of other faculty, who sat in silent shock with the rest of the audience. The bishop smiled down meanly at them as they arrived at the base of the platform. Lore could just make out his poisonous stare of unadulterated hate.

"Sisters, it has come to my attention, from quite a credible source, that the two of you have cast away your sacred vows to the Vitruvian Sisterhood in favor of a life of revolting sin as lovers," he spat the final word. "Do you deny it?"

Sister Fingerton sighed audibly and looked at Martha. "Oh, Martha…"

Martha met her with a steady gaze and nodded. Then, instead of cowering or begging forgiveness, she took Fingerton's hand and turned her face defiantly to the bishop, projecting her voice so it rang out in everyone's ears.

"We don't deny it."

"We don't deny it, Your Excellency."

She met his correction with a silence that seemed to feed his vengeance. His mouth twisted into a leer. "So, you don't deny it?" he hissed. "And you stand here in defiance of Vitruvian law?"

"No, Horace," she used his given name for even more of an affront. "We stand here as ourselves. That's all."

He lifted his hands, their countless age spots as numerous as his sins, and asked with a mocking concern, "What would you have me do then, Sisters? This will not stand."

"I would have you show compassion or understanding or acceptance – or humanity," Sister Martha answered, then turned his own tone back on him, "but since asking that would be like asking a hog to perform *Hamlet*, we'll make it easy on you. Do what you've already planned then, you revolting coward. You small, small man," she spat.

Lore had never seen so much resolve in anyone – to face death and humiliation with such fearlessness. But for what? Why wouldn't you simply lie to save yourself? The bishop glowered for a moment, clearly stunned by the mix of her venom and courage, and then nodded to the galateans. They raised their weapons and unleashed a cloud of fighting yoctos that quickly penetrated the women, tearing up their insides.

During the cutting silence, Lore caught a glimpse of Gideon's terrified face. She saw the girl next to Sawyer clap her hand over the latter's mouth and restrain her from shouting out in protest. Lore forced herself to look once more upon the scene, and she saw Sister Martha's mouth twisted in agony as she clutched her chest and stomach. Blood began to seep from her eyes and ears, and her thick form fell, slapping onto the hard surface like stone against stone.

"Now," the bishop continued, "if anyone else is considering a rebellious act or behavior that openly defies our laws of decorum and propriety, then remember this day."

By the time Headmaster Danforth moved to the platform, all traces of what transpired had been erased, but his pudgy face still wore remnants of horror. Visibly shaken, he wiped the sweat from his brow and attempted to smile. As Lore looked around her, the rest of the faces mirrored his discomfort – save for Bishop Gerathy, Emperor Berclay, and Fallon.

"This concludes our one-hundred and fifty-third commencement of Chersley Bartlett. Year twelves," he began, but faltered. He obviously had some manner of inspirational or poignant speech planned that he now felt incapable of delivering. His face saddened, he managed, "I wish you well in all your endeavors," before hastening off the platform.

Lore wanted to cry but could not, the spark of rage inside her smothered by the icy numbness that accompanied her will to survive. And deep within, she'd answered her own question. This is how it happened and kept happening – the regression, the control, the surrender of integrity of an entire population. People would go along with anything to keep living. Even if it meant living in fear. Like the others, she could only stand and follow the rest of her class, retracing her steps on the white stone, now forever tainted.

"Thank Lucien that's over with," she said, throwing off her robe.

Meeting with her parents and Gideon's family for the reception afterwards had been stunted. Still inwardly reeling from what they had seen, they remained true to social customs and didn't acknowledge it. Instead, they sipped sparkling honey wine and exchanged awkward pleasantries. She still didn't know how she'd endured it without breaking down into cataclysmic sobs. In fact, she couldn't do that now if she wanted to. Her heart felt drained and limp, like a heavy piece of dried fruit. Even Sawyer appeared to be shaken out of her normal feistiness.

The girls were to change and join their parents, Gideon and his family, and Fallon and the emperor for a special dinner in the Summit Tower in the very center of the city. The emperor had it held exclusively for them that evening. Lore hated these formal dinners with the emperor. And this one, she imagined, had the potential to be quite worse.

Lord Berclay had been like an uncle to her growing up. And, while he held steadfastly to all of his father's and grandfather's principles as he expected of Fallon, she never believed him to be cruel. How could he then just sit there and allow his bishop to display that much power?

"Well, you're done. That must be such a relief," Sawyer spoke for the first time since they'd returned to freshen up. "Now all you have to do for the rest of your life is have luncheons and pop out babies. Oh, and pretend to love a man you don't really love."

"You're not making this any easier for me, are you?"

"I'm just a realist is all."

"You're a real drab is what you are."

"We're both drabs in these shitty dresses," Sawyer commented.

They examined their reflections in the full-length mirror. Unlike a night out at Bonne Sante in dresses with fringe, this evening represented the epitome of Victorian splendor. Lore wore a dress of deep violet brocade, corseted, billowing out at the waist, and with capped sleeves. Her gloves were dove-gray silk, as were her slippers, and she wore black diamond chandelier earrings and a matching necklace. Sawyer complemented her hazel eyes with a shimmering topaz gown and an heirloom double strand of pearls.

"I think you both look lovely," Constance chimed in.

"Thank you, Constance," Lore said as the maid put the finishing touches on her upswept hair. "Look Soy, you need to be on your best behavior tonight, especially with the bishop present."

"That old murderous swine will be there? I hadn't thought about that. I hate the way he stares at me."

"He stares that way at everyone."

"Exactly, he's scum. Worse than scum for having Martha killed." She choked on Martha's name.

"You two shouldn't speak so freely," Constance warned, looking around.

"Stop then, this minute," Lore said to Sawyer. "You need to follow my lead, and under no circumstances are you to sneak off and meet you-know-who. Do you hear me? Did you see what happened today?!"

"If I do disappear, no one will notice. Not even you. See you in your buggy," she said and left.

"You've got a problem on your hands with that one, miss," said Constance.

"I've got several."

"A toast," said Emperor Berclay, raising his glass, "to my son and his friends on their academic achievements. And to Gideon and his bride-to-be, our darling, Lorelei."

Fallon raised his glass along with the rest of the party, but his eyes were suspended on her. Lore felt uncomfortable. She smiled and sipped the pink bubbles, playing along with the charade. Gideon tried to look adoring, but his eyes were red and swollen like he'd been weeping.

"Lorelei," the emperor said as though two women hadn't been slaughtered only hours before, "you must be thrilled to be done with the burden of school so you can set up house."

Lore choked on her drink. She watched his personal galatean, Chauncy, a delicate male with silvery blond hair and sea blue eyes, cut his meat for him and sprinkle a special blend of spices on it from a gold filigree box kept in his vest pocket.

"Yes, of course, Your Imperial Majesty. I can't think of anything more sublime than beginning my domestic life."

Next to her, Sawyer attempted to stifle a snort. Lore reached under the table and pinched her leg.

"It is so refreshing to see such demure obedience," Bishop Gerathy interjected, his voice falling in duplicitous notes. "It is a great concern to me and the other bishops that our female population is becoming too...willful." His gaze fell on Sawyer, who preoccupied herself with the stuffed monkfish on her plate. "We are coming to a point where measures must be taken to reinstate the proper balance, given certain past events."

"I couldn't agree more, Your Excellency," Fallon interrupted, "but now is not the time to discuss such matters of state, is it? I think you addressed that enough earlier today. This is the happiest of occasions."

"Yes, of course, Master Berclay," the bishop conceded with a reproachful look.

Lore knew he'd be scolded for speaking to the old man with such condescension, but Fallon didn't seem to fear the emperor's inevitable reprimand.

"Meet us later at Bonne Sante, then, will you, love? We're going for some drinks, but I assume you girls want to change," Gideon said as the dinner tapered off and they bade goodnight to their parents.

"You assume correctly," said Sawyer, who had made it through the evening without saying anything controversial or sneaking off.

Back in her dorm, Lore changed into her best dress – one fringed with real peacock feathers. In the bathroom, she hoped to get a bit of reading in before she had to leave. She felt guilty for not tearing through this material at a faster pace to complete her new education.

"Show your true form."

Within seconds, the suitcase appeared in front of her. She pulled out her recent read, *The True History of the Former United States*, and opened to where she had left off.

It read:

In the past two centuries, natural disasters, pandemics, food shortages, widespread poverty, and violent uprisings around the grossly inequitable wealth distribution have nearly destroyed the United States. Fear opened the door to a succession of increasingly radical leaders. Several rebellions followed and were squelched, but during this time of civil unrest, certain states were allowed to secede. Others were renamed and borders changed. At the end of it, a dictatorial monarchist regime took power. Currently, the former United States is called Vitruvia.

Lore set the book back down, unable to concentrate. At this point in their primping ritual, Sawyer should be banging on the door for her to hurry up. She entered her living room to just Constance tidying up.

"Where is she?"

"She said she'd meet you in your carriage."

Lore knew too well what that meant. Inside her coach, green velvety seats waited for her without Sawyer. She sighed. Sawyer had the nerve to continue an illicit affair with the head bishop in town – even with Martha's blood spilled over the center of the amphitheater – and Lore couldn't do anything about it except hope that her friend came out of the indiscretion with all of her parts intact.

"You know where to go," she ordered Macreedy.

When she arrived at Bonne Sante, Gideon and Fallon were already three drinks deep.

"Where's Soy?" Fallon asked.

Lore rolled her eyes. "Where else? Out playing with fire."

His jaw twitched. "It's almost like she wants Gerathy to catch her, like she's daring him."

"Well, I don't know what else to do with her. She's beyond my control or my influence. Believe me, I've tried talking sense into her."

"You have been a good friend," Gideon slurred, grabbing her hand.

Fallon watched their handholding with a silent bitterness. "Well, aren't you two just adorable?"

Lore scowled at his mockery. Gideon laughed and patted his back.

"We are, aren't we? And I'm so lucky to have you as my best man," he said, hiccupping the last part.

Fallon softened at his friend's genuine sentiment, smiled, and looked away.

"We three have had a fun run of it, eh?" Gideon continued his ramble. "Hey, remember that time in year nine when we were going through military training? You gave Lore your simulator rifle and she shot every one of the yocto-targets in less than thirty seconds. I knew then that I was lucky to be marrying this girl."

"Sure, I remember. She nearly broke my gun."

"It seems like you two have had enough. I'm going to go."

"No, dearest, please don't leave. I'll be better behaved," Gideon pleaded. "Please, I want the three of us to spend time together. Come, love, sit."

"No, I shouldn't have come once Sawyer took off. It breeches decorum for me to be out with you while you're like this, especially with what happened at graduation."

"We're at a secret club, and I'm the heir apparent," Fallon said. "Who the hell is going to find out?"

"I'd rather go so you two can have more time as bachelors."

"Oh fine, I can't argue with you in this state." Gideon rested his head on his arms.

"I'll see you in the morning." She gave Fallon another disapproving look. "Make sure he gets in okay, and shame on you for getting him so drunk. You know he's not like you."

He smirked. "What's got you all upset tonight? Getting cold feet?"

"Do you really need to ask me that?" She bent down close and whispered, "I think you know what's gotten everyone upset, and I can't believe your father just sat there and allowed his authority to be usurped by that wretched piece of excrement masquerading as a man."

He stood, fast and angry, looking around. "Don't you dare speak of my father like that again," he hissed in her ear. "Gerathy works for him, don't forget that. He ordered it to be done that way."

In a flash, Lazarus, Fallon's chief protector, towered over her. The gorilla's red eyes glowed and a fierce growl erupted from the deep recesses of his belly. Yocto-steam blew out of his cavernous nostrils and circled back in.

"No, it's fine." Fallon drew him away. "Lore, friend. Go back."

Though shaken, Lore willed herself to be strong in this moment. When he resumed his place in front of her, she looked into his eyes to see whether or not he approved of such extreme measures. He grabbed the crook of her arm and spoke in a gentler tone, his lips just grazing her ear with intent.

"You know that when I am on the throne, nothing like that will happen. Do you question it?"

She brushed his hand away and spoke with the same resolve as Martha had earlier. "I'm beginning to question everything."

Once again, Lore heard inside voices as she arrived at her door, but she couldn't make them out. For an instant, she debated fleeing since it might be authorities questioning Constance on the whereabouts of Sawyer. If so, it would be the religious police, Vitruvics – vile and menacing sorts recruited by the Bishop from the impoverished lower class. They were rough and usually liked to humiliate when they questioned. She had only ever seen these types of encounters on the street in some of the less desirable areas of the city when she accompanied Sawyer to buy her herbal tonics. Once, she witnessed a young Vitruvic, who looked no more than thirteen, rubbing an old lady's nose on a filthy sidewalk for simply showing too much ankle below the hem of her dress.

"You think anyone wants to see those fat, veined legs, you daft old sow?" he'd jeered, pressing her face into a gutter with his boot as onlookers pretended not to see, or worse, laughed.

That day, Lore had to physically restrain Sawyer from interfering and getting them both apprehended. If the authorities had now come for her friend, she'd have to help misdirect them. She had no idea what Constance knew or might impart, but so far, the maid had proven herself to be a trusted confidante. Slowly, she opened the door.

But the Vitruvics hadn't come. Constance busied herself readying Lore's trunks for tomorrow's journey back home, while Sawyer lounged on a settee like a long blonde gazelle, reading aloud in her husky voice from the book Lore had left unattended in the bathroom.

"Unlike our counterparts in the early 21st century, women today are severely repressed. More than two hundred years ago, women could vote, own property, take multiple lovers and remain single, give birth out of wedlock, take contraceptive measures or terminate an unwanted pregnancy. They engaged in pre- marital sex without fear of being shunned. Considered equals to men, they had a prominent foothold in every major social institution. However, there was still a marked gap between the historic privilege of white women and women of color that remained unrecognized and unremedied in the shadow of white supremacy."

"What do you think you're doing?"

Sawyer and Constance froze and looked up at her.

"What do you think you're doing with these books?" Sawyer brandished the suitcase.

Lore grabbed the book from her. "These are my things. You can't just waltz in here and start using them."

"I know what those are." Sawyer pointed. "Where'd you get them is the question? Do you know how long I've been on the hunt for anything like this?"

"Never mind. It's my business. What are you doing here, anyway? Shouldn't you be out having a dangerously foolish rendezvous?"

"I would, but he's scared while Gerathy is in town, so he cancelled. And I'm making it my business, thank you very much. You go on and on scolding me for being careless. What do you call this? You know how I hate hypocrisy."

"Okay, I made a mistake leaving this out in the open, I admit. But otherwise, it's safe. Watch. 'As you were,'" she commanded, and the three watched the suitcase morph back into a nondescript journal.

"What the devil kind of witchcraft is that?" Constance exclaimed.

"My grandmother left it to me. I've been reading all about True History and it's quite shocking. I feel like for the past twelve years, we've been brainwashed."

"Speak for yourself," Sawyer snorted.

"Maybe not you, but you're the exception. Look at me, I subscribed to all of this: the obedience, the demureness, the acceptance of a marriage I don't want, the unquestioning faith in the emperor. But after today, I don't want to live in a world where I can't write, where I'm considered inferior, where I'm at the mercy of men all the time. Or where even before any of this, it was a world where women like us didn't even stand up for other women. How can anyone ever really be free if that doesn't apply to everyone?"

A familiar sound entered the room, a faint buzzing that then grew louder and ended with a snap. After a puff of smoke, a letter appeared in front of Lore. She snatched it out of the air.

"Who's sending you a manifest so late?" Sawyer gave her a knowing glance.

Fallon had. It read:

My dearest friend,

I hate the way you looked at me tonight, as though I had some part in what transpired at our graduation. Please believe that I did not. Plan to meet me at midnight on the evening of your betrothal dinner in your favorite secret garden. You'll see why.

F

"It's just from my father. He wants us ready at seven o'clock sharp tomorrow morning," Lore lied.

Sawyer regarded her with concern. "So, what's your plan? You want to leave? Escape from your wedding? Try to make it over the Hopespoke border and into Landraven?"

"Miss, do you remember Lottie, the kitchen maid at your parents' house?" Constance asked, her face poised to reveal a great secret.

"Yes, of course. Why?"

"No one knew excepting myself, but she came from Landraven. Her mother had been a maid who'd fled there from another household. She ended up marrying a political leader and had Lottie. A few years back, Lottie's parents died in a violent protest. She said that the members of Parliament are divided there and it's making the masses restless. More and more, the men who come into power want to reinstate laws against women, and there's a rebel group of men who go around wreaking havoc and committing violent acts. So, Lottie came back to Vitruvia for safety."

"What? Willingly come here and work as a servant when you could be free?" Sawyer exclaimed.

"She said that at least here she had a chance. She managed to sneak over the border and sent a manifest to the Seat asking for permission to be placed. The head bishop even met with her for questioning, and she said she told him everything she knew. It seems like a dangerous place, miss."

"It doesn't matter, anyway. I can't run, not after what happened to my grandmother."

"Your grandmother?"

As Lore related the tragic tale of Mathilde without giving away Artemis or his identity, she began to see the hopelessness of her situation. It felt futile to run when the Imperial Guard had the means to hunt anyone down. And breaking a betrothal decree meant harsh punishment for the offender. No, attempting to run seemed like the most foolish thing she could possibly do.

Chapter V

Midnight hung in the air as Lore moved quietly across the still lawn. Her dress, a floor-length gown of mint green silk, rustled against the slumbering blades of grass beneath her slippered feet.

Traditionally, the father of the bride threw the betrothal dinner two nights before the nuptials. Tonight's festivities had already ended, and the entire party planned to remain at the Fetherston Estate for the duration of the wedding weekend.

Lore reached the secret garden, fondly named Alexandra's Way, after her great-great-great grandmother. The entire estate sat on fifty acres of land settled more than four centuries ago by her father's ancestor, Clifford Fetherston, who sat gruffly in portrait in the library. As a child, Lore often escaped to this part of the property to play in the secluded paradise, losing herself in the hidden alcoves, fountains, and wildflowers between its arched canopies and stone walkways.

Just this morning, she had walked there as well and marveled at its daylight scenery. She'd crafted a poem during this brief hour, not scribed on paper, but in her mind while she mused. It seemed to carry something like a sad portent in its words as they unfolded across the sky in front of her.

The Unselfish Heart

No better am I
Than petal to roots.
Though lofty I fly,
A flower that shoots.

I blossom for all,
But you bite through earth,
Protecting my fall
As I bathe in mirth.
Without you beneath
My life force is lost.
I wither in grief,
While you outlast frost.

My love, you and me,
A different pair –
Like flower and bee
Or darkness and fair.
What you seek to steal
I freely bestow.
Since love that is real
Means letting you go.
For an unselfish heart
Knows beauty and pain,
But these clouds will part
And whole we remain.

Small, mesh lanterns floated on the lawn or up in the forest of trees surrounding the estate, their warm glow illuminating the landscape with the alluring whimsy of a fairy revel. These lights also bordered the stone steps leading into this forgotten place. Pausing on the first step during daylight hours in brief meditation, she loved the view of the Boston skyline that this summit afforded.

The dimly lit canopy of this space bathed everything below it in a faint glow. Her footsteps echoed on the stones and a shadow moved in the distance. Lore's heart began its rapid beat once more. What could he possibly have to say to her that hadn't already been said?

"Is it you?" a voice asked, but not Fallon's.

Lore moved further into the darker corner and let her eyes adjust. He stood by her favorite fountain, the one of Juno. This very fountain had inspired her to pick June as her wedding month for good luck.

"Gideon?"

He stepped out towards her, his face pale with surprise. "Lore? Whatever are you doing walking at night?"

"Whom did you think it was?"

"I don't know, my father or Fallon, I suppose." He broke into a grin. "Not my little darling. What are you up to, sneaking around so late?" He took both her hands in his.

Lore reasoned that if Fallon had shown up, he had likely hidden or left, and now might be the time to have an honest conversation with her other best friend and future husband.

"You don't have to pretend so well," she started.

His face fell, not from disappointment, but recognition. "Oh, we're doing this now, then? I'm surprised we haven't done it before."

"I know. It's just that, I do love you. You know that."

"Of course." His eyes were kind and open. "Lore, of all the people on this earth, you're my best friend. And, at least if I have to be made to marry someone, it's you. But I understand what this means for your freedoms, and I am truly sorry. Just know that I will never subjugate you."

"Thank you," she said. "I miss the way we used to be, too. We were so familiar, and now, it's like we aren't even friends anymore. Everything is so formal."

He sighed. "Yes, but part of me thinks this union will be good for both of us."

"How?"

He hesitated. "We can protect each other."

"From what?" Lore couldn't help but wonder if he'd been waiting for someone in the same way she had come here to meet Fallon.

He didn't answer but crinkled his brow in concentration as he decided whether to confide in her.

"You know you can be honest with me."

"If I am…" he began, then fell silent for a moment. "Lore, I know that your heart has always been elsewhere, and I accept that about you. But I–"

Before he could continue, a new set of brisk footfalls sounded on the pavement. Fallon appeared and seemed confused by the sight of them.

"There you are," he said to Gideon, quickly recovering. "I've been looking all over for you. You should get some rest – you and your bride. I didn't realize you had both retreated for some privacy." He smirked at Lore when he said this.

"You caught us," she replied, her sarcasm subtle enough for Gideon to miss.

"Truly, am I interrupting, though?"

"No, no. I'm retiring to bed now. It is late, after all," she said. "Goodnight." She pressed Gideon's hand. "We can finish our talk tomorrow."

"Yes, love, of course. Sweet dreams."

"Goodnight, Fallon."

"'Night, Lore," he said as she moved past him.

She held his eyes, searching for meaning in them, but he stayed guarded in front of Gideon. He smiled politely and bowed. She hoped he would find a way to follow her, so she moved slowly and had made it halfway to the main house when, in the distance, she saw a white mass careening towards her. She stopped. As it got closer, she recognized it as Sawyer, running about in a night dress with her golden locks flying around her head in a crazed tangle of curls. She grasped a manifest in her hand and couldn't control her hysterical tears.

"What is it?" Lore said as her friend halted in front of her, gasping for air between body-shaking sobs.

She handed Lore the crumpled letter before collapsing at her feet. Lore smoothed it out as best she could and held it to the moonlight.

My darling Moonbeam,

I am so heartily sorry for this betrayal, but no longer can I live with the guilt of our sins. For many days now, since the bishop's visit, I've felt as though he knows our secret, as though he has spies in every corner where our frenzied trysts occur.

Instead of waiting in agony for the same punishment delivered to Sisters Fingerton and Rhine, I plan to travel to the Seat tomorrow and confess to him in person. I will never name you. I will destroy all of our manifests, including this, and you should do the same. You have a chance to escape in the meantime, if they should somehow discover your identity. I, however, will take my punishment nobly, and pray that it will be lessened for my honesty.

Forgive me, love. The days I spent with you were the happiest of my life. Be free and Godspeed.

Your Samuel

"He's a fool," cried Sawyer. "You know as well as I do, they can recover manifests. I'll be named."

A knot began once more to form in Lore's stomach, and she knew this demanded immediate action.

"Artemis..." she whispered.

"Who?" asked Sawyer.

"No, hold on. I'm talking to someone. I'll explain to you in a second."

"Lore?" a groggy voice answered.

"I need your help!"

"Of course, what is it?"

As she walked Sawyer back to the house, she relayed their plight to Artemis as quickly and quietly as she could.

"Well, this is it. You have no choice now, Lore. If you want to save your friend, you must run. Grab some nicer men's clothes if you can and come directly to me."

Only moments later, Lore sat in her coach directing Macreedy back to the alleyway in Boston with Sawyer, Constance, her journals, and a bag full of the old suits and shirts her father's valet had planned to donate. Constance watched them from her side of the coach with eyes full of words. Surprisingly, in their desperation, she hadn't given them away; instead, she'd insisted on joining them.

"Constance, what is it?"

"Well, miss, I left out part of Lottie's story. See, there's one thing she didn't share with the bishop."

"What's that?"

Constance leaned in closer to them and lowered her voice even more. "She said there's a lady there who secretly runs things, who's beautiful but terrifying. And, once she casts her spell on someone, they're wrapped around her finger forever. But she maintains a very private profile."

"I've heard of this woman," said Sawyer.

"You have? Where?" Lore prickled that her friend might know something she hadn't shared.

Sawyer shrugged. "In the milliner's shop once, I met a lady visiting from down in the Seat where she runs a boarding house. She told me she knew the woman personally in girlhood. But to me, it sounded too good to be true, like a myth or whatever for women to hold onto. If there really is a woman like that, though, then maybe the rest is true."

"What rest?" Lore asked.

"You mean the Winged Escadrille?" Constance asked.

Sawyer locked eyes with the maid, her face a mixture of incredulity and elation.

"Exactly."

Lore listened while Constance explained what she knew of this mysterious group, but her mind couldn't fully focus. It meandered wildly as though it still wandered through the estate grounds, waiting in the moonlit shadows for Fallon to reach out, take her in his arms and finally kiss her like they've both wanted for so many years. She wondered what poor Gideon would do when he realized she had abandoned him, their wedding, and somehow – most ruefully – their friendship. She wondered if her parents would be too shamed and angry to miss her, even though deep in the pit of her she knew their same sadness and loss.

But in this moment, as she took in Sawyer's grateful expression and felt the scenery of their former lives whipping by them at a breakneck pace, Lore didn't wonder whether or not she had made the right choice in leaving everything behind.

She knew it.

Part Two:
The Winged Escadrille

Chapter VI

Ursula Vandeleur's backstory told that she came from humble beginnings in a small mill town on the edge of Hopespoke bordering Vitruvia. She stood this evening, stately in her gown of crimson silk, and addressed the ballroom in her deep, eloquent voice.

"And now, for the entertainment of our honored guests, I present to you this fantastic spectacle: *The Trojan War.*"

Lore adjusted her elaborate costume and nervous flutters coursed through her. Hushed in the dim lights backstage, they waited for the curtain to open. She caught Avery's eyes and turned hers away. He was staring at her again, Ursula's stepson.

None other than the golden boy of Landraven could be so fitting to play Achilles. Sinewy and handsomely rugged, he stood a few inches past six feet. His eyes, though, wide and gentle, looked at her in such a way that made her heart want to stop beating. But Lore only attributed that to the attachment she assumed came with their experience together. She did not consider it love. And besides, could a person love two people at once?

Lore played opposite him as Briseis, given to Achilles as a concubine after her family and husband died at his hands. Ursula's star pupil, Sawyer, also starred in this production as Helen, the face that launched a thousand ships – and appropriately so, considering all the high-ranking men in the Free State of Hopespoke favored her in the same way the boys at school had. Only here, she could act on all of her urges.

Sawyer's current assignment was Josiah Kilburn. Tall and undeniably handsome, he didn't have the chiseled looks and build of Avery; he possessed a cherubic grace, almost ethereal in his soft mouth and illuminated blue eyes. As the newest and youngest member of Parliament, he'd made his mark as the most conservative and aloof, bringing with him the latest movement of feminine repression. He urged for a reexamination of women's voting patterns, addressing in impassioned speeches their increasing erraticism and fragility. He pontificated on how the structure of society had begun to erode, just as it had in the early 2000s because of the glorification of loose morals and the degradation of family values. Ursula attended all of these sessions but had to remain silent. She started to become visibly unhinged in front of the girls.

She needed someone who could carve her way deep into a man's confidences. While Sawyer may have been artful in this, Lore still worried about her friend's propensity to fall in love. And after weeks, Sawyer couldn't yet confirm his connection to The Society of Gentlemen Against the Rights of Women (SOGATROW), which had become popular throughout the state, especially on the outskirts of Landraven in the poorer villages. There were signs pointing towards this activity in graffiti on buildings and in random acts of violence against women. Sometimes these criminals even branded the acronym SOGATROW into their victims' necks.

The curtain opened, signaling the start of the grand musical. Ursula knew if she kept Parliament diverted with artistic performances and sporting events, they'd be too content to continue their infighting. And those who now comprised the conservative majority would be distracted enough with her girls to avoid upsetting the status quo by passing laws that may prohibit their future pleasure.

None of the men realized the young women attending Ursula's private academy on the grounds of the prime minister's residence, existed, above all else, to bait and trap them. But that's precisely what the Winged Escadrille did. For the last year of Lore's life, she had been trained for such purposes.

There she and Sawyer learned True History, all those years of the former United States they'd been deprived of – the centuries of the wars, unrest, and cataclysms that led to Vitruvia sealing off its borders from most of the world. They learned languages, the sciences, mathematics. They studied academics for twelve consecutive hours three days a week.

They divided the remainder of their time between the liberal arts, military skills, and the art of seduction. Some were excellent singers, others played piano, and others could draw or paint well. Physically they were required to be in the best of shape. And they were all beautiful, yes. Ursula wouldn't accept anyone unattractive. That would defeat the purpose, of course. Before full admittance to the Escadrille, in fact, they underwent additional beautification treatments, permanently removing unwanted body hair or any minor surface imperfections. Sawyer had fought it, but her freckles had to be bleached away. More than mere physical beauty, Ursula looked for something else in each girl taken under her wing – a quality of sorts, a coquetry she said she immediately recognized in both Sawyer and Lore: the ability to make a man want you without so much as trying.

"Your eyes are magnificent," she'd said to Lore during their first private meeting. "They're innocent, but they have that spark as well."

"Spark?" Lore questioned, still nursing the shock of losing Constance.

"Yes, that spark. That spark that says you're innocent, but you can also be naughty."

Ursula stood and moved over to where Lore sat on a tufted chaise. For a woman in her late forties, she carried the taut glow of youth. Shiny chestnut hair framed her heart-shaped face. She had pointy features and her cunning eyes were such an inky brown they seemed black. Tall and long but full in the bosom, she cast an elegant silhouette. But her physical beauty paled when compared to the infectious charm she'd wielded to win over Hopespoke's most powerful men, including her own husband.

She sat close and set a graceful finger underneath Lore's chin, gently turning the latter's face side to side, inspecting it. "Exquisite. Such a delicate silhouette, you have. It reflects the best breeding. I could really use a girl like you. Goodness knows, things are shifting and not in our favor. I need some help turning it around."

Ursula

Ursula stared at a gilded door behind her desk, a tapestry of intricate brass curves topped with an elaborate lock. Lore watched her expression change from pensive and musing to almost enamored, and wondered what secret it held – one too grand to be conceived, it appeared.

"You mean the laws they're trying to pass?"

Ursula turned her attention back on Lore. "First of all, Lorelei, if you're going to be part of this, you must act as though you are nothing more than a pupil at Vandeleur's Preparatory School for Young Ladies. Do you understand?"

"Yes, Miss Ursula."

"Second, as to your previous question, yes." She softened. "I fought during the Great Rebellion, you know. And I didn't just fight for my own rights. I fought for future generations of women – for your rights. I never thought I'd have to fight the same battle again thirty years later." She bent, brushed Lore's hair behind her ear, and kissed her cheek. "So, what do you say, little one? Will you join me?"

"Don't miss your cue like in rehearsal," a voice whispered.

Lore snapped back to attention to find Avery standing close behind her, so close that his breath heated the back of her neck.

"I won't."

He shifted in his plated armor. "I can just tell you're drifting off. What are you thinking of?"

"Nothing."

The stage manager motioned him out from the other wing. He squeezed past Lore, and she could smell his cologne, a citrusy musk. In addition to his good looks, charisma, and mellifluous baritone, he had also just accepted a promotion as head of the Prime Minister's Guard.

Soon, she'd have to join him onstage. She scanned the audience, the insides of her stomach roiling with nerves. All of Parliament had come, and out of the three hundred of them, surprisingly, less than one-third were women. Some of the men brought their spouses to Ursula's lavish affairs, but most came alone.

For this occasion, Ursula had transformed the ballroom into an affluent Grecian city. Urns and columns decorated every corner and carved statues of deities presided over the action like silent beneficiaries. The stage had been constructed in a semicircle that flowed out to immerse the audience in the action. She commissioned only the most up-and-coming young artists to help create these imaginative productions.

A long banquet table, laid with an endless variety of foods, sat along the full length of one wall and rivaled the rest of the elaborate scenery. A towering silver fountain like the one at Bonne Sante held court over everything, continuously flowing with sparkling wine. An array of girls who'd not been cast in the show served hors d'oeuvres wearing topless sheaths, gold jewelry, and their hair up in braids.

Lore wore her own sheath, her modesty protected by a golden breast plate to match the ribbons that wound through her labyrinthine mass of braids and glossy ringlets. But something felt wrong. In the moment before the applause rang out, a strange hush fell over room like a fog cloud as the last note of Avery's song reverberated in the space. Lore looked up to the balconies – empty for this occasion – only to see shadows moving along the walls. She looked back at Avery, who stood frozen through the cheers, focused on a point high above everyone's heads.

He glanced over at Lore and nodded once as a different kind of cue. Lore turned and ran to the back of the stage where the arms were hidden, shouting code to other members of the Escadrille and the Prime Minister's Guard as she passed. Bodies sprang into action like so many moving parts of a machine. They'd had many drills in preparation for an occurrence like this. Members of SOGATROW had infiltrated the prime minister's residence. They were under attack.

"Everyone, get down!" Avery shouted at the audience. A small explosion followed this warning as one of assailants dropped a handmade bomb into the crowd.

Lore grabbed the double-barrel Goliath, Avery's preferred weapon of choice, and his special heat sensor goggles. She took two delicate Renard pistols for herself and the atomic magnifier wristlet.

"Here," she said, handing them to him with her eyes still on the balcony.

He slung the copper goggles over his head and continued his surveillance. In the crowd, Ursula's face burned red with fury, though she ducked into the corner furthest from danger.

"There's two of them." He fired up into the balcony.

Lore held the magnifier up to her eyes and squinted at the balustrades. She couldn't see much of the perpetrators, but she could see enough. One had a bright green streak through his spiked hair, like a skunk. Suddenly, time morphed and her memory placed her back on the border of Hopespoke almost a year ago.

Artemis had already been turning over ideas for a proper escape plan for Lore in the months following her marriage, but their need arose earlier than he had ever anticipated. In fact, the very scenario he'd dreaded had started to play out. Disguising them as wealthy merchants and providing them with a more discreet carriage in place of Macreedy, to whom Lore had bade farewell and sent back to her parents' estate, would have to be the immediate solution.

"There's an area of the Vitruvian border where the energy field is weakest," he instructed them. "It's called the Van der Wall. It's not under guard because no one knows about it except privileged military personnel, specifically the man who happened to engineer the border force." He thumbed his own chest. "I'm just not sure these disguises will do without arousing suspicion on your way there."

He looked glum while observing them in the amber light of his dingy apartment. In truth, Lore thought they looked ridiculous and didn't quite see how this plan would work. Nor did she like the idea of even pretending to be a wealthy merchant, who, from her experience, were the worst kind of people. Fortunately, the caste system of the monarchy barred them from purchasing titles, although they were able to send their children to private schools where they could afford it. At Chersley Bartlett, Lore found the children of merchants to be the most elitist and the cruelest towards servants and anyone considered to be beneath them.

He shook his head. "This isn't going to work."

"What other option do we have at this point?" Lore asked, the ill-fitting top hat slipping down over her eyes. Inwardly, she chided herself for not changing into a more unassuming dress and making Sawyer do the same before they'd left.

"If only I had more time." Artemis looked around the room full of clocks and sighed at the irony.

"Are you working on something?"

"There's something, all right. I'm just not sure it's quite safe yet. I haven't tested it on myself."

"Does it have to do with innocuous concealment?"

"Clever girl."

"Only with humans?"

"Innocuous what?" asked Sawyer, her tone beseeching.

"It's the molecular engineering he uses to disguise the suitcase as the journal."

"How would that work on humans, then? Would we become dogs or something?"

Artemis glanced warily at the ginger cat. She had recently given birth to a litter and guarded her sleeping kittens in a warm corner.

"Close."

Lore still didn't quite remember her time as a kitten, but now it seemed surreal. Artemis drove them the twenty-nine hours to the Van der Wall himself without stopping, only by the grace of a special stimulant he had engineered for such an emergency. The three of them sat in a basket meowing involuntarily and sleeping most of the way.

"This way, if we do happen upon a member of the Vitruvian Guard, they know who I am. I can easily say that I had heard rumors of servants escaping through the entry point and I wanted to see if I could make it more secure," he said, speaking to them as he drove.

The wall itself didn't look like a clear border as Lore had expected. They drove a few miles into a beautiful wooded area, and Artemis pulled the car to a stop. He got out and carried the basket with him for a short while until they reached a low brick wall. The silence of the trees proclaimed the absence of any other human.

"I told you no one knows about this place."

Setting down the basket, he uttered the necessary words. "Show your true form." Suddenly, they were back. Constance immediately vomited.

"That's a normal reaction." Artemis comforted her as she keeled over a second time. "How do you two feel?"

"I'm a little dizzy, but I'll be okay," admitted Lore.

"I feel fine," Sawyer said, smoothing the wrinkles out of her nightgown.

"Well, here you are. Free," he said, giving her a sad smile.

"That's all? We're free once we cross the wall?"

"That's it. Now what you need to do is walk about twenty miles in that direction." He pointed behind her. "It's deep forest, but at the end you'll find yourself on the outskirts of Landraven – the outskirts. That means you shouldn't speak to or interact with anyone until you're safely in the capital center, if you can help it. You'll know when you are. Stay south and you'll run right into it. If you do interact with anyone, under no circumstances should you reveal your real identities or how you came to be here. Say that you're ladies from a neighboring town – Summit or Kent – and that you were visiting a friend."

"Shouldn't we have a weapon?"

"That's the one thing I have so many of and that would be of no use to you here. Hopespoke has its own protection against Vitruvia, should the Seat ever decide to invade. They have engineers who, in recent years, have put up a force field that renders our weaponry unusable. I know that crazy Hawfinch is trying to figure it out, but he's always come up short. Take these, though. They may end up being of more use to you than weapons." He handed her a bag of clumsily made jam sandwiches.

"Artemis, will I still be able to communicate with you?"

The old man shook his head.

"No, not that, either. There's no communication possible between the two countries. There are barriers, but even though I know how to override them, there's always a chance our words could be intercepted. No, Lore, my sweet girl, I sincerely hope to never hear from you or about you again. I will take it as a sign that you survived."

Lore reached over the wall to clasp the old man as tightly as she could. In that time, she pretended to hug everyone she didn't have the chance to say goodbye to – Sister Martha, her parents, Fallon, Gideon, her grandmother. She let go and looked at him once more, understanding fully that he was the last thread connecting her to that world. When she severed this bond, there'd be no return.

"I'm scared to leave you."

His eyes flooded with tears, but his smile offered reassurance.

"Go on then, girl. Saint Lucien be with you."

The morning light painted a hazy pinkish orange across the sky. After what felt like several miles of walking, the way became thicker, branches swept past them, scratching arms, catching on dresses like jagged claws trying to keep them from freedom. The canopy of trees held a cacophony of birdsong, and Lore wondered what sounds may pervade this wood by twilight. Feeling her own exhaustion, she took inventory of her companions. Constance huffed and puffed next to her, and Sawyer had lost her sprightly gait, dragging her feet along the underbrush.

"Perhaps we should stop for a rest? Maybe eat some of these sandwiches?"

She slowed down and noticed that the ground beneath her feet had faded into a pathway of rounded river stones. Moss sprung up between the rocks, defining the way even better in bright patches of green. Then, music started in haunting celestial notes, faint at first, but then swelling into a crescendo as a device wound its way to them from somewhere further down the snaking path. The tiny clockwork owl halted in front of them, and a sign sprung up out of one of its wings that read, "Someone in this wood has noticed you. Please follow me."

Lore hesitated. "What do you think? This could be a trap."

Constance tried to answer her but bent over to vomit again instead.

"It could be. But it could also be someone who might help us," Sawyer offered, picking branches from her uncontrollable nest of hair.

"I could use a rest, miss," Constance managed through heaves.

Lore nodded and followed the owl. It had somehow waited for them to come to a decision, and now turned around and zoomed off towards its home. The river stones ran parallel to a lovely brook trimmed by wildflowers and slightly downhill into a well-concealed valley of tall pines.

The pathway ended in front of a curious stone cottage, its six windows lined with different clockwork creatures – squirrels, birds, chipmunks, foxes. They all cocked their heads as the visitors approached. Smoke blew out of the chimney and made designs in the air, spiraling its way into forms of woodland creatures and flora like it had a mind of its own. Five rocking chairs sat out on the porch.

The owl teetered through a small opening at the base of the front door. They watched as he reappeared in a vacant spot in one of the second story windows. A sign nailed to the wood read, "Come in. We've been expecting you." The intoxicating scent of a proper breakfast lingered in the air and greeted them as Lore gently pushed open the door.

"Hello?"

Sunlight illuminated the two figures milling about in the main room. A middle-aged man bent over the fireplace, turning over sausages in a pan, and a little old lady scooped porridge into bowls. At the sound of Lore's voice, they both looked up and smiled as if she and her companions were long-lost relations.

"Good morning to you, ladies," the man said in a pleasant but reserved tone.

He had bright, clever eyes, but a sadness lingered in his countenance, in the way he drew up his mouth into a smile that seemed also like a frown. To Lore, he seemed vaguely familiar, like a face from an old photograph. He set down the pan on the long, wooden table in the center of the room and approached them with his hand outstretched.

"My name is O, and this is my mother, Em."

"Welcome," said Em in a much more robust manner than Lore had expected.

This older woman had a healthy glow, and a golden light seemed to shine through her brown skin, the complete opposite of her own grandmother's pallid sallowness. Her bone white hair sat in two neat buns behind her ears, and eyes that twinkled like twin stars completed her. This is what freedom looks like, thought Lore.

"How did you know we were here?"

The two glanced at each other.

"We've been living in this forest for decades, see," began O. "We know it so well that nothing escapes our notice."

"That doesn't really answer the question," said Sawyer.

O half-laughed. "Let's just say, we have our ways. And it looked like you needed a good rest and some food. So here we are, offering up our bounty. Will you accept it?"

Lore looked at Sawyer, who nodded, and Constance, who still held her upset stomach.

"I don't think we have much choice because our friend is ill. We certainly appreciate it."

"Can you eat, dear?" Em asked Constance.

The maid looked sick at the sight of the food and then glanced madly about the room. Row upon row of little clockwork creatures lining the walls all the way to the ceiling stared down at them. Sweat began to pour down the sides of Constance's face.

"Come, love. Have a rest. I've a nice bed all made up for you." Em, albeit small in stature, put an arm around Constance and steadied the girl before walking her out of the room.

"Will she be okay?" Lore asked when Em returned.

"Oh, yes. I gave her one of my special tonics and put her to bed. She's burning up with fever, but those herbs will bring it right down. She just needs a day to sleep it off."

"Thank you so much."

"And just what are three young ladies doing in the forest all alone?" Em smiled as she asked this question. "And one of you dressed so fancy, the other dressed for sleep, and the other a maid. It looks a might bit strange, don't you think, O?"

O gave them a quick once over. "Sure does, Mum."

Lore started into her story of Kent like Artemis had instructed, but she could tell from their expressions they weren't convinced. Em shook her head and chortled, showing two deep dimples on either side of her mouth.

"Now, now. Don't be afraid. You can tell us the truth. Are you in trouble? Are you running from something?"

"You could say that," Sawyer admitted. Lore gave her a reproachful look.

"Well, it's not my fault you're a wretched liar," Sawyer shot back. "We escaped from Vitruvia."

Em and O exchanged another look.

"Really, now? Well, that's quite a feat," said Em. "So did we."

"You?" Lore asked.

"Yes, thirty years ago now."

"Why stay so close to the border?" Lore asked.

O laughed. "It may seem like we're close to the border, but technically we aren't."

"What do you mean?"

He smiled at her, warm and easy now, alluding to his own cleverness. "You can't expect us to reveal all our tricks. It's safe to say we've been hidden quite well all these years. How's that for an explanation?"

"That's dog shit," said Sawyer.

"Such words for a young lady," started Em, "in this day and age."

Sawyer shrugged.

"Yes, it's this blatant lack of decorum that warranted our swift departure," said Lore.

"I had quite the trash mouth on me growing up, too. But back then, women spoke freely."

"Back when?" Sawyer nestled herself next to Em on the table bench.

"Oh, way back when women were still free. Me, I'm ninety-one years old. I knew freedom for the first twenty-three years of my life."

"Will you tell us your story?" Lore asked, thinking it might be interesting to record.

"I will, but it's a very long story. Perhaps after breakfast. I think it would benefit you to stay with us for a rest before you go on your way. You seem like you've had a hard time of it."

"Where exactly are you headed?" asked O.

"To Landraven."

"What's your purpose there?"

"To start fresh, I suppose. There's a place we heard about called Leviathan's Flask."

"So, you want to get noticed, then?" he asked, his question curt.

Lore glanced at Sawyer.

He held up his hand. "Please, don't think there's anything you know about that I don't." With those words he left the room.

"Don't mind him. He gets in these moods. He'll go out by the barn and have his thoughts, and at dinner he'll be a new man." The old woman began doling out eggs, sausages, and biscuits.

When they had finished eating, Em perched on a piano bench lined with plum velvet and fringed in golden tassels. The garishly painted upright piano lit up the room in a wild kaleidoscope of flowers. She dusted off the yellowed keys with a bit of her dress and noticed an old picture of herself in a weathered frame resting on top of the instrument. She plucked it down and spun it around to show them, holding it up next to her plump face. A younger version of herself smiled back at them, her dark hair swept up in a bun and a white veil floating like wispy clouds in the air around her. She wore a simple dress of white silk, her shoulders and arms bare.

"I sat for this picture on my wedding day, sixty-eight years ago now." She set it back in its place, and her nimble hands worked the keys into a soft, enchanting tune to accompany her narrative. Clockwork animals from all over the house made their way down from their assigned spots on the walls and arranged themselves around her as she played.

"That same year, Lord Henley came into power. Had I been married any later, I'd have been forced to wear traditional Victorian dress. Instead, I had one month of a normal life before he turned everything upside down. You see, we had lost some rights during the previous two centuries and we all knew it. They took away our right to vote in 2164 when the United States of America became Vitruvia. Back then, there had been brutal wars, famines, illnesses, waves of tornadoes had decimated crops, and what seemed like endless natural disasters vastly decreased the country's footprint from what it used to be. In fact, the entire world had experienced these changes in a similar way.

People were so scared. People were starving, desperate, downtrodden. Social issues became less of a focus when voting in politicians. And so, the conservative majority grew at an alarming rate as True Faith, which you might recognize as the established religion of Vitruvia, began to surface and gain a following. Some think this happened because other religions began to die off and people needed something to believe in. I think it was all because that crackpot Lucien went and got himself martyred. People were just crazy over him for whatever reason – probably because of his handsome face.

"I learned from my mother in my very early years that a hum of protest rang out when the first demi-emperor and his public-elected Council revoked their right to vote. But just a slight rumble. At that point, society felt too collectively grateful for being fed that they didn't have the will to fight this battle. Women were happy to be alive, to have their husbands and their children.

"But life moves in cycles, you see, and slowly things began changing back with the ebb and flow of it. Women could still work and have careers even. We started becoming more active in politics and movements sprung up among both men and women to reestablish a more democratic system. A new generation of suffragettes surfaced like there had been in the years before 1919, myself among them. And then, the Henley Era fell upon us with the new emperor selecting his own Council above the public vote. I have no doubt that, where you're from, you learned how Emperor Henley came to have such a transformative effect on society as a new ruler. To throw a nation into complete cultural upheaval just for his obsession with a past age seems implausible. He accomplished it by igniting a fourth World War. He sealed Vitruvia's borders – no one in and no one out, save for True Faith missionaries. He cut off much of our international trade, keeping just enough with a select few countries. And he pulled us out of all the world organizations, making his burgeoning distrust of our allies quite clear."

"We were taught in school that Orsia attacked us," Lore offered. "They sent cyber bombs into the Seat."

"Humph!" Em paused as she introduced a complicated riff. "I tend to think your own Council staged this attack. In any case, a month after my wedding, my life began to change. My husband, Richard, and I were the children of merchants and both in medical school in New York. Truth be told, I had a bit more talent than my love, but that became irrelevant when I and all the other women in my program were expelled.

"My career options decreased to only one: herbalist. I simply stayed at home waiting for him each day, cooking and cleaning – the way Emperor Henley intended it. We were all made to burn our clothes and adopt the Victorian dress. Each morning, our maid laced me up into a corset so tight it pinched my spine. And the one domestic task required of me above all else, I couldn't perform. Babies. Well, now we know Richard is the one who lacked the means because I had my O later in life – in my second life, I like to call it.

"After Richard became a successful surgeon, he suddenly wanted to open an herbalist boutique in the shopping district for me to run. I obeyed because, at that point, I had no choice. During this time, you see, many men realized that they had the whip hand over their wives. If your wife defied you, in fact, you could lodge a formal complaint with the Council and the religious police would come and punish her as you wished. One of my dear friends, Regina, had been refusing to sleep with her husband because of severe abdominal pains one week. He called in two Vitruvics and had them rape her in front of him to teach her a lesson. She died shortly after from her injuries.

"There used to be a quote long ago, 'Power corrupts; absolute power corrupts absolutely.' Between the emperor and the male population, those initial years of the Henley Era were the hardest for women. And they were doubly hard for me and other women of color – which had been the case in previous decades, unfortunately the ones we were being forced to revisit while burying every inch of racial progress. The Malady, as he called those years between 1910 and the start of his reign, was never to be spoken of. Although, to be sure, just like every other aspect of our freedom as a people and nation, these hateful sentiments had already been bubbling up to the surface with the rest of the tyrannical ambitions. I'm guessing that, as products of your environment, indoctrinated to believe not just your inferiority to men but our inferiority to you, this is a truth of which you may still be unaware. And it will be a brutal truth to learn how women like me have historically been betrayed by our lighter peers."

"We're not entirely ignorant of true history," Lore interjected. "I was gifted some forbidden books and a few mentioned American slavery and the centuries of inequity that continued even after it was abolished."

"I never thought it made any sense that people of color were treated differently," mused Sawyer. "Some are wealthy merchants, sure, but most are confined to the Turbine and the nits. And none are allowed in the Tree Vale. At this point, though, the whole country is so far brainwashed no one knows the truth anymore – save for the very old, and if they speak up, they're just cast off as crazy and thrown in a home or prison."

Em sighed heavily, and Lore imagined she was thinking that could have been her reality had she never escaped.

"I'm shocked they didn't revoke our marriage since Richard was white. But I think they mustn't have cared so much if mixing happened within the lower classes. And besides that, truthfully there weren't enough of us left to be considered a threat to the population. Many had fled after they revoked women's suffrage because it was a signal that our own oppression may return as it were before."

"I'm so sorry, Em," Lore offered, unsure of what else she could say. What could anyone say to ease the burden of such a widespread evil? And what could be done to change it for good this time?

While Lore ruminated, Em continued her story, "So, back to my experience. Richard bought a building in a block of quaint storefronts below and apartments above, and I opened Madame Finglass' Herbal Tonics using my maiden name. And shortly thereafter, my husband, ever pious in his life as a medical surgeon for the True Faith Clinic, began using my business to do illegal operations on young girls and women who found themselves in a family way. He went by the name Dr. Godwit, and he got away with it, too, for decades. I think he paid the Vitruvics to stay away.

"I didn't question his actions. I simply ran my establishment with as much integrity as I could, and I became close friends with Stephen, the man who ran the trinket shop next door." Here she looked over her shoulder and winked at them. "And soon after that, I had O at forty years old. Well, Richard didn't know what to think of it, but it didn't matter. He'd become so embroiled in balancing his double life that it slipped his mind that we were no longer very intimate – though we still had enough contact for him not to question it.

"O became my little helper in the store, and soon enough, he bonded with his real father over their shared passion. Stephen made his living as an engineer of sorts. He built all these little creatures. They look like clockwork, see, but they're programmable automata – less life-like versions of the galateans. He called them maillardets. O had a knack for the programming aspect and the two of them spent hours together in Stephen's workshop.

"Some of the happiest days I spent there were finishing up at my shop, going upstairs to cook dinner, and going back down to the workshop to fetch O, but first peeking in to watch them poring over their work with their heads just touching and such identical concentration. Richard usually arrived home very late, and so I would include Stephen in our dinner plans. As we sat eating and laughing together, it seemed like we were silently agreeing that we three should be a family.

"Of course, when O came of age, I told him. He had never been close with Richard, who always expressed disappointment in the boy's lack of passion for the medical industry. Richard, himself, had become more and more absentminded and clumsy. He had botched a surgery at the hospital that resulted in a death and they forced him to retire. He took this quite hard and told me he would never practice again, including the girls. He could no longer trust his hands, he said.

"One day, a pair of young girls came in together, the younger pregnant by a half-brother. Well, Richard felt so sorry for them he agreed to do it, but he botched it so badly, even with my reluctant supervision, that the poor dear almost bled to death. And that signaled the end for him. Devastated that he had lost his life's skill, he soon lost his will to live. Shortly thereafter, he died – wouldn't eat, wouldn't get out of bed. I tried to comfort him, but he only thanked me for being a good wife and asked me for a special tonic to help him drift off. I complied with his wishes to the last.

"And then, just when the timing aligned for the three of us to be a family, the Great Rebellion happened, but that," she abruptly stopped playing and shut the lid with a snap, "is for another day."

Lore woke in a panic, but the smell of something decadent and full of spices reminded her of the magical place they'd stumbled upon. She began to make out the forms around her. Sawyer slept across from her on the quilt-covered sofa, the sunset shining through the curtains and casting a hot orange glow over her hair. Lore remembered now that Em suggested they take naps while she worked on her tonics in the other room and then prepared dinner.

Swinging her legs around, she inspected the comfortable day dress Em had given her. No corset nor layers of elaborate undergarments pinched her middle and restricted movements. She even liked the rich plum fabric with tiny white and poppy flowers on it, and delighted in discovering its pockets. Someone had also lovingly put her hair in two braids. She stood and admired her reflection in a hallway mirror. A hummingbird maillardet with emerald stones for eyes hovered by her ear, the tiny mechanisms inside it whispering, "Come out to the barn."

She quietly slipped out to the backyard, stopping to smell the variety of roses adorning the bright flower garden. A lone bird fountain cast a crooked silhouette in the middle of the splendor. Off next to the barn stood several beehives, buzzing with activity.

She walked in and the smell of warm wood and animals greeted her along with something else – a pungent blend of smoke and spices. A few goats sat snoozing in a stall to the right. Another stall adjacent harbored a doe-eyed cow. Lore had never seen one up close and approached with care. It didn't seem frightened and instead batted long eyelashes and nuzzled her hand. A silver tag on its pink collar read: Delilah.

To the left, dozens of dusty glass jugs rested on shelves that stretched to the ceiling. On the hay-strewn floor stood a large copper mechanism that looked like a round stove on legs. From the top, a thick pipe connected on one side to a freestanding metal vat. Out of a nozzle at the bottom of the vat, a liquid dripped methodically into a glass jug set below it.

"Up here," a voice descended from a higher point.

She looked up; a ladder next to the stalls led into a hayloft. Lore guessed the rings of smoke being sent into the air above her were from O.

"Can't you come down?"

"I'm comfortable. Why, are you afraid?" He snickered. "Or could it be that you don't think it's appropriate to lumber up into a hayloft with an unfamiliar man?"

"I'm certainly not afraid."

"So, the latter, then. Well, I can assure you, I wouldn't dare try anything because I'm a gentleman and my dear mama raised me in a proper way. Also, poor Delilah there would go mad with jealousy."

Lore laughed.

"Have I set you at ease? Come up, then. Don't be shy."

O lounged on a pile of hay, his suspenders down around his waist, shoes off, and shirt-sleeves rolled up. He held a long, slender pipe of knobby wood and took long swigs from a jug the color of molasses. He offered it to her.

"No, thank you." She sat across from him, though not too close, the straw pricking at her bare legs.

"Please, you must. I make it myself. There's honey in it, molasses, nutmeg, and cinnamon. Just try a sip."

Lore swilled the jug around and sniffed it before sampling the contents. Its sweet burn pleasantly tickled her throat and she had a bit more.

"It's lovely. What do you call it?"

"Woodlock Nine, because it tastes best after nine years." He reclined back on the hay and put his arms behind his head.

"Woodlock," she repeated, trying to recall how she knew this name, the same as she knew his face. He recognized this and nodded at her.

"Come now, you can do it. You're a smart girl."

"Of course! You're Oliver Woodlock, aren't you? There are wanted posters everywhere in Vitruvia with a reward for your capture."

He applauded her. "I'm only trusting you because you seem to be an outlaw of sorts, too."

"I suppose I am. You must spend a lot of time up here."

He snorted. "That's an understatement."

"It's been just you and your mother?"

"No, my father lived with us for much of it. He died a few years back."

"I'm so sorry."

"You know, it's funny. When we fled Vitruvia, I had just turned twenty-one. I had my whole life ahead of me. Now I'm fifty-one and I've accomplished nothing but daydreaming up here in this hayloft of what might have been. Most of the time, I don't mind that – especially considering what happened to bring us here. Fortunately, we've been able to have a peaceful existence."

"Is that why you asked me up here? Because you wanted to tell me something?"

He sat up now, more animated, and looked directly in her eyes. She noticed how young he looked for his age. He barely had wrinkles and his messy dark hair only harbored a few distinguished streaks of gray.

"Yes, to be honest. There's something about you that makes me want to talk. You've this frank little face and big honest eyes just like our cow." He laughed. "But should I tell you what I know? What good would it do, anyway?" He sank back down.

"Maybe it would unburden you, at the very least."

"Are you to be trusted?" he asked the beams of the roof more than her.

"I can promise you that I'll keep what you tell me to myself."

He looked back at her and sighed. "You said you're making your way to Leviathan's Flask, and I asked if you're trying to get noticed. Are you?"

"Yes."

"Well, I know her – the woman you're trying to attract. I'm probably the only person in all of Hopespoke, other than the people who work at that club, who know that's one of her spots."

"Who is she?"

"She's the reason I've hidden in these woods for three decades. She's the reason I'm personally responsible for so many deaths." He pinched his eyes shut like as if to block out an image, then took another long drink.

"How is that possible?"

"I loved her. I would have done anything she'd asked. Back then, I still worked with my father. He ran a trinket shop next to where my mother sold herbal tonics. By trade, he made a living as a toymaker, but to me he was much more – an engineer, a creator. And I, his programmer. I can make any object come to life. You see, there were places in the nit, underground parlors, where people like me got together to have competitions."

"The hummingbird just now – how did you put your voice in it like that?"

"It's just a matter of transferring energy. I can be sitting up here and, through this technique, something near you can be moving." He looked at her. "How do you think God works?"

"God?"

"The Great Creator. How do you think you and I are talking right now? You think we're responsible for what these shells we're trapped in do? No, dear. This is the one true principle I use in my programming. My creations are just like me – they're being controlled from another plane of existence. It's just like how our souls reside somewhere else and can't be harmed by the physical things in this world. Life is breathed into us all from the same divine breath. There's only really one player in this game, see."

"That's an amazing concept."

"It is, isn't it? Well, I became known in this circuit. And soon, I started a group with two friends, Bathorn Claven and Trimble Osprey. We called ourselves Perchloric Octopodia. We were the best cyber pirates of the age. We could hack into any yocto-system and reprogram it for our own purposes. We kept this well-hidden at first, but then Trimble liked to brag, and people began finding out and hitting us with requests. I called it quits for a spell. I didn't want my parents discovering my involvement in something so seedy. And then, she sought me out, this girl. This girl that I had seen once before at my mother's shop.

"She found me hanging around one of those nocturnal cybercades – the interactive billiards – and she took me into a dark corner. 'I know your secret,' she said. 'Instead of telling people, I'll tell you mine because it's better than yours. But only if you promise to help me.' Well, how could I refuse her? She had no idea, but I wouldn't have refused her even if she hadn't shared hers." He looked at Lore now, embarrassed. "'I can't pay you in money,' she said to me, 'but I can give you whatever else you want.' 'I promise,' I muttered. And then she slips this into my hand."

O reached under his pile of hay, pulled out a black mask in the shape of a cat's face, and handed it to Lore. She inspected the item, admiring the painted gold whiskers and pink nose.

O continued, "I knew right away this signified her part in the rebel group. I asked her what she needed of me, and when she made her request, my blood ran cold for I knew the intention behind it. It was murderous. And still, I couldn't refuse her.

"So, on the fifth of January at noon, I hacked into the Starter and reprogrammed all the galateans in the Seat. You see, having a personal galatean marked the elite. It proved to be my greatest challenge, but I did it, and I showed up on that day to witness my genius and then flee with my new love. At first, it worked. We were able to storm Lucien's Basilica during the havoc of the galateans turning on their masters. The leagues of galateans in the Vitruvian and Imperial Guard all now fought in our favor. But then, something happened – something truly terrifying. The engineers in the Seat took back control of the Starter and they programmed the galateans to turn on the crowd. Blood soaked the streets, people screamed, limbless bodies writhed in agony. I began frantically searching for her, knowing she'd gone to the Imperial Chambers. In the second I stopped to catch my breath in front of a window, I saw the carnage on the great lawn –" His voice broke here. "Thousands of them, just killing – killing everyone in the main square, not just the rebels. They pulled innocent people out of their homes and shops and autos. Men, women, children, animals. I zeroed in on one, and I wish I'd never looked, but I made myself look. Along with two others, it had cornered a young family. One held the father in an iron grip while another ripped the baby from its mother's arms – a small baby, probably only a few months old. It threw the baby on the hard ground and stomped on its head, dashing its brains everywhere. At the sight of this, I found myself nearly paralyzed because I knew the grisly reality of what it meant."

"What do you mean?"

"Don't you see? It meant that, all along, the monarchy had this power. You don't just create code like that on a whim. You have it written. The galateans had always been their backup plan in the face of rebellion, and they had the ability to turn them bad just like that – like the flicking of a switch. I should have suspected it. All this death fell to me and, believe me when I say, it has properly haunted me these past thirty years."

"How did you get out of there?"

"I managed to escape, but without her. She had promised to run away with me. She'd whispered such sweet visions of a future during our heated meetings, and, like a fool, I believed her. Of course, these were lies. I returned to New York and explained my sins to my parents. The Seat still hadn't recovered from the decimation, but the emperor's desire for justice took precedence above all else. Rumors told that something of great value to him had been stolen. Broken and vengeful, he intended to find the one who'd hacked into the Starter. He ordered his Vitruvics to comb the regions looking for anyone with that kind of talent. If they ever came across Trimble and Bathorn, I could be named. My mother suggested we make our escape to Hopespoke while we still had a window. On our way down, we heard tales of the rebel leader heading down this way herself.

"We settled here, close to the border to keep tabs on both countries. No one can see us, though. I have a special field up around us. We're seen when we want to be seen. You'd be surprised as to how many people wander through here and give us useful intel. Runaway girls, deserters from the Vitruvian Guard looking for better lives. But some of them we avoid. Some are dangerous and would happily turn me in if they recognized me. There are more and more men coming across as well to join SOGATROW. Even some of the Vitruvian Guard are in on it. I can hear them talking, though they censor themselves even in these woods. Somehow, they find the weak spot in the border and they cross over. Once even, a young maid came through trying to reach Vitruvia. Mother helped her find her way across."

"You mean Lottie?"

"Yes, I believe that's what she called herself. How do you know that?"

"She works at my parents' estate."

"Well, she provided a lot of useful information."

"How did you find out where this woman ended up?"

"Well, we do venture into some of the surrounding towns now and again, the poorer ones, for food and whatnot. We trade wares with some of the people. Not too much because with a Vitruvian warrant for my arrest, it's risky. There are still ways for some to communicate. There are hackers here just like anywhere. And I knew her face, unlike most people, who only saw her in her mask. A few years after we settled here, we went to a great parade in Landraven, disguised ourselves, but I spotted her, and she saw me. If you want to get her attention, all you need to do is walk into Landraven wearing that." He pointed to the mask Lore still held. "It's what I had on that day, and she knew me. Tell her Ollie sent you. She'll take care of you. She owes me that at least."

"Do you still love her?"

"My one mistake was valuing love over my work. I could have used my talents to somehow make the world a better place, but here I am wasting them."

"But do you still love her?"

He took a drag of his pipe and blew a heart of smoke into the air that twisted and danced until it evaporated.

"Does that answer your question?"

They stayed protected with O and Em for two restful days, and Lore found herself quite remiss to leave. Em had made them each another travel frock, packed them some sandwiches, and gave them enough Hopespoke money in case they needed to buy anything. She hugged them as though they were her own granddaughters.

"Remember my advice." O touched her shoulder and then set down the maillardet owl to lead them back to the path.

They walked the remainder of the ten miles in silence, stopping once to eat some sandwiches. Em had cut off the heels of Lore's dress slippers for her, but they were still uncomfortable. Sawyer's bedroom slippers weren't much better. And though Constance found herself able to move at a normal pace, she still didn't feel completely well. After about five hours, they landed on a narrow road lined with a few stores. There weren't many people about, save for one or two passersby. They stood, not speaking, unsure of where to go.

"Miss, I'm powerful hungry," Constance finally said.

Lore scanned the dingy town center. She'd imagined quite a different version of Hopespoke. Where were the scenic towns? The welcoming citizens? This appeared to be an unfriendly and industrial place. By the looks of storefronts and signage, they'd landed in Covent Mills. Up the road, Lore spied an appropriately decrepit diner. The Jolly Sandboys: Grub like the Good Ol' Days, the sign read.

"That seems like as a good a place as any."

A few worker types filled the stools at the counter, sloughing sandwiches, pie, and a black sludge that passed for coffee. The red vinyl booths sat empty save for one.

"Girls, you can sit where you like," an old waitress said, barely looking at them.

They chose a booth near the door. In a corner, Lore could see two young men watching them. They wore Victorian style suits made of studded leather and mesh. One of the men had a shaved head and inkings up his neck, but the other had black hair with a green stripe through the middle of it. He wore eyeliner, which made his electric blue eyes stand out even more. They kept staring until the girls finished eating and lingered out front debating on which way to continue. Suddenly, green hair stood in front of them.

"Hello there." He bowed. "I'm Cage, Cage Mooney. And this is my friend, Zeke Wilderspin."

"I'm Philippa. This is Nelly and Mabel," Lore answered.

"A pleasure." He bowed again. Zeke nodded, but didn't speak.

"We couldn't help but notice that you seem a little out of sorts. Are you lost?"

"We've been visiting a friend and now we're on our way to Landraven," Lore said. If anything, maybe these men could point them in the right direction.

"Landraven, you say?" Cage looked surprised.

"That's right, what of it?" Sawyer asked, cocking her head in defiance.

"Oh, nothing at all. It's just that we can lead you the rest of the way. We're on our way back there and it can be a little confusing and wayward in these small towns. It's not the safest place for women in these parts right now. You may have heard."

"We have."

Cage looked concerned and lowered his voice. "Most of the attacks happen on the outskirts of Landraven, in fact. It's our pleasure to escort you, especially if you want to reach it quickly. Our mode of transport is best." He nodded to two unreal contraptions.

They looked like bulkier versions of some of the scooters people rode in New York. The rims of the wheels were large clock faces with ticking hands. Cage watched her befuddled expression with amusement.

"These are Time Benders. I don't have an extra helmet, but you're welcome to mine." He tossed her a hard leather shell. "Your friends can ride with Zeke. He has the sidecar."

Cage helped her on and situated himself in front of her. "Better hold tight."

And then, they were flying. Lore had never felt this kind of freedom before and, as they wound through the streets, she nearly forgot the danger.

"I need to stop and fuel up," Cage shouted back to her after a while. "These mites burn up like nobody's business."

Lore noticed the barrenness of road; lined by thick woods, nothing existed save for the self-service pump. She tried to ignore her uneasiness.

"Where in Landraven would you like to go?" Cage asked as he refueled.

"We're trying to go to Leviathan's Flask."

He stopped and looked up at her. "How do you know about that place? It's pretty underground."

Lore shrugged, trying to appear innocent. Cage watched her face carefully and rubbed one of his mutton chop sideburns with a gloved hand.

"Where did you say you were from again?"

"I didn't."

"Well, where are you from?"

"Summit."

"Summit?"

She nodded.

"They evacuated Summit last week because of a really violent protest. Several women died at the hands of SOGATROW. You must have known that."

"That's why we were staying with our friend this week," piped in Sawyer.

"Is that so?" Cage turned to her slowly. Zeke stood next to him now and, at once, they both dropped their gentlemanly facades. "You know what I think, Zeke?" Cage said without taking his eyes from them. "I think we've got three little liars standing in front of us – and you know how I feel about liars."

He pulled something from his breast pocket and waved it in front of their faces. Lore could only make out a few of the letters across the top of the badge – S-O-G – before he stuffed it back within the leather folds of his suit.

"We're officers of The Society of Gentlemen Against the Rights of Women. It is our responsibility to detain any female arousing suspicion, especially ones who look like Vitruvian runaways."

Lore glanced at Sawyer for an answer but found a frightened face that mirrored her own. Only Constance, at this moment, sprang into action. She kicked the lanky Zeke in his groin with her hefty leg and then ran in the opposite direction, snatching the keys off of Cage's bike before she did.

"HEY!" he screamed, running after her.

"Take the other bike, miss! Take it!" Constance yelled as Cage caught up with her and kicked her in her back.

Zeke started coming to, and Lore knew she only had an instant to act. She grabbed Sawyer and swung herself onto Zeke's bike. Turning back, she saw Constance's last act of loyalty to her. As Cage grabbed her hair to pull her off the ground, she put the keys in her mouth and swallowed them.

"You bitch!"

Cage's blue eyes lit up with rage and he reached under his tailcoat. The roaring of the engine dulled the pistol shots, but they still sounded in her brain. Sawyer held on tightly and Lore could feel the hot tears spilling on her shoulders while she sped down the road as fast as the machine would go.

In a few more miles, the grayness of the industrial villages melded into more scenic residential neighborhoods, and then, across an arched bridge of steel, Landraven rose out of the mist like a majestic vision. Lore knew she had to survive in this new world – not just for her grandmother and Artemis, but for Constance, her once-nemesis turned savior. A lump rose in her throat as she looked upon this beautiful skyline, wishing the maid were sitting next to her in the sidecar where she belonged. But dwelling on sadness didn't count as a plan, and she needed to form one.

"We need to ditch this bike and buy some new clothes."

"Well, we spent all the money Em gave us on lunch," said Sawyer.

"Then we'll have to try and swap what we have for new things. It shouldn't be too difficult. We still have your pearls – they're real." She reached into her satchel to make sure they hadn't fallen out in the fray. No, they were there, nestled between her journals. Her fingers closed around them.

They decided to leave the bike in a vacant alley, but not before trashing it and slicing its tires with a knife they found in the sidecar compartment. They had to act quickly because the streets ahead seemed bustling with people and activity. Lore could hear music in the distance, the same type of gritty jazz band that played at Bonne Sante.

"In here, this one," Sawyer said, pulling her into a shop called Miss Natasha's.

"Hello, young misses…" said whom they assumed to be none other than Miss Natasha in a bell-like tone before she trailed off awkwardly at the sight of them.

The fashion in Landraven had not escaped the influence of the mandated dress code present in Vitruvia. People looked like hybrids of sorts. Edwardian influence dominated, but with a punk element about it – the edgy hair, leather, gunmetal, and tattoos sported by some. However, in stark contrast, they paired this with a daintier daytime look that included rounded collars, cardigans, and T-strap heels. And the men who didn't look like Victorian pirates dressed in wool slacks, sweater vests, and bowties, three-piece suits, pocket squares, spats, and bowler hats.

Miss Natasha ended up being an empathetic sort who took pity on the obvious refugees. She even sprung for them to be cleaned up at Yoshi's Salon, Spa & Beautification Palace adjacent to her shop before she fitted them with appropriate outfits.

"Do you happen to know where Leviathan's Flask is?" Lore asked as casually as she could.

"Never heard of it," said Miss Natasha, while hovering around her with a steamer to get any last-minute wrinkles out of her petal pink dress.

Outside the shop, Sawyer moved quickly.

"Where are you going?"

"Just follow me and get your cat mask on."

Shops and street peddlers lined Bellamy Boulevard, the main thoroughfare of Landraven. The mood in the air felt celebratory as families dressed in their best – layers of frilly white dresses, lacey parasols, heavily ornamented hats, seersucker suits and spats – cavorted between the different activities. Lore felt this couldn't be the city in its normal state. A large banner sweeping across the width of the street that read, "Landraven Exposition and World's Fair: 2282" soon proved her suspicions to be true. Closer to the center of town, she spied an enormous pavilion set up with columns around it, the people flowing in and out to see the curious exhibitions, inventions, food offerings, and performances.

"Soy, look, it's marvelous!"

Presiding over this grand event, a gargantuan Ferris wheel slowly made its way around so riders could enjoy the sights below. Sawyer paused to appreciate its undeniable majesty, but soon resumed her errand, moving through the streets as though she lived there. In a more congested area, people lined the streets to watch a parade. Someone shouted, "Make way for the prime minister's motorcade!"

Lore fished the rumpled cat mask out of her new satchel, grateful that, like Sawyer's pearls, she had held onto it. She secured the elastic around her face and watched as a sleek, black coach with tinted windows drove past them. People cheered. Some booed. Guards armed with strange weapons marched next to the car. They wore embellished metal helmets with crests that made them look like Spartans. Lore caught the eyes of the young man leading them, and he looked curiously at her through her cat eyes.

The coach slowed almost to a stop by where she and Sawyer stood. A window rolled down and she met another pair of eyes – sharp black ones – only for a second. They narrowed and then the window rolled back up. After the motorcade passed, the crowd dispersed.

"Here it is, Stanhope Street," Sawyer muttered to herself, continuing their journey without missing a beat.

From there, Lore followed as she crossed over to Perch Square. Turning left, she marched down a small, brick alley to a dead end. In the right corner, stairs funneled down.

"Soy, tell me what this is!" Lore asked, quickly following her down to the cryptic violet door.

"It's Leviathan's Flask, dummy."

"How did you find out from her? She wouldn't tell me a thing!"

"Because I know how to talk to shopkeepers." Sawyer smiled and knocked at the door three times long and two times quick.

Someone threw back a slot in the wood and asked, "Who is gently rapping, rapping at my chamber door?"

"'T'is the raven," Sawyer answered.

The heavy door swung open, revealing a shadowy foyer absent of anyone to greet or direct them – even the mysterious voice had vanished. They walked slowly through the cavernous room, lit in an eerie, emerald glow with stone walls and private booths, the music loud and thumping. Lore passed by a sign that stated:

Leviathan's Flask: serving rebels since 2208

They hunkered down into a rounded booth. Lore removed her mask and set it on the table. A portrait of a skeleton with long black hair wearing a deep violet dress hung on the wall above them. Their presence had already been noted.

"Can I join you?" a girlish voice asked.

This girl couldn't have been more than a year or two older than they, but to Lore, she seemed leagues more sophisticated. Her ivory corset had a lace overlay the same deep mauve as her gauzy miniskirt; over this she wore a striking emerald leather jacket and a long cascade of vibrant auburn hair spilled down her back. Creamy stiletto boots buttoned all the way to her mid-thigh. Most luminescent, though, were her glowing bronze complexion and the soft, brown eyes offset by a rosy, bow-shaped mouth.

"Of course." Lore gestured to the cushion next to her.

"I'm Eva Darnay. And you are?"

"I'm Lore. Lorelei Fetherston. And this is Sawyer Hillbury." Lore scanned the room. Artemis had said they could safely share information there. "We came from Vitruvia," she added.

Eva smiled. "Hey, this isn't my first rodeo, sweetheart. I think I know a pair of lost little girls since I was one myself."

"You were? From Vitruvia?"

"Yes, from the Granary – just your typical farmer's daughter in braids and overalls."

"How'd you do it?" Sawyer asked, sipping her fizzy cocktail and then sneezing as bubbles flew up her nose.

"Easy, my father and some of his friends were illegally transporting part of their harvests to Hopespoke when they had enough of a surplus. You know, the farming here isn't as good. Something happened to the soil during the disasters, and it's never been as fertile as it used to be. He had a convenient back-alley deal with the Vitruvian Guard. They'd get a cut and so on. One day, I just got sick of everything and hid myself in a truck full of corn."

"And what happened?"

"I met someone who helped me out, took me under her wing, so to speak."

"This someone. Would you introduce us?" Lore asked.

Eva looked them both over in a calculating way before she answered.

"That's why I'm here. She saw you from the prime minister's car today. She's his wife."

Eva Darnay turned out to be the captain of the Winged Escadrille. Lore wondered if she ever regretted recruiting them since Sawyer went on to steal all of the leads in Ursula's blockbuster productions and Lore...well, technically she hadn't stolen Avery since he swore that he and Eva were never an item. Lore didn't even think it could classify as stealing since no actual romantic relationship existed between them. But Eva did seem to nurse unrequited feelings for the prime minister's son despite his glaringly obvious preference for Lore.

At the present dire moment, none of that mattered and the same Eva had just thrown her the magnifier wristlet. Lore concentrated again on the balcony, but all movement had stopped.

"Avery, let me go up."

"Are you insane?" He peered through his goggles, Goliath poised and ready.

"Please, I know one of them. They're SOGATROW. Remember the story I told you about my maid?"

He glanced sidelong at her. During one of their ordered times together, she had shared more than she wished. But she couldn't help it; he was so easy to confide in.

"They're the ones?"

She nodded. "Please let me go. I won't kill them. I'll incapacitate."

"You'd better, then."

Lore slowly climbed the stairwell leading to the top balcony of the grand ballroom. She paused to listen, but no sound came. A surprise ambush would be to her benefit since Cage may likely die of shock when he saw her. Slower still, she made her way. All those years of sneaking up behind Fallon may have paid off. Her Renards, in addition to being lightweight, were also silent.

Cage sat in the center of a row with his back to her, reloading his weapon. Zeke peeked over the edge, ready to throw another explosive into the crowd below. Lore moved a few rows behind them and crept her way into the middle until she stood only feet from them. She waited a few more seconds.

"You have the vial on you, right?" Zeke asked. She had never heard him speak before and he had one of those voices that didn't fit his looks. High and squeaky, it made him seem like a human rat with his long face and pointy nose.

"Of course, I do." Cage grimaced. Lore could see that Avery's fire had struck him.

She wasted no more time, but rose from the middle of the row, her two Renards pointed with deadly accuracy at her targets.

Chapter VII

"Lore acted with amazing gumption today," Avery said to his stepmother, now once again her cool, composed self.

The attack had ruined the event, but fortunately no members of the Parliament were injured. Ursula stood, still in her crimson gown, her face creased in deep concern. They sat in her private chambers, the large drawing room and library where Lore had first met with her. Her mind wandered back to that initial meeting.

After she'd agreed to be part of the Winged Escadrille, Ursula clued her in to how things worked for the debutantes, as she liked to call the new recruits.

"The other girls might give you a hard time, especially if you're a standout talent in any area. They don't mean any harm by it, and you have to just let it slide off your back or else they'll think you're weak and lose respect for you. Can you handle that?"

Lore nodded, even though doubt washed over her like a soft but constant sprinkling of rain.

"And the other part of this, well, it's a delicate matter. We have to test you in a certain way to see what you're ready to experience and what might need to come at a future date. From the talk I had with Sawyer, I know she can just go straight to work on certain assignments, but you –" She placed a hand on Lore's and smiled in a most maternal way. "You're an innocent, aren't you? A quintessential Vitruvian virgin. Yes?"

Again, Lore nodded.

Ursula sighed. "Well, it's best that your first encounter be with someone most trusted. I will arrange it, and you must trust me and not be afraid. All right?"

Lore thought for a moment and then nodded a third time, secretly wishing she had met with Fallon that night. After all, wouldn't it have been better for her now had she known what it meant to be with a man? Instead, she would be losing her virtue to a stranger instead of someone she loved. And she couldn't risk Ursula's disappointment if she refused. Besides, she knew a little of the ways of love from Sawyer's tales. Her grandmother had also left her some books that weren't entirely informative, at least not in the way of True History. A couple of them brandished covers of men and women in dramatic embraces and described such encounters in great detail so Lore had a decent idea of what should happen.

"Can I ask something?"

"Of course, darling."

"Just to be clear in my purpose here at your school. Am I expected to –"

"My dear, no." Ursula cut her off before she could finish her question. "No. Goodness, that would be a regression of ourselves as women, wouldn't it? Gracious. Let me explain something to you. Hopespoke is a liberated and sovereign country. You may have already heard that it used to be a state called Texas hundreds of years ago when Vitruvia still bore the name of the United States of America. Ironically, Texas had always been quite a conservative state. By the time borders were redrawn and it seceded to become Hopespoke, it had grown to be more liberal, although still not enough to fully benefit our gender. We were free, yes, but in general, treated much like second-class citizens.

"The education system here failed as well, and that is entirely reflected in the ignorance of most. It's an issue that I'm constantly addressing with my husband. My point is, powerful men like those in our Parliament, those who are highly educated and come from old remnants of pedigree dynasties – well, they've never been exposed to such accomplished ladies as those who are my pupils. They'd have to fly to Orsia to find such an anomaly. You see, you girls are rare jewels and you should never have to share yourself with a man in that way to charm him, to win him over, to...extract information. Each of you should be able to do that with the sheer impressiveness of your minds. However, certain scenarios may arise, and you'll need to be prepared. These men, you must realize, are just as dangerous as you are. But the most important thing is that you should never be perceived as anything but a student. I would expect that you use all of your charms to keep up that guise."

Lore nodded, feeling a slight relief, until Ursula asked her next question.

"Speaking of guise," she said, holding up the cat mask, "would you like to tell me how you came to be in possession of this?"

"Yes, I'm sorry. I'm supposed to tell you that Ollie sent us."

At this name, Ursula started. "Ollie? You saw him?"

"Yes, he and his mother helped us after we were left at the border."

"Really? And what did he tell you about me?"

"Nothing."

"Nothing? Not one little thing?"

Ursula examined her like a ripe fruit waiting to be peeled. Lore put on her best dumb face.

"No, he just said if we wanted to get noticed to wear this around Landraven and mention him to you."

"Interesting." Ursula ran her fingers over the mask and smiled a little before she dismissed Lore.

"Well, I hope you're no longer worried about your stay here. All will be well for you, trust me."

Ursula assigned Avery to her. Lore received a manifest from him a few days later telling her to stay behind from that evening's reading hour to wait for him in her apartment.

The girls – as diverse a group as Lore and Sawyer had ever been exposed to – lived in a structure built on the prime minister's grounds called Chambre des Anges. Under Ursula's direction, one of Hopespoke's premier architects had designed it to resemble a grand French chateau. Each girl kept her own modest apartment, which included a bedroom and bath, a small kitchen, a living room, and a balcony overlooking the gardens. Lore and Sawyer easily assimilated to this life since it mimicked their years at Chersley Bartlett, but their new peers made it difficult in other ways at first. The taunting began one day over breakfast.

"So, you're a virgin, eh?" asked Clementine Shotter during the morning of Lore's scheduled encounter. She had deep amber skin, wise green eyes, and spoke in a lilting tone that almost sounded like singing. But otherwise, she seemed standoffish and appraising like the rest of them.

"Yes," Lore answered directly. After all, why lie to them? She avoided Clementine's incredulous look by feigning more interest than she felt in the smoked salmon, avocado, and berries in front of her.

"Well, I'm sure as shit not," interrupted Sawyer, partly to save Lore from more awkward interrogation, but mostly to establish herself within the ranks as quickly as possible.

Clementine exchanged an amused glance with her friend, Jesseny, and then turned back to Sawyer.

"That so? 'Bout how many did you have before you got here?"

"About seven or so."

Lore wondered if she was lying. Either way, Sawyer definitely didn't seem to be making friends with the same agility as usual.

"Or so? What does that mean?" Jesseny asked, braiding her golden hair into a messy fishtail.

"Some of them couldn't get it up for you?" Clementine doled out the punchline, and the table erupted into laughter.

"Funny, how many did you have, then?"

"Nine," Clementine said.

Lore noted a dimness in the girl's eyes when she said this, but Sawyer missed the subtlety.

Instead, she snorted. "Whatever, two of my seven were at the same time."

"Really?" Clementine put her palms at the edge of the table and slowly stood, not taking her eyes off Sawyer. "Because nine of my nine were at the same time."

Sawyer fell silent along with the rest of them. They watched as tears spilled down Clementine's cheeks. After a few moments, she sat with her head in her hands. Eva said nothing but put an arm around her and handed her a glass of water.

"What happened to you?" Lore asked in a small voice.

Forty heads turned to look at her, all wearing the same expression of shock and reproach, as if to collectively say without speaking that you don't question a member of the Escadrille when you're just a debutante.

"How dare you be so insensitive," Eva admonished.

"No, it's okay." Clementine gingerly wiped her eyes. "I've never actually talked about it with any of you. Maybe it's time." She glanced back at Sawyer, who'd been thrown off by the display of emotion. "You want to guess what happened to me, Goldilocks?"

Sawyer shook her head, tears starting to well in her own eyes. Later that day, Lore resurrected her old journal from among her belongings and wrote down as much of Clementine's story as she could remember.

"Nine on one, that's how it goes down sometimes in LaFontaine. It's east of here on the border of Underhill, a place discarded by Vitruvia and secretly helped by Hopespoke, though not enough to make it prosperous." She added the last part so Lore and Sawyer would have a reference point. "Bad things can happen to a girl in a place like that. That's what happened to me one night when I tried to visit my great aunt, who lay dying a slow death in a damp cottage by the water of the Beauchamps inlet.

"The time before that when I'd visited her, she looked at me with strange eyes like she could see into the future. And she said, 'Clementine Dempsey

Shotter, you done paid yo respek to me. Nuff now. If you come again, sum'n bad gon befall you. No mo. You hear me?'

"'Yes ma'am,' I said.

"No one thought she would last the night, but she did. She had a strong spirit. And did I listen to her warning? No, like a fool I wanted to be there when her spirit left her body. I wanted to see if I could witness it happen like in the old stories that my grandmama used to tell me. So, I went. But when I arrived, she had already passed. Her face had turned green and her eyes looked out in front of her, beyond all the mourners, as though she were seeing something beautiful off in the distance.

"On my way home, I remembered her warning from the day before. The streets in this part of town were dark and dotted with several taverns and places of ill repute. Tucked down an alley sat a known whorehouse run by a ruthless woman named Madame Vistoire, and I passed by as quickly as I could. But then, it happened. No sooner had my great aunt's warning shot into my head than I felt a hand close over my mouth and the sharp point of a knife pressed into my ribs.

"'Don't you dare try to bite or scream, whore, or I'll cut out your tongue and break out your teeth with a hammer,' said a voice that my ears recognized. He dragged me behind a building where others waited.

"'I caught one!' the voice rejoiced, and drunken slurs joined in.

"He threw me to the ground and as he kicked me in my side and flipped me over, I recognized him – my brother's best friend, Harlowe. Harlowe had fallen in with a bad crowd of men, the kind who go around stealing and raping, selling drugs, blackmailing. This seemed like an initiation of sorts. Find a whore for them to go at. Only I wasn't a whore from Madame Vistoire's. I was the daughter of a well-known doctor. For a second, I thought Harlowe recognized me, too – that he might let me go. I don't quite know if he did or if he'd drunk too much to realize his mistake. He'd always tried to court me and I rejected him, so maybe this had become a win-win situation for him.

"In any case, after a brief moment of hope, he slapped me so hard across my face I almost blacked out. Later, I wished I had. I wished many things as he threw me onto a dirty mattress next to a dumpster and, one by one, they defiled me. But mostly, I wished to be dead." Clementine paused for a moment in her narrative.

"What happened to them?" Sawyer questioned, rage burning in her face.

Clementine looked up and smiled. "That's just it. Nothing. You see, one of them was the son of the town's judge. And he sentenced them each to a week in jail because he blamed me for loitering outside a known whorehouse late at night when there are drunken men around looking for women. My father also believed me to be at fault and blamed me for ruining his reputation. So, I stole some money from his safe one night and left for Landraven." She looked at Eva and laughed. "Then I met this bad bee and my life has been a cake walk. Sure, there are men to deal with, but most of the time, there's no need for anything but a little flirting if you know how to properly mystify a fellow. They're easily tricked."

"Well," Jesseny interjected, "we can't all wield the voodoo like you do."

"Actually, Ursula has scheduled a test of sorts for me tonight. I received a letter this morning that I should return to my apartment after dinner and wait for him."

"Who is he, cher?" Clementine asked.

"Well, she told me it would be someone trusted. So, it's her stepson, I guess."

Eva's face blanched. "Avery?" she asked slowly. "Are you sure?"

"Yes, the manifest came from him. Why? Is that bad?"

"No." Eva smiled, shot a look at the others, and stood. "It's just fine, Lore. I'm sure you'll have a very pleasant first experience. If you'll all excuse me."

As she walked away, Lore could see her poised expression morph into one of terrified doubt.

"Did I do something wrong?" she whispered across the hushed table to Clementine.

"No child, you're just about to have a rendezvous with the unofficial boyfriend of the Escadrille's captain. That's all."

Lore sat in her living area, unsure of what to expect when Avery arrived. Someone had left a bottle of wine with two glasses and a modest dress for her to wear. Delicate, white lace with a pretty scalloped neckline and capped sleeves made the top half, and then it billowed into a deep pink tulle, ending just above her knees.

She jumped when she heard his timid knock. He stood there, dressed quite casually in a pastel plaid shirt, his sleeves rolled up, and light pants. He looked apologetic, and something in the way he moved and spoke reminded her so much of Fallon – even the light bit of scruff covering his face.

"Good evening."

"Good evening," she answered.

He smiled as if to point out the obvious. "Are you going to invite me in?"

"Of course, please come in."

They sat next to each other on the plush sofa, and Lore tried to steady her hands as she poured the glasses of wine.

"Is this the first time you've had to do something like this for your stepmother?" she asked. She couldn't help it. She wanted to know how many of the girls he had actually been with.

"No. Once before she asked me to," he answered. After a pause, he added, "She only saves me for the special ones."

"I see."

They each sipped their wine. She could feel him sizing her up, but she forced herself to look at him. He had big features – striking wide eyes of muddy hazel that gave him an openness and shone golden in the light; full, well-formed lips; and a solid, straight nose. He'd combed his dark hair back, but the ends curled up like a duck's tail at the nape of his neck.

As Lore admired him, he leaned over, took her wine glass, and set it down. Then, taking her in his arms in one fluid motion, he gently kissed her. She nearly cried from the comfort of such an embrace.

"We don't have to do anything if you don't want to."

"I'm a little nervous."

He smiled and backed away.

"Maybe this time, we can just kiss a bit. And talk a bit. And drink this bottle of wine. What say you?" He freshened her glass.

"Okay. Is it me?"

"Don't be silly, Lore. I just want to know your story. I've been curious about you. I want to know how you got here. So?"

Lore sighed. "It's a long story. First, you tell me something."

"All right, what do you want to know?"

"What was it like growing up with Ursula as a stepmother?"

"Humph," he snorted. "What a question to ask."

"Well, I'm curious. I mean, where I'm from, she's a legend – a myth, really. It must be intimidating to be attached to such a person."

"I suppose, but she came around so early in my childhood that I can't remember life without her. And here, she's not known as a legend. Although, in recent years, some rumors have flown about, but they're mainly treated like radical conspiracy theories."

"So, was she more like a mother to you, then?"

"No, not that, either. She's always been too focused on her career to be maternal."

"Her career?"

"Yes. Sometimes, I think she set her sights on my father more because she wanted to learn from him than that she actually loved him."

"Really?"

"Of course. He had an ideal career and a spotless image. He's beloved by all. She began to emulate him and, as soon as I was old enough, I noticed this about her. She'd study him – his mannerisms, the words he chose. And then, later in the day, I'd see her regurgitating his demeanor with our servants; she was a copycat, a perfect mimic."

"Interesting."

"Yes, and sure enough, she began imitating him so well that he'd just as soon let her lead in his stead. And he did so, in secret, of course."

"How do you mean?"

"Oh, for years he consulted her on every executive decision. It's safe to say that, for the last decade, Ursula has been the true prime minister of Hopespoke – and a great one, at that. But, if anyone ever found out, especially now, it would be an utter disaster for him."

"What a shame."

"Yes, and with the more conservative upswing in our own cabinet, he's muted her influence. She's basically powerless at this point, and it's shaken her to her core. You're witnessing a true nadir in her life."

"I'm sorry to hear it. I have the utmost respect for her."

"And she deserves it, a woman like her who pulled herself up from nothing. But please remember one thing about her."

"What's that?"

"She's a constant observer and always plotting eight steps ahead of everyone else. She never acts arbitrarily. There's always a reason."

They met three other times before anything serious happened. A true gentleman, Avery never pressured her to do anything. But as they shared more of their backgrounds, their interests, their mutual love of writing, Lore found herself wanting something more.

"You should write down your story," he said on this occasion, swilling a glass of scotch and looking irresistible in another colorful plaid shirt. "It's amazing, really. And here, women can be published."

Lore suddenly thought of her journal, not the blank one given to her by Artemis, but the one she had already recorded so much of her story in. The idea that she could freely use her talent here and that Avery had been the one to remind her of this kindled something within her that she hadn't felt since her time with Fallon. It bubbled up inside as a big feeling, but a simple one. Joy. Euphoria. Serenity. This person existed here with her in this moment and, in this moment, in this place, she could also be the person she wanted to be – her truest self. She set her own wine down this time, grasped his face in both hands, and kissed him. He understood this signal.

"Are you sure?"

She kissed him again in answer, slowly and sweetly.

He pulled away. "There are things – things you don't know about me that might change your mind."

"I know all I need to know right now."

He stared at her for another brief second and then reciprocated her kisses, finding her tongue, cradling the nape of her neck to pull her in closer. Suddenly, he scooped her into his arms and carried her to bed.

"She was careless, though," Ursula said now, giving Lore a reproachful look. "She nearly killed them."

"But she didn't. It was brilliant what she did."

"So, what are you suggesting, Avery?" Ursula demanded.

Prime Minister Vandeleur sat touching his little gray beard and allowing his wife to do all the talking. Their argument appeared to have mesmerized him, his white pompadour bobbed back and forth, as though he were at the theater.

"I'm suggesting she be made head of the military unit of the Escadrille. We need our best people up front. Lore has excellent judgment and she's a sure shot. I don't see where the question is."

Ursula waved her hands. "Fine then, Lore can lead the military unit in the Escadrille. That's not the issue here. The issue is, how did they get in? How did they get in, and what were they planning to use on us?"

"It's bio warfare," Avery said. "That's what our scientists told me. It's such a complex agent, in fact, they haven't been able to surmise its intention," he finished.

"SOGATROW. We need to put an end to them." Ursula held her chin as if to force her own mouth closed while she schemed. "I want to know how they were able to cross the barriers here."

"We're still looking into that."

"Look harder."

"A few towns away, there's a place we believe they convene. I think we should send a small group to investigate. The more knowledge we have if they attack again, the better."

"Knowledge is all well and good, but I plan to have the full battalion surrounding this place."

"Dearest," the prime minister began. "You're all riled up. Calm down."

She glared at him with hawk-like perception. "Don't patronize me, Archibald. Say what you mean."

He smiled patiently and continued, as if speaking to a child about to throw a tantrum. "You know we can't have the full battalion surrounding the property. That would be noticed and severely questioned by Parliament. We have our own security, and we have Avery's unit here, but that will be all."

"You would leave us like sitting ducks, then?"

"I hardly think we're that. SOGATROW, from what we've gathered, is nothing more than a few cells of hooligans."

"Clearly not. If two of them were able to get in here with a biological weapon, then I'm afraid we have no idea what else they're capable of or what kind of financial backing they're receiving," she spat.

"That is my final word on the matter, dear. In the meantime, send out some of your girls like Avery suggests. If they uncover more damaging evidence of a valid and severe threat, I'll reconsider how much security is warranted. Now, if you'll excuse me, I would like to have a discussion with my son." He left, ushering Avery out.

Ursula finally sat down. She didn't look happy. In fact, the way her chest heaved up and down like an injured bird surely conveyed the opposite of the calmness she mustered as she regarded Lore and Eva.

"You girls will need to put together a small unit, not too exotic as we don't want to arouse suspicion. I would say it should be the two of you and Jesseny. Sawyer won't be able to go because if Josiah's involved, she'll be recognized, of course. Lore, you can circle back with Avery for his thoughts. Thank you." She stood again and turned to look out on the grounds, her trembling hand lingering on the handle of that mysterious, gilded door.

"You're sure a favorite of his," Eva's voice rang out behind her as they left Ursula to her thoughts.

"Whose?"

Eva now walked up close to her, looking down into her eyes. She tipped her index finger under Lore's chin to appraise her face.

"You know who. I don't blame him. You are quite a pretty, little thing."

Lore sighed. Even though what had happened between her and Avery those months ago hadn't been repeated, she still felt a sense of guilt about it because Eva had always been kind to her. And Eva had her own secrets.

"Don't you ever wonder why you haven't been assigned to anyone?" Eva now asked, still pressing her finger under Lore's chin, letting her nail dig into the soft flesh ever so slightly.

Lore had wondered this and what manner of report Avery had given Ursula. The latter grew colder with her on passing, as though Lore had disappointed in some way and any enthusiasm for her potential abilities had vanished. Clearly, Sawyer had become Ursula's favorite for all of her zealous conquests and valuable information. Lore did excel in military training, though, and that redeemed her to an extent.

But in the same way Sawyer had been placed on a pedestal by Ursula, Avery silently doted on Lore. She blushed when the others pointed out how he watched her during rehearsals, when he paid her a kindness or a compliment, or how their stage kisses seemed like real, passionate ones secretly coveted and hungered for by both.

And poor Eva had begun to fade into the background. Sometimes the girls who had been there before Eva mentioned her rocky beginnings. Soon after she'd been recruited, she disappeared for some months, and then returned as though nothing had happened. This was also the time when she took her place as leader and began to show a true propensity for seduction.

Jesseny confided to Lore one night that Eva's relationship with Ursula had still been shaky since that start six years ago. Not many remembered this because, at that point, members of the original Escadrille like Trixie Webber, Louisa Gunman, and Genevieve Choate were coming of age and marrying. Ursula had grown desperate to reinvigorate the group.

"I have a theory," Jesseny said. She and Clementine had joined Lore on her balcony in the twilight hours of a warm spring eve. Magnolia blossoms drifted in the air around them as they sipped minted lavender tea. "I think she had a baby."

"Mm-hmm," agreed Clementine.

"But we all take contraceptives."

"Sometimes there are accidents," said Jesseny. "I had an accident once and she made me get rid of it. But I think Eva fought her."

"What happened to the child?"

The two girls looked at each other, and Clementine shook her head ever so slightly as if to signal discretion.

"No one knows," said Jesseny. "It's a secret, I guess."

"She ain't the only one with secrets." Clementine looked out in the direction of the prime minister's mansion. "That woman, I will ever be grateful to her, but there's a bit of unnatural something in that office of hers behind that golden door. Every time I'm in there, I feel like the Devil's right on the other side of it."

"Maybe it's a portal to Hell," Lore said, but her friend didn't appreciate the joke.

"Listen, cher, I take this very seriously. I know about these things and I tell you she's got something from the other side in that room. She shuts herself up in there talking with it. And it talks back. Many of us have heard it, but no one has ever had the guts to try and get in there to see what it is."

Lore felt her face growing cold at this story. Maybe the night closing in around them made her wary of this macabre subject. Jesseny quickly changed the subject back to Eva.

"But anyway, Eva, she's beat, we think. She peaked years ago and now she's on her way out. It seems like that's the way she wants it, though."

Lore knew why Eva hadn't taken too much offense at Sawyer's usurping of her throne. Or, at least, she thought she did, and this conversation corroborated her assumption. This discovery happened some months ago as she walked about the vast grounds. An English garden had been planted in one corner, remote like the one on her parents' estate, with wildflowers, stone walkways, and hidden corners. Lore began walking there during her free time, hoping to run into Avery and steal a moment with him, even though part of her fought against that feeling. She needed some closure after what had happened between them – or what hadn't. She wanted to ask him what he'd told Ursula that caused her to become so distant and unimpressed by anything she did. But she also wanted to be alone with him to tell him what she couldn't openly say in front of the others when they were all together during rehearsals or assemblies – that she'd started writing her story, and all of their stories.

While she walked, thoughts of her family, Gideon, and Fallon flooded her mind. She wondered what a world would be like where she could have been close with her parents. Or a world where she could have married Fallon, published her writings freely, and still been best friends with Gideon. She began taking her journal with her and jotting things down, notes about the girls' lives, tidbits they'd shared with her. That day after Clementine splayed out her past on the table for all to see, Lore had become like a human confessional.

She'd been writing about Jesseny's life in the Turbine on the day he approached her. She sat in a stone alcove by a cast iron fountain, scribbling away feverishly:

Jesseny Albright began working in the meat factory at four years old. While other children didn't even begin lower school until a year later, she stood in a line wielding the sharpest of knives to make her quota of cuts. The meat never seemed to stop coming down the line, faster and faster in bloody hunks as the day went into its twelfth hour. People screamed because they ached. The adults, especially the older ones, screamed worse than the children. But one little boy she remembered didn't scream at all, even when he nearly severed his hand.

"I remember his face so well. He had dark hair and eyes, and always a somber expression. Even when his mother still lived, he never screamed nor complained, but worked as fast as he could, sometimes for both of them when she felt weak and needed a break. She was so beautiful, a rare type you don't often see in a place like that. Everyone gossiped about one of the lords being in love with her and fathering her little boy.

"Then one day, she hadn't come in with him. And I asked him about her absence. He just looked at me, looked through me really, with eyes so sad. But he said nothing. That same day, he almost sliced his whole hand off. He didn't make a sound, just looked down at the blood spewing all over him, and then once more at me – right in my eyes. The foreman flew into a rage and dragged him outside. Later that day, after my shift, I went to look for him. His blood still stained the

ground in back of the factory, but he'd vanished. I never screamed again myself after that, even though I had more than one good reason. I never made a sound. But from that day forward, I started to plan my escape."

"Hello," the small voice said.

Lore glanced up, thinking she'd imagined it, but in front of her stood a little boy.

"Hello, who are you?"

"I'm R.J. Who are you?"

"My name is Lore. Do you live here, R.J.?"

He nodded and then pointed to the servants' quarters. "Oh, I see. Your parents are servants here."

"Yes, do you go to Miss Ursula's academy?"

"I do. How old are you?"

"I'm six today."

"Today? Happy Birthday. You're very tall for your age."

He smiled. On closer inspection, she couldn't help noticing his wide golden eyes that were so much like Avery's and the shock of deep auburn hair that hung in those eyes like someone else's she knew. As a thought began to form in her head, Eva came into the alcove and stopped short at the sight of them. She held a mechanical toy train tied with a bow.

"Eva!" R.J. ran to her and wrapped his spindly arms around her middle. "For me?!" He snatched the train.

"Hey, buddy." She bent and kissed his head, her own dark red hair mingling with his. "Happy Birthday."

In that instant, Lore confirmed the hypothesis she'd been forming.

"He's my maid's son," Eva said flatly.

"It's sweet that you remembered his birthday," Lore said, standing. "I'm just leaving."

Now, as Eva still held onto her face, Lore imagined she might be recalling the same moment along with the reality that Lore had kept her secret.

"Look, I didn't mean for anything to happen with Avery," Lore began, "but it's been a year and it only happened once. If he favors me, it's not because of anything I've done. I hope it won't cause a problem between us."

Eva smiled again, only it ended in a frown. "No, we're good. And we have more important things to do."

Chapter VIII

Lore ran as fast as she could, keeping pace with swift Jesseny, while Eva fell behind, clutching her side. The pale outlines of drab, box-shaped residences whirred by in the darkness, and the absence of streetlights gave the night an even more crepuscular presence; only the waning moon cast its ghostly light on gnarled branches and other frightening shapes. Eventually, they reached more rural territory where the buildings stood farther apart, and this made Lore nervous. She thought back to that forest-lined road she had ridden down on the back of Cage's Time Bender.

"Over here!" Jesseny ran up to a house that seemed abandoned. Many of the windows were boarded up or barred; not even a knob graced the door. She halted in the archway, catching her breath while Lore helped Eva.

"You're badly hurt," Lore said, observing the red stain rapidly spreading across Eva's beige satin glove.

"Here." Jesseny pulled off her hair sash and fastened it about Eva's waist. "That should stop it for a little while."

"Thanks."

"Let's go in and see if we can rest for a bit, gather our bearings. It'll be safer to head back out in daylight."

Jesseny cautiously pushed in the door. Moonlight flooded the front hall and another archway opened to a parlor, but the house was far from abandoned. There were people in it, their eerie shadows cast on the walls, the sounds of labored breathing. Chairs lined the room and dark figures sat without making a sound.

"What is this place?" Lore whispered.

"I don't know, but it stinks like horse shit. Here's a light switch."

As Jesseny flicked it on, the living room took on a faint, sallow glow. The women in the chairs and on the tattered couches opened their eyes, startled. They made soft moaning sounds like sad lambs and closed their eyes again. They were all emaciated, like bony specters dressed in hospital gowns that were once white, but now soiled beyond recognition, some of them practically falling apart from the layers of filth. The skin of their arms and legs bore bruises of all shades – from yellowing plum to peacock green; some even had black eyes and bald spots with scars where their hair had been ripped out.

"Shit, look at this." Jesseny had come close enough to one woman to see the letters branded into her neck: SOGATROW.

Lore looked at this poor soul and instantly knew her even though she appeared as a gaunt, skeletal version of her former self with hollow cheeks and dark circles under her eyes.

"Constance?" she murmured.

"You know her?" Eva asked.

"Yes, she worked at my parents' estate. She came here with us. I thought they shot her when we were attacked." She put a hand on the maid's shoulder. "Constance, do you know me? It's Lore."

The eyes looked at her with a spark of knowing but soon went dead again. Lore gently touched her face where a fresh purple bruise made her pale skin even whiter.

"Over here," Jesseny called from across the room.

She had found a kitchen, but it wasn't stocked with food. She leaned into the fridge staring at hundreds of those tiny vials, all nearly full to the brim with an emerald liquid.

"I know what this place is," Lore whispered, terror gripping her stomach again, twisting it around like someone squeezing dirty water from a sponge. "It's a test site for that chemical they have."

"You mean the women they attack, who go missing...they bring them here and give them this?" Jesseny thought out loud.

Eva clenched her fists. "Then they come back and abuse them." She locked eyes with Lore.

A week ago, Lore recorded Eva's full story as they sat planning for the surveillance mission that had gone so horribly awry earlier. When Eva asked about the journal she always carried, Lore read part of an earlier entry to her.

"So, do you want my story?" Eva asked. "I told you I hid in one of my father's black-market corn trucks one day, but that's not all of it."

Lore nodded and Eva went into a long retelling of the following events.

"I lived right over the Hopespoke border in a place called Sully Falls, named after the waterfall in the town center. It was a beautiful town, but we couldn't enjoy it. We were farmers, working like dogs to produce enough food for the gluttons in the Seat and the Tree Vale. That's how everyone felt, really. Sure, sometimes we had our annual dances and we were allowed to celebrate St. Lucien's Day, but mostly, we toiled. Even in the winter, the men set about repairing equipment and the women busied themselves canning the remainders of the season and teaching True Faith to the children.

"My father was a drunk by necessity. They all were. A farmer's life is hard. It's backbreaking work, and then, if your harvest comes up short, there is the threat of fines and punishment — like having your sons drafted to the front lines of the Vitruvian Guard during a time of war with Orsia. That happened to us once and my eldest brother, Trent, never came back. Some people said government had fabricated the war, and they simply killed the young men or used them for testing. They said this mostly because of Johnny Pickford. His daddy came up short one year, and they hauled Johnny off, kicking and screaming. And three months later, he showed up again in the center of town, skinny as a corpse and with strange marks all over his skin. He kept ranting on and on about a lab and a man trying

to suck his soul from his body and put it into a galatean. Of course, his family snatched him up and tried to hide him, but it was no use. The Vitruvics showed up and wasted no time hanging him in the town square, right in front of the lovely falls. They beat him badly, too – beat his face right to a pulp so even his own mother wouldn't have recognized him. And then for good measure, they took the family's next eldest son, leaving only little Hannah.

"So, you can understand the pressure my own father felt, having lost a son already. My brother Trent had been kind and gentle, and my younger brother, Rory, took after him. He even looked like him, same dark blond hair, dimples, gray eyes flecked with dark green. But the other two, Seamus and Carlton, they were right bastards like my old man. And the same way my father would beat on my mother when he drank too much, they would beat on me. Mercilessly, really. And if my mother tried to defend me, they'd ridicule her.

"Rory stuck up for me time and again, knowing they would turn on him. And I didn't want him to be hurt on my account, so I'd often provoke them and refocus the violence my way. Rory did teach me to fight, though. We were both slight, but scrappy. The other two were just big and dumb. Rory knew how to fight. He used to sneak down to the cage-fighting matches some of the men held in secret.

"Then one day, Seamus and Carlton decided to just wail on the both of us. They were drunk and mean for no good reason. The harvest had thrived that year and father was even being kind to mother, not just gruffly civil. We were in the barn brushing the horses when it happened.

"'Look at the two lovebirds in here,' Carlton spat.

"'What nonsense are you spewing now, brother?' Rory set down his brush and grabbed a pitchfork. I could tell he had had enough.

"'Aw, look at this. What you gonna do with that pitchfork, boy?' Seamus taunted, moving closer.

"'I don't rightly know. I was thinkin' of shovin' it up your fat ass, but I know you'd probably like that.'

"And that was it. In a flash they were both on him.

"'Run, Eva! Go!' he yelled. So, I did.

"I looked back once and saw what they had done. Carlton held him while Seamus drove the pitchfork into his stomach. I ran. And when I got to the field, I saw one of father's trucks leaving for the border. The driver wasn't paying any attention, so I scrambled up on the back and buried myself in the corn. I thought, this is my chance, and Rory would want me to take it."

She paused here, wiping the tears away before she continued.

"Before the truck pulled into the warehouse, I managed to jump off. I had heard tales of Hopespoke, of underground places a girl could escape to. We whispered about it in domestic classes at school. So, I immediately found my way there on foot. It took days, but I knew how to be out in the elements. I had pinched a few ears of corn, so I made fires and roasted them. When I finally arrived at Leviathan's Flask, I must have looked a mess. I had on overalls and a filthy plaid shirt. I smelled like horses and dirt, my hair in knots. Patrons gave me the once-over and not in a nice way.

"And then I heard a voice. 'Can I join you?' it said.

"I looked up and saw my first true angel: Trixie Webber. Her signature white-blonde pixie cut had a hot pink stripe running through the left side of it. She sported a short leather jacket over a shiny, pastel pink dress that puffed out around the hem like cotton candy. She emanated dark sweetness, and I immediately wanted to be just like her.

"'Yes,' I answered.

"'You look lost.'

"'I am.'

"'In more ways than one, I bet.'

"'How do you mean?'

"'*Please, this isn't my first rodeo, sweetheart. I think I know a lost, little girl since I was one myself.*'"

"Those are the words I said to you when we first met. I had always wanted to use them, to be like her. She saved me. She brought me to Ursula, and I felt like I'd landed in heaven on earth compared to my former life – like I had been given a second chance. Of course, I was a virgin. Ursula sent Avery to me and…well, you know. I thought I felt something for him, but then I started receiving assignments to other men because he'd recommended me for it. Obviously, he didn't feel what I had felt. And looking back on it, I think I only felt that way because he was my first. This might be the case for you as well, if you have feelings. But it seems like he reciprocates."

Lore didn't dare ask about the months of her disappearance after all that she had divulged.

"I'm not sure what my feelings are, quite honestly," Lore admitted. "There's another boy back home. Someone I can't entirely forget."

"I know how you feel," Eva said, touching her hand. "There was a boy like that back home for me, too."

"What was his name?"

"Johnny Pickford."

Earlier that evening during their surveillance mission, Eva's past caught up with her in such a way that Lore began to fear she'd summoned it by transcribing her story. They had gone undercover to Hephaestus' Den, a gentlemen's club that employed only female servers and an alleged spot frequented by SOGATROW enthusiasts.

Jesseny had once worked there herself and successfully bribed some of the mamzelles, as they were called, into having a night off in exchange for their uniforms. Some wore sexualized gents outfits – cropped jackets with tails over bustiers, cravats, short knickers, top hats, and monocles. Others dressed like demons in corsets, capelets of crimson feathers, and frayed gauzy skirts.

A cavernous building that had once been a railway station housed the club, one intimate lounge winding into another. Dark woods, fireplaces, studded mahogany chairs, bookcases, and billiard tables filled the space along with remnants of the station that hung from the brick walls like industrial nostalgia. Avery and a few of his men had come, too, in their own disguises, mainly dark and plain so they didn't stand out among the crowd. In her naughty gents outfit, Lore could feel him watch her as she walked around passing drinks, and she could see him tense whenever a man tried to grab her. The men there all seemed to be waiting for something to happen. And then the amber lights flickered, and a familiar voice came over a speaker – light, crisp, and condescending.

"Good evening, my good brothers of SOGATROW," it said. "I want to inform you that we've succeeded in infiltrating the prime minister's residence. It seems our men were careless enough to get themselves caught, but the key point is that we have reached initial penetration. It is only a matter of time before we can wage a full overthrow of the government, setting to order this morally orphaned land and reclaiming the pristine life. We shall wait until another of their whorish gatherings of excessive indulgence is planned before we make our next move. All of you will be needed."

Lore nearly dropped her tray of Smoking Satyrs.

"This is your leader, signing off." And then it went silent.

She had heard that voice before. As her mind began to place it, a commotion in her periphery stole it from her. An enormous man had grabbed Eva by the arm. He tried to peer into her face, but his level of inebriation made focusing a challenge.

"Eva?" he growled. "Is this little Eva?" Next to him, another man of equal stature chimed in.

"Well, look who we found, Carlton. Our right little slut of a sis who done run off on our family like a thief in the night." He stood menacingly.

Avery and his men edged over, but Eva didn't need anyone else to save her.

"I knew I'd run into you someday, you monsters," she said coolly. "Tell me, how did you avoid prison after you killed Rory?"

The man whom Lore assumed to be Seamus grinned from ear to ear, showing the brown insides of his rotted mouth.

"No, no, my sweet. You're mistaken, see. You killed poor Rory. You was mad because you tried to seduce him and he wouldn't play your dirty game, so you plowed him with a pitchfork, you did. He told us with his last dying breath. Now what kind of peach goes and does that to her own kin?" He grabbed her roughly. "You're wanted for murder back home, and we'll be the ones to take you there."

"Or not," Jesseny said from next to Lore, throwing a dagger the length of the room that landed squarely in the center of his hand.

He howled in pain as Eva yanked it out and plunged it into his eye. Chaos erupted. Avery's men started a brawl to divert the attention off the girls. One of his larger fellows began flipping over tables. Jesseny had daggers hidden all over her person and moved like a phantom through the throng of men. Lore pulled out her Renards and began aiming for legs, knees, and arms. One man almost caught her around the waist, but a bullet to his foot stopped him.

She could see Carlton bent over Eva. She ducked her way over through the masses of fighting men. He'd taken the knife from his brother's eye and gotten her good in the stomach. He pulled back his arm to strike again when Lore shot him straight through the head. She dragged Eva to her feet, and they ran.

"What's that noise?" Jesseny whispered.

It sounded like they were no longer the only visitors in this terrible place. A chorus of drunken laughter echoed through the house. Lore peeked through the kitchen door and watched as three young men entered the scene, dressed like dandies, only in an overly exaggerated way that seemed ironic.

"Who turned this light on?" one said to the room of women, whose eyes fluttered again like moths.

"All right then, let's check on these birds. Were we supposed to bring food today?"

"Lucien if I know," the second said.

He stopped in front of one young woman and flicked her on the cheek with his dirty fingernail. For good measure, he flicked her again on the other cheek.

"These ones really won't put up a fight, will they?"

"Got no fight left in 'em," the first man said, biting hard on another woman's arm, and then biting down hard on each of her fingertips. The woman didn't move. She just opened her eyes and turned them upward to look at her assailant in the most passive way.

"What should we do?" Jesseny whispered. "This is making me sick."

"We need to get Eva out of here."

Eva was doubled over in pain, the bleeding had seeped through the sash and coated the spaces in between her fingers as she held her side.

"I feel weak," she said through labored breaths.

The third man moved closer to the kitchen. "I'll go get the medicine. You two decide which one we should have our fun with tonight and make sure she's cleaned up a bit."

"Shit."

"Quiet," Jesseny whispered, sidling up next to the door, dagger in hand. As the door swung inward, she grabbed him and slit his throat before he could even make a noise.

"This way." She motioned, dragging him across the floor. "We have to wait until the other two come in here looking for him and get them the same way."

Eva had slumped down and passed out in a corner. Lore panicked, looking around for any kind of feasible exit, but there was nothing. Barred kitchen windows and a bricked-up back door hinted that, perhaps, when they first brought these women here, they needed to be locked in.

"We have to get her out of here, Jess. She's slipping from us every second." Lore knelt and wiped the sweat from Eva's face with a coat sleeve.

"What's all this?"

In a second, the two men had entered the kitchen. Jesseny acted quickly, throwing a knife at the first. It landed in his shoulder. He yanked it out, leering at them.

"What fresh tarts are these?" the first one said. He looked back and forth between them with delight. "You lost? Hmm?" He inched closer, even though Jesseny had her hand poised around another knife. His eyes moved slowly to Lore. "Betcha didn't know what kind of place you was wanderin' into? This is a bad place where bad things happen to little girls."

"Bad things are about to happen to you," Jesseny said, not a note of fear in her voice. "Like what happened to your friend over there." She tilted her head to the corner where they hadn't seen the condition of their mate, who continued to leak red all over the white tile.

"That so?" He eyed them both. "Cedric, you take the lemon tart and I'll have chocolate."

They moved fast. Cedric, broad and bulky, had a heavy chain on him. He whipped it at Jesseny, knocking the knife from her hand and then charging at her. Lore had herself to worry about. The first man had grabbed her by her hair and forced her to her knees.

"I know just what I'll do with you," he sneered, getting behind her. He began tugging at her knickers, leaning with all his weight on her back while he forced his hand to her front to unbutton her pants.

She looked over at Jesseny, now pinned beneath Cedric while he slit open the seams of her trousers with her own knife. Lore tried to remain calm. She had one bullet left, and she knew where she had to put it. The Renard rested in her breast pocket. She slid it out while he continued to pull her hair with one hand and expose her bottom with the other. Her underpants were now down around her knees and he marveled at the unmarred, alabaster skin. Lore thought back to that night with Avery after he'd carried her to her bed.

"I can't," he had said, looking down at her, an unbearable deference in his eyes.

"Why not?"

He hovered above her, his face only inches away. "I don't want to ruin it by taking you this way."

"Ruin what?"

"Us."

"Us?"

"Yes, I want to know everything there is to know about you before we share our bodies. And I want you to know everything about me. I want to crawl into your soul and live there for a while – possibly forever. Do you see?"

"I see. I think that's beautiful."

But for all his initial overtures and ongoing regard for her, he'd still kept a distance between them. And now, on this grimy floor, Lore would know disgrace if this shot wasn't accurate. She tucked her arm between her legs as he readied himself.

"What in bloody hell?" she heard him mutter as he saw the tip of the gun pointing up at him from her nether parts.

Bloody hell is right, she thought, and wasted no time pulling the trigger. His blood spattered all over the dirty white cabinets in front of her like bad art. She sloughed him off to see that Eva had come to and was using all of her strength to beat Cedric. He pushed her back hard and she collapsed against the counter, but Jesseny had reclaimed her knife and plunged it into his gut as he turned his attention back to her.

"Let's get out of here. Help me with her."

Lore refastened her knickers and helped Jesseny carry Eva outside while the women fluttered their eyes again like stationary moths.

"Look, they came in an auto. Let's take it."

They hoisted Eva into the backseat. Lore wanted to grab Constance, too, but couldn't hope to do that and save her friend. She silently vowed to go back there; she would demand it when they arrived home. Holding Eva's head in her lap, she watched the black silhouettes of trees against moonlight casting shadows of light across her beautiful face.

"I never thanked you," Lore spoke, trying to keep Eva from slipping away.

"For what?" came the weak response.

"For saving me – and Sawyer – just like Trixie saved you."

Eva smiled slightly and then her eyes held Lore's with their meaning before she spoke one last time. "Say goodbye to my little boy for me."

Chapter IX

"How could you have done this? You've humiliated me!"

"I recognized his voice. What did you want me to do, hide it until you were able to figure it out?"

"You're wrong, it can't be him. He's in love with me. I almost have him convinced to align with the more liberal side of Parliament."

Lore faced Sawyer in the meadow. They were supposed to be running lines in preparation for the fête of all fêtes that Ursula had arranged to entice SOGATROW into another attack.

Eva had been in the ground only one week and a hush still fell over the entire Chambre des Anges. Her absence was profound. They had gathered around the grave on the day of her burial. Covered in wildflowers, she looked like a beautiful sylvan queen, and they couldn't bear to begin piling the dirt onto her face. Instead they sat together, all the girls, Avery, and some of his men. They read poems and passages that she loved, sang her favorite songs, wept, and consoled one another. Ursula allowed them one day of grieving. She even came for a little while, sporting puffy eyes and maternal loss.

The following day she demanded they begin a rigorous schedule of practice for her newest brainchild production. A marvelous musical presentation of Shakespeare's comedy, *Twelfth Night*, only set during the Roaring Twenties. Lore, now much a favorite, had been cast as the plucky heroine, Viola, opposite Avery's brooding Orsino. Clementine played the beautiful Olivia, and Sawyer had been demoted to the supporting role of Mariah, the maid.

Every light was ablaze when they'd arrived back at the prime minister's residence in the dead of that night, the entire house in a panic over what may have happened to the girls. Avery and his men had escaped with intel enough to prove Lore's suspicions true. Josiah Kilburn, aside from being a mole and poseur, also served as the voice of SOGATROW – and what's worse, he had Sawyer completely fooled. Lore could imagine why.

"And tell me, are you in love with him?" she asked now.

Sawyer looked away.

"This is your problem, Soy. Look at all the trouble you've caused yourself because you fall too hard and too fast. You give your heart away like it's nothing."

"At least I use my heart for its higher purpose and not just to pump blood."

"Eva's dead because of him. I watched her leave the world because of men like him – like the men in that horrible house."

"And you left Constance there."

"You know I would have taken her if I could! Ursula forbade us to go back. I begged her."

Sawyer shrugged and strode away.

"You haven't told him anything about us, have you? About the Escadrille?" Lore shouted after her.

"Don't be stupid," she answered without turning around.

This didn't set Lore at ease. She knew Sawyer and she knew Sawyer's story well, as well as her own. In fact, her friend's tale happened to be the first she'd ever documented in her forbidden journal, now showing its wear and creased from all the openings and closings. That she knew about Sawyer's life remained one of the only reasons she tolerated her friend's capricious behavior.

Sawyer Hillbury is a gorgeous girl, her piece begins. She is one of those girls whom other girls envy but can't help liking despite themselves. It's because she has no idea how beautiful she is, and she does nothing to artificially enhance it. It's because she gets into trouble constantly. It's because she's always in good humor, even when she's not.

It's the reason I'm such good friends with her. And it's also the reason I feel a strong urge to protect her. I always have, since we were little. When someone is that raw and real, you want to protect them. Sawyer is unspoiled, even though by Vitruvian standards, she's mightily corrupted.

I worry for her constantly, though. And sometimes her friendship feels like a duty more than a pleasure. But mostly, it's a pleasure. We are silly together, even in bad times. We often make up words for things, we laugh, and we talk about deep, philosophical issues that no one else I know likes to think about, save Gideon and Fallon. Sawyer doesn't judge. She is open and honest. There are no trifling matters with her, no pettiness. Everything she is and feels is out there.

And that quality of openness about her that I love so much, is dually the source of my concern. But because I know the reason for this is why I protect her. It isn't her fault. Although, many will say that simply because you've had a hard time of it in your youth, that doesn't excuse bad decisions as you grow. Still though, to have a father and be shunned by him, is all the cause of Sawyer's unhappiness.

Her mother died in childbirth and the coldness of several different nannies is what reared Sawyer. None of them understood her unfettered charisma, so they abandoned her. Her father is a vainglorious cad who cared more about his newest velveteen waistcoat than the perennial loneliness of his only child. So, Sawyer sought love in others...in anyone. Especially in men, because with the exception of her father, she never wanted for their attentions.

Aside from some antics with the boys when we were in lower school, the first man to pay her significant attention appeared during her thirteenth year. He ran a laser ink parlor in one of the lower districts. I hated that she would sneak off from school and frequent these seedy parts of town, but I couldn't stop her, so I often accompanied her. At least, after this first circumstance.

His name was Drassilis Rinn Mara. The worker types in the nit were different than those who worked in the factories of the Turbine, Fallon once told me. These types looked down on that kind of forced labor, but they themselves were beyond the compulsory morals of the factory worker. They were freer, grittier sorts.

SAWYER

Drassilis or Drass, as he went by, had Sawyer under a spell from the beginning. So different from any of the boys we went to school with, Drass had hair the color of sand that he wetted and spiked up in sharp peaks. Black ink covered almost every inch of his body. From out of the waist of his trousers, tiny naked women climbed and clawed their way up his torso and also up his arms, each with a name down her back, marking all of his notable conquests: Drusilla, Veronica, Rebekah, Marguerite...the list went on. Further up his torso, they began morphing; their arms and legs took on a serpentine quality until they fully turned to snakes that wound their way up his neck and stopped, their forked tongues rimming his jawline like a permanent beard.

Sawyer had wandered into his studio one day by accident, mistaking it for an herbalist shop. He had been having a slow day and busied himself by perusing a dirty mag. When Sawyer strode in, overconfident for her age, he wasted no time seducing her. After a brief initial banter, he locked the shop, took her in the back, and ordered her to undress. He told Sawyer her unmarred flesh beckoned to him. It had been years since he had seen a naked body with no inkings. Not so naïvely, she obliged him. She knew what would happen, she later told me, but she didn't care. She only wanted to be touched – by anyone. It might as well be this man who embodied everything filthy that people like her father despised and shunned.

He wasn't gentle. Men like him never are, Sawyer says. She's been with a few others of the same ilk, like a moth inching closer and closer to fire until its wings get singed. I wonder if, like my friend, the moths inherently know they're about to get burned and still can't stop themselves. Sawyer was a virgin, had only just gotten her first period a few months earlier, and yet he drove into her without restraint. He bit her all over the flawless skin on her breasts and back.

It hurt the first time, as expected. It hurt worse the second time when what seemed like a fresh wound felt newly opened. By the third time, she grew to like it, to move back against him as he moved in her. She liked the biting. It meant he wanted to claim her as his own, and she allowed it. He taught her things – how to properly pleasure a man with her mouth, how to pleasure herself, how to allow herself to be pleasured. It all made her feel alive, she said. Pain and pleasure mixed made her feel human.

What didn't make her feel human, though, was when he bedded her in his shop and didn't warn her about the presence of his sick three-year-old daughter, who then walked in on them. What didn't make her feel human was when she became pregnant, and Drass went ballistic, forcing her to kill the baby with Madame Claudette's Lunar Pills, which contained a toxic mixture of pennyroyal, tansy, and savin. They worked, though Sawyer was dreadfully sick for three days, and we had to fib and say she had food poisoning on top of bad cramping.

She stopped seeing Drass after that, but he had already done his damage. It makes me think of the people who go to the inking parlors and are covered in designs. There's one instance during their first visit when they're completely bare, and once there's ink, they can never return to that original state. So, they just keep adding compulsively to their collection, as though maybe they can achieve the same type of singular, solid purity if they can cover every inch of their bodies instead. And that's how Sawyer lived after Drass took her innocence. Only the ink wasn't superficial – it had embedded itself into her soul and could never be removed.

Lore walked off in her own direction to the garden where Eva's grave stood. There she found little R.J., staring at the headstone that had since been erected, a simple marker of rose quartz. A single flower sagged in his hand and his little shoulders shook as he wept. Lore put her hand on his shoulder, and he jumped, turning to face her with tears running down his fair cheeks.

"I'm sorry."

But he didn't answer, he only wrapped his arms around her waist and buried his head. Lore instinctively grasped him close and let him cry for a while. When he stopped, he looked up at her with Avery's wide eyes.

"Why did she have to die?" he finally asked.

Lore's heart broke for the innocence in his child's voice even though she had asked herself the same question almost every day since it happened.

"I don't know. Sometimes, there aren't reasons why things happen and they just do. And we don't really need to understand them in order to have feelings about them," she told him, saying the first words that came into her head.

"Oh." He buried his head again.

"Her last words were about you, you know," she offered.

He raised his head. "Really?"

"Yes. She told me to tell you goodbye."

A fresh wave of tears came over him and wetted her dress. She stroked his head. "See, she loved you, R.J. She loved you most of all, and it's okay for you to be sad right now."

He sniffled and looked up at her again.

"Is Lore your real name?" he asked.

"No, Lore stands for Lorelei. What does R.J. stand for?"

"Rory John," he answered shyly.

Lore now felt her own tears spilling down her face as she hugged Eva's little boy, but a movement a few feet away jarred her from it. Avery walked over and took R.J.'s hand, appraising Lore's face in his intense way.

"Your mother has been looking everywhere for you," he said.

"Bye, Lorelei," R.J. said, not taking his eyes from her.

"Bye, then." She bent and kissed his forehead before Avery ushered him away back to the servants' quarters.

Later that night, the trouble began. Lore couldn't sleep and decided to walk about the grounds again. She knew it wasn't entirely safe, but she considered it a kind of informal patrol. Ursula had other officers stationed at key points of entry, possibly even Avery. Here in the garden, she felt a stillness as she moved, an eerie stillness like time had stopped and all the life had been sucked from the air.

In a grouping of spruces a few yards away, she could make out two figures illuminated by the moonlight. At first, she assumed it might be one of the girls having an illicit tryst with a guard, but as she drew nearer, she could see Sawyer's unmistakable golden tendrils as she threw down a large rock and sobbed into her hands. Beneath her, a man lay motionless.

"Sawyer?"

The offender looked up, squinting and unable to control her breath. "Lore...I...he," she gulped through tears.

As Lore entered the clearing, she could see the unconscious man's angelic face that bled from above his right eye. It was Josiah Kilburn. Once again, Lore felt overcome by the instinct to protect Sawyer.

"What have you done?"

"I confronted him about everything. He got so angry. He started to choke me, so I grabbed that rock and hit him. It was the only way I could get him to stop."

"We have to get him out of here."

"How?"

"I have an idea, but we can't get caught."

Minutes later, Sawyer had successfully tempted the young male guard at the garage with an herbal tonic that put him to sleep while Lore removed the cream tarp from the forest green buggy she and Jesseny had used to escape. They had rolled Josiah's body through the wooded area bordering the gardens and to the edge of the private drive that led to the estate. How they would get through the gate would be another matter.

"What are you going to say?"

"Depends who the guard is."

It was Avery and he looked angry as he shone his light on them and approached the car.

"What's the meaning of this, Lore? You know we're under strict guard. How did you even get this auto? Did Lester let you at it?"

"Don't blame Lester. He fell asleep at his post," said Sawyer.

"Avery, I know this seems careless and stupid, but I need you to trust me," Lore pleaded.

He pointed his light in the backseat to see nothing but mustard upholstery. "What are you up to?"

"Please, I need you to trust me."

"And what will I say if anything happens to you? What will I say if someone finds you missing? I'm the only one here who could let you in or out."

"Well, you can't be at your post every second, can you? We'll just be a couple of hours, I promise. No one will even miss us."

"Are you completely mad? It's two o'clock in the morning. Do you really think I would send you out into the night when there are men just waiting to do horrible things to girls on their own? Do you know how unsafe it is?"

"I need to do this. I'm asking you to trust me, as a friend."

"Give me a reason, a good enough reason, or I won't let you out."

Lore sighed. "We're going to rescue Constance."

"That's a foolish idea you've gotten into your head," he sputtered. "It's reckless is what it is, going back to the scene of a crime. The Spokes could have discovered those men by now. They could be on the lookout for this very same auto."

Lore didn't speak. She hadn't considered any of this. Next to her, Sawyer began to break down in a fresh wave of regret and frustration that she tried to conceal by turning the other direction and clasping her hands over her mouth.

"What if," Lore began, wracking her brain for a negotiation point. "What if we took an official coach? No one on the street would dare stop us – not the Spokes, not SOGATROW."

He seemed to give a little, his face softening as he mulled it over. Even Sawyer stopped her crying and looked hopeful.

"Still though," he said, "if something went wrong."

"Avery, please, there has to be a way."

"There is. If I go with you."

"You can't."

"There's something you're not telling me," he said slowly.

"Please, we don't have much time." She wondered when one of the night guards would discover Josiah's body. They had to get it out of there.

Avery pulled his head out of the window and stood back, throwing his arms up. "You're the one wasting it. Let's turn around. I'll have Larkin or Christian cover my post, and we can take one of the coaches."

She looked at Sawyer. The latter shrugged and said, "It's either this or leave a dead body in the woods."

"Okay," Lore told Avery. "But there's something we have to show you once we switch cars."

After they were equipped with a new auto – Avery had decided it might be best to take an unmarked coach – and he had reprimanded them for drugging poor Lester, they pulled onto the drive and took him up the opposite side to the place where they'd dumped Josiah.

"Who the hell is that?" he asked, pointing to the body.

"It's Josiah," answered Sawyer. "He attacked me."

Avery looked at Lore. "And how did you get dragged into this mess?"

"I was out walking, and I came upon them."

"Out walking? In the middle of the night?"

"I do it when I can't sleep."

"Do you even know how bad this looks? This is a member of Parliament!" he yelled. "So, this is your brilliant plan, then? Take him and dump him at the same test site where you just killed three other men?"

"Yes," Lore snapped. "Those other men deserved it and so did this one. Why shouldn't he be dumped there the same way those women were?"

His mouth formed a tight line as he tried to think of any alternative plan that made more sense, but after a moment, he shook his head. "You think he won't be missed? They'll find him and there will be a full investigation."

"Well, then it's a good thing your father runs the country."

He couldn't argue with that.

Lore watched the fire double itself in Constance's eyes as the maid turned to look back at the burning building, watching the months of her torment turn to ashes. Lore held her chapped hand and, every now and then, the maid looked at her, trying to discern. Her senses seemed to be awakening since they pulled her from the wreckage.

It took longer than Lore thought to find the unkempt house again. The fire had only just started when they arrived. It could have been a faulty fuse, or it could have been a SOGATROW-intended arson for the bodies of the three men were gone and only the pink-stained floor spoke of their demise. The women remained, fluttering as they entered. Only when they moved Josiah into one of the back rooms, tied him to a chair, and began to drape a sheet over him, Sawyer noticed the smoke coming from under the doorway of the adjoining room.

"This place is about to go up in flames. We need to get out now," Avery yelled, dropping the sheet.

"I'm not leaving a second time without Constance."

And then Josiah came to. He blinked a bit and looked around until his eyes focused on Sawyer.

"You – you did this, you bitch."

In a second, Avery held a pistol to his head. "You're about to die, Josiah. You have two choices – either burn slowly with the victims you consigned to this hell pit or tell us who you work for and I will mercifully shoot you in the back of the head. What'll it be, then?"

Flames tore through the wall and Josiah smiled at them; his wild eyes lit by the blaze. "I'd rather burn. And my name isn't Josiah. It's Ganymede."

"Suit yourself. Run!" Avery ordered them.

"Constance, she's there!" Lore pointed across the room.

In one fell swoop, he grabbed Constance and slung her over his shoulder. They ran to the car, parked around an unlit corner. Now, as they pulled up to the prime minister's gate, someone waited for them. The silhouette of a tall figure stood against the placid backdrop of a crisp dawn breaking over the estate. As they drew closer, they could see Ursula's face, normally so composed, now looked twisted in anger. She walked around to the driver's side of the car and ducked her head in the window.

"Meet me in my chambers," was all she said before she strode back through the gate.

They drove past her and she continued walking back to the manse, her face once more an unreadable mask.

"Don't blame them. It was my idea to go," Sawyer blurted out moments later.

Ursula ignored her and addressed Avery. "I expected more of you than this," she said.

Lore watched him, unsure of whether or not he would reveal what had transpired.

"With all due respect, Ursula, you have no idea what you're talking about in this case. And it's probably best you remain ignorant to the truth. Just be assured, some matters troubling to you as of late, have been set to rest. Additionally, we rescued Lore's maid from a burning inferno."

"How dare you speak to me like this? Who do you think I am?"

"I think you're my stepmother. Am I incorrect?"

Now she stood, the fingers of each palm splayed out before her. "No, you're not incorrect. But you forget your place, my dear."

Avery stood to face her. "My place is as head of the Prime Minister's Guard. I work for him, not you, Ursula. I think you've forgotten that your place is as his wife. And understand, it's within my duties and my rights to act in whatever way I see fit to protect him, his household, and the people of Hopespoke. What I did tonight, I consider a military action, and that's something I will discuss with my father in the morning. You should be thanking me for preventing your charges from putting his and your reputation at great risk, not treating me like some schoolboy who's gotten himself into mischief." He stormed out.

Ursula moved around to the front of her desk and leaned back against it, appraising them with flashing dark eyes.

"Understand that I'm most displeased, especially with you, Lorelei. Going forward, I want no more shenanigans from either of you. Your maid can have sanctuary here, and we will have someone work with her for rehabilitative purposes. But I expect no more surprises – only unbroken focus on this show. Do you understand?" She enunciated each syllable of her last question.

Lore and Sawyer both nodded.

"Good. I would go get some rest if I were you. It's going to be a long day."

It sounded like hundreds of bombs exploding at once. Lore's eardrums vibrated with the deafening roar as they ran to the windows of the grand ballroom to see the commotion. What she saw when she looked into the vast yard of the estate nearly knocked her backwards. She turned to Avery, who stood next to her at the same window. She could see panic in his face. They weren't prepared for something like this.

"What is this?" she whispered.

"This is the end of us, that's what. But we aren't going down without a fight. Let's go." He turned and ran for the stage to retrieve the artfully hidden weapons.

Lore followed. They had expected an attack similar to the initial strike – disorganized but maybe involving more members of SOGATROW as the meeting had indicated. With their leader, Josiah, mysteriously missing, speculation dictated they may not even make a strike. Never had anyone imagined a full squadron of Eckener atomic zeppelins and flying aces in Hawker planes.

Only two days ago she felt as if she'd reached the pinnacle of happiness. They'd been alternating between rehearsals and military training, and, in one instance, she and Avery had gone to the garden to practice a scene.

"What dost thou know?"

"Too well what love women may to men owe:/ In faith, they are as true of heart as we. /My father had a daughter lov'd a man, /As it might be, perhaps, were I a woman, /I should your lordship."

"And what is her history?" He leaned in closer, placing his hand on the stone wall behind her. His breath smelled like citrus and mint.

"A blank, my lord. She never told her love, /But let concealment, like a worm i' the bud, /Feed on her damask cheek: she pin'd in thought/And with a green and yellow melancholy/She sat like patience on a monument, / Smiling at grief. Was not this love indeed?"

Here he stopped her lines with a kiss. His lips were soft, and she felt a longing when he pulled away.

"Well, that's not in the play," she joked, but he didn't laugh.

He kissed her again. This time she expected it and reciprocated, touching his face, tracing her fingers below his jaw and around to the back of his neck, pulling him closer into her. When the kiss ended, he stepped back and looked at her.

"I'm in love with you. I have been for months – since you arrived here, really." He said this quite seriously.

"But why then, after you'd said you wanted to know everything about me, did you pull back?"

"Ursula – she saw right through my feelings for you and she forbade it. She said being in a relationship with me would distract you from your education and growth. But I think we're past that point now. Lore, do you think you might be in love with me, too?"

"Yes." Only in her lack of hesitation did she realize the true depth of her feelings for him.

Now he held both her hands, kissed them, and grinned from ear to ear.

"Lore, when this is all over, I'm going to ask my father permission to marry you –" He stopped. "That is, do you ever think of marrying me?"

"Yes." Again, her answer came out before she could even think about it.

He kissed her. "We'll go away from this place and have our own house somewhere, maybe out in the countryside. Would you like that? A sweet farmhouse on a nice piece of land? A cottage by the sea?"

"I would love that."

Her happiness glowed upon her like a halo. Even Ursula noticed it during rehearsals and demanded that she focus less on emoting and more on logistics. While this show needed to be a spectacular performance in all respects, just like every preceding production of the Escadrille, each scene also had to be practiced to include their reaction to an attack, which meant rehearsing strategies and drills simultaneously with the acting.

Now, as Lore grabbed her trusted Renards and magnifier wristlet, she thought of how, in just seconds, she'd suddenly been swept so far from that idyllic future with Avery. And this made her furious. The play had ended, the celebration following it wound down, and, thankfully, their outside guests had left – not just members of Parliament, but the upstanding and elite from the community. They'd gathered to have a toast amongst themselves, partly in relief as an attack seemed unlikely at this point.

The planes landed and ladders descended; men spilled out of the machines like swarms of ants. The Escadrille and Avery's men formed a barricade around the side of the prime minister's residence, facing these unknown enemies.

Lore stood with the girls in the center of the ranks, her hands poised on the pistols in their holsters around the low waist of her fringed, sequined dress. She laughed inside, thinking how the pure sight of all these girls dressed as flappers and holding weapons must look to SOGATROW. But no, this couldn't be SOGATROW. She could see the insignia now on the sides of the aircraft. It was the Vitruvian seal, the emperor's emblem. She moved forward, breaking the line, and began approaching a young pilot who walked towards them.

"Lore!" Avery shouted. "Lore, what are you doing? It isn't safe!"

She waved him off and began running to the young man. The pilot stopped as he got a better view of her, removing his goggles. He took off his cap and shook free his familiar nest of blond hair.

"Gideon?!"

"Lore?!"

She ran the rest of the way to him and found herself swallowed up in his embrace.

"Are you ever a sight for sore eyes!" he exclaimed. "What are you doing here?" He took another look at her. "What are you doing with guns?"

"It's a long story. But I'm so happy to see you. You're not SOGATROW."

"SOGA–what?"

The leagues of men behind him had simply formed themselves into ranks and stood motionless until a tall but portly older man, whom Lore recognized as Gideon's father, came forward. General Henry Thaddeus Danaher sported an iconic white moustache that had earned him the nickname "White Walrus" among the officers.

"Great Lucien. Is that you, Lorelei?"

"Just what is the meaning of this?" the prime minister's voice cut in behind them. He and Ursula now approached, along with Avery.

"Might you be Prime Minister Vandeleur?"

"Yes, I am. And who are you, sir, and why has your squadron decided to land on my lawn?"

"I'm Commander Danaher, with the Vitruvian Air Force."

"Vitruvia?" Ursula went white.

"How in the devil did you cross over the borders? We're protected. There are all kinds of shields in place!" he shouted.

"Please, allow my father to explain," interrupted in Gideon.

The White Walrus took that as his cue. "Well, frankly, we've been dabbling with some technology to allow us entry into your country, but it hasn't been for the sinister purposes you might assume. For years, our emperor wished to become allies with you, set aside old feuding, and join forces in order to pose a united front against threats from Orsia. Just recently, we succeeded in breeching your security."

"Where is your emperor then, if he is so anxious to be allies? Why doesn't he come himself?"

"Unfortunately, that's exactly the reason we're here," said Gideon. "The emperor is dead."

Part Three:
The Takeover

Chapter X

"Dead?" Lore whispered. "Then Fallon is to be crowned?"

"Yes," said Gideon, somber now after a hushed conversation with his father. The White Walrus nodded at him to continue. "And you'll be coming with us, Lore."

"Excuse me?" said Avery, stepping forward. "She'll be doing no such thing."

"What is it to you, son?" the prime minister asked.

To Lore's relief, Avery didn't respond. It wouldn't be safe at this point to reveal their plans.

Gideon smiled faintly and turned back to Lore. "Lorelei Henriette Fetherston, you are under arrest for crimes against Vitruvia in breaching Vitruvian marital law and aiding the escape of a criminal."

"Gideon, you can't mean this. We're in Landraven. I have sanctuary here." She looked back to see where Sawyer had gone. Luckily, she was out of sight.

"Excuse me, I'm Ursula Vandeleur, the prime minister's wife. We were anticipating an attack today from an organization known as SOGATROW, which explains our heavy military presence; but your arrival is most shocking. My husband and I would very much appreciate it if you would let us adjourn to the house to discuss these new developments."

Gideon and his father exchanged a glance that said they weren't at all used to women taking the lead in negotiations. Nevertheless, for the good of this new alliance, they each bowed graciously to Ursula.

"Very well, Miss Vandeleur," said the White Walrus under his moustache, "but please ensure that the young lady in question does not leave the property."

"Of course, sir. You have my word." Ursula took Lore by the shoulders and led her party back to the estate.

Ursula paced her chambers with a frenetic energy typical to her usual demeanor while the prime minister, Avery, and Lore watched. In the meantime, Sawyer had sneaked in, still clad in her maid's costume.

Ursula stopped and stared at each of them. Lore imagined if she used one of Jesseny's blades to split Ursula in half, she would see all manner of elaborate cogs and wheels operated by the tiniest of goblins. The mistress looked back and forth from Lore in her fancy dress to Sawyer in her maid's outfit a few times before a slight smile crossed her mouth.

"Lore will have to go," she said.

"Father, you can't possibly allow this!"

"Avery, please. Your stepmother must have a good reason." Archibald looked at her expectantly.

Ursula shrugged. "I don't trust them, that's all, and I want a girl on the inside. Lore is the obvious choice considering her past. But I want another girl accompanying her," she said, eyeing Sawyer again, "as her maid. They won't deny her that. I assume she'll be under some sort of house arrest. It can't be Sawyer because she's already known there. Jesseny will go instead."

"And what will happen to Lore?" Avery asked. He'd been brooding in the doorway.

"We'll eventually get her back. This is temporary, I'm sure." Ursula smiled at her.

"I want to go with her," Sawyer spoke up. "Please."

"It's too dangerous, my dear. You're known there. Infamous, from what you've told me."

"I'll disguise myself. My hair, I'll cut it and dye it. Some of the others can come with me and we can stay with that woman I know in the Seat who owns a boarding house," Sawyer said.

Boarding house. That's right, the woman Sawyer spoke of was the same one who claimed to have grown up around Ursula.

"That's not a half-bad idea. Call a meeting of the Escadrille later today and we will discuss arrangements. Since there's communication possible between the two countries now, I don't think we'll have a problem contacting her. You remember her name?"

"Yes. It's Madame Ermengarde."

Ursula granted her a smile. "Excellent, then. I'll leave it to you to coordinate. As for you, dear Lore, I'm sorry you'll be leaving us, but believe me when I say this is not forever. One of the house maids will pack your belongings, and, in the meantime, I'd like a word with you in private. If you will all please excuse me now, I need to speak with my husband. Lore, wait for me in the hallway. We're going to go for a little walk."

The three exited, leaving Ursula with the prime minister. During the time that Ursula spoke, a kernel of recognition clicked in Lore's mind like a timer, connecting the presence of Vitruvian forces with the death of Josiah Kilburn. As she stood in the hallway, it went off like an alarm in her brain. She hoped to be incorrect, but it didn't seem likely.

Avery was talking to her, grasping her hands. "I won't let them do this to you."

"No," she answered him, though her mind still spun on this one thought. "Don't you see? I have to go. There's no other option."

He looked anxious, desperate. "Lore, tell me you love me."

"I love you."

His eyes filled with worry. "Do you want to go because of Fallon?"

"Of course not. I don't even know that I'll see him. He'll be emperor now."

"He'll need to choose an empress soon. There will be pressure."

"I doubt it will be her, if that's what you're worried about," Sawyer butted in. "Technically, she's a criminal."

Avery threw her a scathing look.

"Avery, I don't know what's going to happen, but I feel compelled to go. I just had a troubling thought." She glanced at Sawyer. "Do you remember what Josiah said right before we had to run?"

Sawyer shook her head.

"He said his name wasn't Josiah, but Ganymede."

"So what?"

"So? Remember Bishop Gerathy and the stories about him? With his young boy servants, all called by that name until they were too old, and he traded them in for younger ones?"

"Oh!" Sawyer exclaimed.

"What?" asked Avery.

"I believe Josiah was working on behalf of Vitruvia, at least on behalf of Bishop Gerathy. They're behind SOGATROW," Lore explained, "and their presence here right now is highly suspicious. I'm not sure if they can be trusted."

"I think this is something you should make my father and Ursula aware of. This is a serious threat," he advised.

"I'll tell Ursula when we take our walk."

"I need to go speak with my men," Avery said. Before he left, he took her face in his hands and kissed her. "Whatever happens, sweet, please think of me."

Lore felt a cloying ache on his departure, an ache that, as usual, she couldn't indulge. She turned to Sawyer, grateful for the distraction.

"You don't have to do this, cut and dye your hair, just because of me."

"Please, I want to. You protected me all those years, the least I can do is make sure you're okay. Besides, I want to get back into Ursula's good graces."

"I'm sure you'll prove yourself worthy."

Sawyer smiled. "I'll go tell the girls."

Lore stood waiting outside the grand door to Ursula's chambers, listening to the rise and fall of the voices inside. There seemed to be a heated symphony of discord between the prime minister and his wife. When he finally flung open the door, he paused to take a handkerchief and wipe the sweat from his brow.

"Good luck to you," he said and stormed off.

Through the crack in the door, Lore could hear muffled voices. She pushed it open, but no one sat at Ursula's desk. The voices drifted from underneath the curious door behind her desk. Lore made out a sentence before she decided she'd better leave.

"Tell me what to do, you're the only one I can trust in the world," pleaded Ursula.

Moments later she emerged, like a carefree butterfly newly coming out of its chrysalis. "There you are. Come now, I want to show you something."

Lore followed her purposeful steps through the darkening night, passing the sleeping army on the lawn. Beyond the garages rose a large building that housed the prime minister's airship, *Cloud Nautilus*, which stood majestic as they entered. But next to it, sat quite another, larger and sinister, made of cast aluminum with an aged brass finish. Carved into every inch of the vehicle, complex and beautiful spider webs wove an eternal web.

"This is *Arachne's Armor*. She hasn't been on her maiden voyage yet. I'm saving that for a very special occasion. But I do come here sometimes and sit in her when I need peace and quiet. Will you join me?"

Lore followed her up the ladder. The interior looked as extravagant as the inside of her manse, each nook and corner decorated with elaborate furniture, tapestries, art. Ursula became looser and more relaxed as she walked, taking on a fluid gate in favor of her usual hurried stomp. She wound her way through hallways, past bedrooms and parlors, until they came to a lounge area, replete with a long mahogany bar. Intimate arrangements of chaises, velveteen sofas, and damask conversation chairs surrounded it, and an elaborate chess table took center stage.

Ursula made her way behind the bar. "What'll it be? Whiskey or wine?"

"Whiskey, please."

"Really? I took you for wine, like me. I'd planned to open this special reserve. It's a very old Bordeaux from hundreds of years ago when part of Orsia still existed as France."

"Wine is fine," Lore said, wandering over to the chess table.

"Do you play?"

"Only a little," she answered. Fallon had taught her when they were sixteen, and after she learned the game pretty well, they made a wager.

"If I win, I get to ask you anything I want, and you have to answer the truth. If you win, you get to ask me," he'd said, staring at her like he knew she would lose and he had something very particular he wanted to ask. Only she didn't lose.

"Checkmate."

His face fell, but he honored their bet. "Ask away, then."

She thought a moment before asking, trying to scour her mind for what she didn't know about him. One matter, he never discussed with them.

"Tell me about your mother."

His eyes flashed at her and she thought he might strike all the pieces onto the floor, but he didn't. Only later, did Lore understand it wasn't anger reflected in them.

"My mother was good-hearted, which made her beloved by everyone in the factory and in our village. She'd go out of her way to help even the lowest of the low. And her inner goodness made her outer beauty even more predominant. A rich man loved her, though I never met him. Sometimes he sent her gifts – impractical indulgences like jewels and furs. She'd sell them and use the money to help the most impoverished in our community.

"She tended to the old and the sick, eased them to sleep or prayed with them in their final hours. Her incessant caretaking of others made her weak and sick herself. My mother was what some might refer to as an angel on earth." He looked up at her with wet eyes. "And she was so good that she had to go back to heaven."

"I'm sorry if my question brought you pain."

"Well, it did." The testiness in his voice melted into mischief with his next request. "And because of that, I think you should answer the question I had for you."

"Oh, really, is that how you're playing it?"

"Playing it? You asked that question of your own free will. I'm merely exploiting your mistake, just like you did mine when I moved my bishop to the wrong square."

"I see how it is."

He laughed. "You know what they say – don't hate the player, hate the game."

"I hate this game, that's for sure, though I could never hate the player."

"You're adorable when you're trapped. Do you know that?" He reached out and grabbed both of her hands over the chessboard, interlacing his fingers with hers.

"Stop it."

"And now you're blushing, even more adorable."

"Ask your bloody question, then."

"Okay." His smile faded and he looked at her for a few moments before speaking, his gaze soft. His question came out in a whisper. "Do you dream of me?"

"What?" she breathed out, suddenly flustered.

"You heard me."

"I mean, in what way?"

He smirked, then grew serious again, staring at their entwined fingers while he spoke.

"In the way I dream of you. Of us – meeting underneath a moonlit sky and running wild together across the Universe; flying through time and space, laughing at the vastness of eternity laid out before us like a cosmic blanket; combing stardust from your hair and kissing it off your lips as we perch in the petaled branches of an indigo tree on a planet all our own. You're in my dreams, Lore, all the time. It's where our souls meet. Don't you remember all these hours of slumber that we've passed in our own blissful half-awake?"

Hot tears forged their way slowly down her cheeks at his poetry. She did recall this gossamer place between sleep and awake, but until now she'd thought it a product of her imagination alone.

"I'll take that as a yes." He gently set down her hands, kissing each one before he did so.

Ursula had just asked her a question.

"Excuse me?"

"I said, would you like to have a game?" She set a brimming glass of wine in front of Lore.

"If you wish. Is there something you wanted to talk to me about?"

"Let's play first and talk later."

"Care to make it interesting?"

Ursula took a long drink, watching her through the duration. "What have you got in mind?"

"If I win, I get to ask you anything I want, and you have to tell me the truth. If you win, you get to ask me."

"I thought you said you only played a little, Miss Lore."

"I do. But this challenge doesn't bother me because I have nothing to hide."

"We all have things to hide, some more than others."

"Then no to the bet?"

"I didn't say that. But there is one question I'll never allow."

"What's that?"

"You must never ask me what's behind the golden door."

The checkmate didn't come as easily as Lore had expected. Even fully intoxicated, Ursula had an unshakable talent for masterminding her moves. But with patience, Lore wore her down. She accomplished this by refilling Ursula's glass and opening a second bottle of the reserve.

"Well then, you may be a very worthy opponent, Lore. I'll make note of that for future reference. Now, what is it that you want to ask me?"

Since Lore couldn't ask the question she truly wished to ask, she thought of the next best thing. "I want your story. Your real story."

"Sometimes it's funny how things work out, isn't it? You see, that's exactly why I brought you here tonight." Ursula slumped against her chair. "Tell me first, though, about this boy Fallon who is to become emperor. Are you in love with him?"

Lore wondered if Ursula had gotten this information from Sawyer or Avery. She guessed Sawyer had divulged the private details of their entire journey in one of her weekly dialogues with the mistress. All the girls were so used to spilling the secrets of others, it would be natural to do so.

"I was. Or thought I was."

"And now?"

"I don't know. I haven't seen him in a year. I suppose I still have love for him. We were childhood friends. Best friends."

"I was in love once, long ago." Ursula's tone grew listless, but she soon recovered. "I will tell you my story, Lore, because what I'm asking of you demands an explanation."

"What are you asking of me?"

Ursula set down her glass and took Lore's face in both hands. "I'm asking you to free Vitruvia."

"And how am I to do that?"

"Help me to claim my rightful place as empress."

"How..." Lore trailed off, but she knew what Ursula meant. It was the same level of heinous as the request she'd made of O all those years before, only somehow worse. "You can't ask me to do that. Not that."

"You're the only one who can get close enough to him. Lore, you could be head of my new Council. Women would be free. They would be able to publish books. There would be no more restrictions. You would be the mother of the new world, replacing St. Lucien. I would make sure of it. Don't you trust me, Lore? Haven't I done right by you and Sawyer? I took you in, I gave you a home, safety, an education. Haven't I done more for you than any man ever has?"

Lore hesitated.

"Maybe then, my story will inspire your allegiance. Let me start from the beginning."

Lore and Jesseny left with the Vitruvian Guard in the dead of that night because Ursula didn't want any fuss or opposition in the morning. They were already going to be in a mess trying to calm the public in the very possible event that this had been leaked to the Hopespoke press by a desperate servant or an unseen, straggling guest.

Before departing, Lore sent two manifests: one to Avery containing overtures of love, and another to Ursula with information on her future location and the astonishing news she'd had from Gideon as his father's airship, *Windspinner*, took off.

"Lore, it's me." He knocked on her chamber door as he unlocked it.

She looked up with reluctance. After her discussion with Ursula, this forced journey home failed to be bittersweet, only bitter, and nothing could ease her burden. What would it be like to be put on trial in front of the entire Council for thwarting her ordained marriage? What might her parents say to her, if they even spoke to her at all? And Fallon, what would he think of her now? But the expression on her former betrothed's face seemed anxious; his eyes held a conspiratorial glow like times in lower school when they'd steal snacks from the school kitchen after curfew.

"What is it? Do you need to handcuff me or something? Locking me in a room isn't enough?"

"Please don't be angry. My father ordered your arrest. He and Mother are still furious at you for what you did. But I have something very important to tell you."

"Speaking of parents, how are mine? Are they all right?"

He screwed up his face. "Were they ever really all right?"

"You haven't earned the right to tease me." She tried to sound firm but couldn't suppress the grin that only he could bring out in her.

"Let's just say your mother is playing her part with the skill of a hundred bad actresses."

"Hey!"

"If your mother were on a stage, it would be so covered with tomatoes that you could make enough ketchup to feed all of Vitruvia."

"What about my father, though?"

He shrugged and grew serious. "He's genuinely sad, lost even. You will have some repairing to do in that respect." He sat down next to her and whispered, "Can I trust you?"

"Of course. You know you can."

"But you're a different person now. I can tell. I knew it when you came running out into the army of an opposing nation with no fear in your face.

Before, you would have never thought of doing such a thing. You're brave, Lore."

"Not really, I just knew Vitruvian weapons wouldn't work here."

"Ha, not true, actually. Old Hawfinch finally figured out how to break through the fields."

"Don't mention that creature."

"He is a creature, but there's also a sad story there."

"There's not a story sad enough to excuse the atrocities he's committed. But yes, you can trust me. I would say that you can trust me even more at this point. I keep the secrets of many others. I'm like a little locked box."

"You must promise not to share this with anyone."

"I promise."

He leaned in even closer, right to the edge of her ear. "I'm leading an underground Resistance against the Seat."

"What?!"

"It's been in the works for some time, but with the emperor's death, now is the time for us to act. Fallon isn't the blood heir."

"You still haven't told me how Emperor Berclay died."

"It seemed like a sudden sickness, a very aggressive virus, but I have suspicions."

She looked into his face. "You know nothing of an organization named SOGATROW? The Society of Gentlemen Against the Rights of Women?"

"No, never heard of it. Why? What are you thinking?"

"Can I trust you?"

"More than anyone."

"It's a group that's been waging attacks against women in areas of Hopespoke. They tried to attack the prime minister's residence and release a type of biological weapon. Then, during a reconnaissance mission, we found a test site full of women who all seemed to be affected by this same agent.

But the man behind it was a new member of Parliament, and before he died, he told us that his real name was Ganymede."

Gideon's blue eyes darkened, and he knew her meaning. "You think the Bishop is behind it?"

"I have a strong feeling. But I don't even know whether those myths about him and his valets are true."

"Oh, they are, Lore. They are. I know that for certain."

"How?"

"Fallon mentioned it once after graduation when he had fully moved into the Imperial Chambers. Bishop Gerathy's quarters are close to those of the emperor, and one day he came across the latest Ganymede. You won't believe who it is."

"Who?"

"Father Hollengarde. What merciful punishment for the dalliance with Sawyer – indentured servitude. I suppose he's lucky Gerathy liked the look of him, otherwise, you know what the outcome could have been."

"This all makes so much sense. Your father said the Seat has been experimenting on cross-border communications for a while – that proves why, doesn't it?"

"Lore," he started, "there's one element in all this you haven't quite explained to me."

"What's that?"

"You and those girls from Ursula's school. You stood out there in the yard as if you were part of the military, fully armed and ready for war. Tell me, what kind of education have you received here?"

Lore sighed and repeated his initial question once more. "Can I trust you?"

"Don't keep asking that when you know the answer."

"It's a bit more than a preparatory school. Perhaps we can help each other. But it would require me sharing what you just told me with a few trusted people."

"If you think so, then I need you to give me full disclosure."

"I will. But first, tell me this. You really aren't sore with me for leaving before our wedding?"

He took her hand. "No, not at all. My only injury was that you didn't tell me. I'd have kept your secret. Hell, I would have come with you. Do you remember that last night when I mentioned us protecting each other?"

"I do."

"Well, I meant that I always knew you loved Fallon. But that was okay, because I never loved you that way, either. You and I, we loved the same person. That night that you found me, I overheard him tell his valet he meant to go for a walk in the garden, and I rushed to get there before him. I had planned to tell him because even if he didn't share my feelings, I needed him to know. When you appeared, I knew that meant he loved you as well and so, I thought it better to just keep my secret where it could do no harm."

Lore let his meaning sink in and felt her heart break twice; once for his pain, once for her own. "Oh Gideon, I had no idea. All those years, I felt like we paraded it in your face, but that maybe you didn't care if you had no real love for me. This is much worse – you did care."

"No matter. You know," he whispered, "I thought Sister Martha's murder happened because of me. Earlier that year, she found me crying and she knew why. She knew what I was. I had always been so ashamed of the way I felt inside. And she took my face in her hands and said, 'I hope someday you and I can live in a world where it's okay to be us.' I swear to Lucien I could feel some presence, some yocto-spy. So, I said, 'I'm sure I don't know what you mean, Sister.' And then, at graduation, they were shot."

"I'm sorry." She hugged him. "That couldn't have been your fault. And I'm sorry about Fallon."

"It's fine, and it's not the case anymore." He released her and wiped his eyes. "I'm actually with someone now. He's another leader in the Resistance, and quite conveniently, serves in the Imperial Guard. But if anyone found us out, we would pay the same price as Sister Martha. That's why I'm waging this war, Lore. So that you and I can be free to be who we want."

"And what of Fallon now? Is he much changed?"

At this, he grew somber. "I'm afraid so."

"In what way?"

"Since you ran off...in almost every way."

Chapter XI

It was fortunate for Lore that all of Vitruvia, including her parents, were too entrenched in their own grief over the death of Emperor Berclay to acknowledge the crossing of a wanted criminal into their great nation. As a member of the elite class, Lore avoided the certain humiliation of being handed over to the authorities and moved directly into a holding chamber within Lucien's Basilica. This mammoth structure spanned six blocks in the center of the Seat and housed all governmental proceedings related to the Council. It also held the Imperial Hall, where the emperor and head bishop resided, and the Military Technology Center, which lived in its bowels. Several acres of lush grounds that included cherry tree orchards, stables, and a succession of landscaped gardens separated it from the rest of the official government buildings.

"The emperor's funeral is today," Gideon informed her before he locked her and Jesseny in the chambers. "Fallon knows of your presence and has demanded that your trial take place before his coronation."

"Why is that?"

"He says he has a special job for you."

"What in Lucien does that mean?"

"I can't imagine, and of course, he isn't forthcoming with me. You should also know I've spoken with my father and told him I'm not pressing my case against you for breaking our betrothal. This means you'll be protected from the Council's harshest sentence. I explained to him your reasons for flight, and I told him I believe it speaks well of your character to have made such a sacrifice for a friend."

"Thank you."

"But if Sawyer is caught within these borders, there will be no mercy for her. She should know that. A special member of the Imperial Guard has been assigned to you." He smirked. "You'll be under constant surveillance." He finished, shaking his head. "Goodbye, then. I know it is burdensome to be locked up in a room for such a long time. Try to be patient." With that, he shut them in.

Jesseny smoothed out her starched gray uniform, then lifted her skirts to readjust the dagger belts encircling both upper thighs. "So, do you have a plan for how we can communicate with the girls and Avery when they get here?"

"Sort of, but it's contingent upon one very crucial element."

"What's that?"

"It's hard to explain. I'll have to show you." She gently pulled her close and pressed her right ear against Jesseny's. "Artemis?" she called, saying a silent prayer that the old man would answer. "Artemis, are you there? I could use your help right about now."

"What's supposed to happen?"

"Let me try again." She began to sweat in her panic. "Artemis?" she called louder.

After a moment, a hushed and broken voice answered back. "Lore? Is that you or am I going mad?"

"It's me. I'm back, under arrest and in a holding chamber in Lucien's Basilica. I need your help."

"Not as much as I need yours."

"What do you mean?"

"I'm in Lucien's Basilica as well."

"What?! Where?"

"I've been here for months. I'm in a subterranean laboratory, the prisoner of a mad scientist."

"Don't worry, I'll get you out of there. I have to. Can you tell me anything of your whereabouts and how to get there from the holding chambers?"

"There are many holding chambers, all in different locations in the Basilica and under ferocious watch."

"I think we have a slight edge. First of all, Emperor Berclay's funeral is today."

"What? The emperor is dead?"

"Yes. I don't know much about it, but I think it means this place is fairly empty."

"Of course, of course. But there will be some guards, mind you."

"I have a girl with me here as my maid. She'll be the one coming to find you."

"Well, she must be very careful. But let me think, let me think..." His mind began waking up. "I know these blueprints like the back of my hand since we always had to be prepared for an Orsian attack. You're of the ruling class, so they most likely have you in the holding chambers in the Imperial Hall. In that case, I've been in there on several occasions when we've had to interrogate misbehaved aristocrats about divulging military secrets. That's a comfortable little apartment. Would you call it comfortable?"

"I think so. There are a few rooms to move about in."

"If I recall, there should be a poorly fastened vent in the bathroom, ground level and adjacent to the toilet."

Jesseny left her side to inspect the washroom. She poked her head out and nodded. Then, Lore heard a bit of commotion as she wrenched the vent off the wall.

"It's a tight squeeze, but if you crawl through the ducts straight for about five hundred feet, you'll come to an intersection. Go down. That will let you out in one of the laundering rooms. There you can likely find something to put on and at least disguise yourself as an official employee – a lab coat would be most ideal in this situation, of course. Once you've done that, walk out of the laundering room and turn left. At the end of this hall is a utility staircase. You can take the stairs all the way to the basement. Don't use the elevator because there's more risk of running into someone. Once you make it to Military Technology Center at the very bottom, you'll have to hide until someone exits, unless you can think of a clever excuse to enter. If no one is there, that means the door is locked and it requires a full facial scan to gain admittance. So hopefully, someone stayed behind. I'm in a cell to the far left near Hawfinch's workstation. It appears to just be a closed metal door and it says, 'Staff Only.' No one knows I'm here, not even the other workers."

"Sounds easy," Jesseny said. She had sidled back up next to Lore and listened.

"Who's that?"

"That's my friend, Jesseny, the one who's coming for you."

"And tell me, what will I do if she succeeds in rescuing me?" He laughed.

"That's easy. You'll walk out the front door."

"We'll see about that."

A moment later, Jesseny positioned herself at the vent. "I don't know what this is about, but I'll try to recover this man for you."

"I'm sorry to ask such a thing, but if anyone can do this, it's you."

Jesseny grinned. "I know," she said before disappearing into the narrow darkness.

It was true that if anyone could carry out such a task, Jesseny could. That's how she escaped the torment of the factory – through a vent. Lore reminded herself of the story as it had been recounted to her:

"The siren ruled our lives in my village. It sounded at four in the morning to signal the start of the day. I lived in a home for wayward girls because I'd already lost both parents to hard factory living. It seemed like they actively tried to work us to death because there were always younger children to fill the shoes of the old.

I slept in a room alone because I had been there almost since birth, and the man who ran the house, Mr. Chamberlain, favored me. He said I looked the same as his dead daughter. Sometimes he even called me by her name, Cora. His younger sister and her husband also lived and worked at the house.

"After the first siren, we had fifteen minutes to be outside for work. The foremen stood on boxes outside and screamed our names to take attendance. Tardiness warranted a five-minute beating on the factory floor in front of everyone.

"Work began at half past four and we worked straight until five in the evening with only fifteen minutes for lunch, which every day consisted of the same gray gruel made of mashed up animal parts and potatoes about to go bad. After work, we could have ten more minutes to wash the day's grime off, and thirty minutes for dinner, which usually consisted of boiled gray meat and mushy vegetables. At six, everyone assembled by the windows to hear a regional cast of Bishop Pawnsworthy reading from the Book of True Faith for an hour before the last siren sounded and we were to be in bed. Of course, the adults had a later bedtime, but most were so spent from the day's toil that they joined us.

"In the hours between the last siren and the first, I didn't sleep much. I lived in constant fear of my door creaking open in the night and Mr. Chamberlain's brother-in-law sneaking into my room. He was a wiry sort, frail and weak-chinned, who received neither love nor respect from his own wife. She'd belittle him quite audibly whenever he made the smallest mistakes in the bookkeeping. And while he seemed to follow her around like a doleful terrier, rumors swirled that she repelled any intimacy with him and even made him sleep in a separate chamber.

"For us children, it was unusual to see a woman exert so much of her will over a man without being punished for it. People speculated it was because Mr. Chamberlain regularly contributed much of his dead wife's money to the bishop's fund that his sister went unchecked for abusing her husband. But he was lonely, her husband – George. And a young child has no defenses. So, he chose me since I conveniently slept alone and not in a room of seven others.

"It started when I turned eight. He'd sneak in at night and slip into bed with me. At first, he pretended to tuck me in. He'd read me stories and stroke my hair,

kiss my head, and leave. After a while, I trusted him and looked forward to his visits. Until about a year after his first visit, he came in drunk and forced me to kiss him. 'Don't you dare scream,' he said, 'or I'll strangle you and then kill myself.' I stopped resisting because I knew he meant it, and despite the wretchedness of my life, I still wanted to live it.

"The abuse continued in varying degrees. Pinned under him, I would look up at the walls, the ceiling, anything to distract myself from what was happening to me. One night, I was gazing at the wall at my left and noticed a vent above the chest of drawers. It was small and tight, but I was small for my age. After he finished, he cried into my neck. I hated him. I hated his weakness. And still, even in my wrecked innocence, I pitied him. The next night, I used the tip of a small knife to unscrew the vent and hid inside it as he came in. He fumbled around with the sheets looking for me. He scrambled under the bed. Soon, he began sobbing, grabbing at my dirty clothes and shoving them up to his nose. Then, he knelt by the bed and began to pray. I could only hear a faint whisper, but it sounded like he prayed for death.

"For the rest of the week, I did the same thing. I watched him search frantically for me, cry, and then pray for death. Afterwards, I explored the duct as much as I could and as quietly as possible. Aside from some dead mice carcasses and dust, there was nothing. Except, as I crept further along each night, I saw that it eventually dropped down at a right angle. I knew the root cellar was below my room because I often heard the maid's voices floating up when they were down there gossiping or sneaking around with the male servants. And I knew the root cellar had an exterior door that let out on the side of the house that bordered the dirty river of sewage and waste.

"The next night, I took one of my favorite knives home with me – long and curved, perfect for slicing flesh. It felt icy cold pressed up against the skin underneath my shirt. George, of course, still visited my room regularly, hoping to find me. I could have simply escaped and left him, praying and pining. But I thought I should give him his wish so he wouldn't harm the next recipient of the single room. As I watched him once more ravage the bed looking for me, there he came upon my knife. He took it up in his hand and looked wildly around the room, wondering where I could be. Finally, his eyes landed on the vent. I sat

behind it, looking back at him through the darkness. He knew I was there, but he didn't come for me. Instead, he kept hold of my gaze while he plunged the knife into his groin. He didn't cry out in pain; he stayed as silent as I had.

"I waited until he bled out, recovered my blade, and then slid down into the cellar, saying my own prayer that no maid would be there to catch me. The house slept. I let myself out the door and right into the dirty river. Moonlight guided me as I clung to the edges, holding my nose as I went. Even that filthy water seemed to be washing my soiled life clean. It carried me out of town and emptied me into a bigger river, once known as the Mississippi. I scavenged at the edges of villages with other hobos, until I reached the remnants of Underhill – formerly Louisiana – land believed to be so unlivable it's not monitored. I took up with a family of wanderers until they tried to force me to marry their eldest son, which didn't suit me at all since I preferred his sister. He also had a way with knives, and we dueled over whether or not I'd consent by throwing blades at apples twenty feet from us. He missed two out of three, and I sliced every one right down the middle so that the seeds fell out whole and perfect with nary a nick.

"And so, I left them, crossed into Hopespoke and found work at Hephaestus's Den. Then one day I ran into Louisa Gunman, who had just retired. She recommended me to Ursula. Ursula liked my looks, sure. I had the same long tresses like sun-bleached corn she'd just lost in Louisa. But she liked my skills even more. She said, 'Oh good, I could use a girl who knows her way around a knife.' I was in, like that."

Lore waited hours in angst. She assumed moving through the vents took time, especially for the distance – and then, there was the risk of her being caught anywhere from the laundering rooms to the stairwell. Even if she made it to the lab, there could be no telling how long she may have to wait before performing the remainder of the rescue. Lore only hoped that the low security would render this mission possible. But just in case, she knelt by the narrow bed and said a quick prayer.

Several hours later, Lore had fallen asleep when an angry knock came at the door. She shot up and ran to open it. A tall and broad young man stood, holding a squirming Jesseny with one hand and Artemis with the other. The latter looked as sick and weak as he'd sounded.

"Oh, Artemis."

"You look well, dear."

"Let him go. Can't you see he's sick?!" she shouted.

The young man released them and turned on Lore, his brow creased, and his eyes opened as wide as possible, screwing up his otherwise handsome face.

"What's the meaning of this, miss? Do you have any idea how much trouble we could all be in?"

Irritated, Lore hooked her arm through Artemis' to hold him up. "First of all, please tell me who you are."

He looked taken aback. "I'm Alaric Kitt, an Imperial Guardsman... Gideon's friend."

Lore felt instant relief. "Well, for your information, this man has been held here against his will for months. I demand his immediate release, and I want Lafayette Hawfinch indicted on kidnapping," she barked.

"And just who do you think you are?" His eyes grew wider with humor. She could immediately see why Gideon liked him.

"I happen to be the daughter of Lord Clarence Fetherston of the Tree Vale, and I want justice for the wrongs committed here."

"Look, I understand you, but you don't know how it is here. Hawfinch is like a God, especially with the bishop. The only way I can help you is by letting him go and pretending this never happened. But you can't overstep your bounds here again, not before your hearing." He put a large paw on her shoulder and squeezed.

"He needs to leave now," Jesseny said, squirming out of the lab coat she'd procured. "Hawfinch is here. He was in another room, though, and all we could hear were screams, but he may discover very soon that his prisoner is missing."

"How did you get caught, then?"

"Alaric caught us trying to use the lift. I just didn't think he could make it up all those stairs."

"Very well," Lore conceded. The situation had turned out much better than she'd planned. She hugged Artemis and whispered, "I said you'd be able to walk out the front door, didn't I? Go to Madame Ermengarde's Boarding House for Young Misses. It's in the nit. They'll take care of you there."

He looked at her again with clear eyes that seemed to have just woken from a nightmare. "My, it's good to see your face."

Lore touched the old man's cheek. "It's good to see yours, too. Now get out of here while you still can."

Chapter XII

An elaborate pink carriage drawn by four large yocto-cats wearing pink bows around their necks paraded Lore through the Seat before her trial. People of all demographics lined the streets to watch her – young and old, male and female, aristocrats, merchants, dregs, Vitruvics. She felt the same awkwardness as she had walking in her grandmother's funeral procession, only now she'd become the sole spectacle.

Her mother sat weeping audibly in the front row of the assembly room. Lore watched as Miranda leaned on Clarence's shoulder and shook with grief. By the attendance, it seemed as though all of the Vitruvian elite had fast recovered from the emperor's death and were now obsessed with the latest drama: the trial of Lorelei Henriette Fetherston, the fallen daughter of Lord Clarence Fetherston of the Tree Vale. Her father had properly adorned himself in a vibrant forest green velveteen, a color emblematic of his region, but his face wore an expression as solemn as if she had perished.

Despite their now surreal existence – her long-suffering mother and foppish, aloof father – part of Lore wanted to run to them. But she couldn't even do this because her hands were bound by yocto-tethers. She once more wore a corset under her dress and had never felt so cornered in all of her life.

The panel deciding her fate included two bishops – Gerathy not among them – and six lords, three of them close friends of her father. She sat in a wooden booth on a dais while the panel sat opposite on a raised platform, looking down at her. Fallon and Bishop Gerathy sat in a private balcony, situated above everything in the uppermost right corner of the hall like spectators at the opera. She couldn't see Fallon from where she sat, but she could feel his eyes boring into her. Lore had been afforded no representation and only had permission to speak when asked a direct question. Instead, she had to listen to the panel, to hear their reprimands, and to accept her just punishment.

"Lorelei Henriette Fetherston," began Bishop Faraday, who presided over the Tree Vale. He had white hair that fell to his shoulders and a soft avuncular expression, which made his next words seem quite out of character. "You are here to be tried for a breach of Vitruvian marital law, of disrespecting and disregarding our traditions. Given your status as the daughter of a lord and a member of the aristocracy, this kind of infraction is most troubling."

There he stopped and Bishop Monnegan, who presided over the Granary, took over. Tall and lean in contrast to Bishop Faraday, he had a withered look about him and cold, black eyes like two dry lumps of coal.

"It's the wish of the panel that you receive the most severe form of punishment allowable at your status, which would be one year in rehabilitative incarceration followed by a marriage reassignment, preferably returning you to Mr. Danaher, if he would have you. However, because he has asked to remit his grievance as a Council item, we are unable to proceed in this."

"Would Lieutenant Danaher please approach the panel?" Lord Kawleigh asked.

Gideon stood, stately in his uniform. "Yes, good members of the panel. I thank you for honoring my request."

"But tell us, son, why will you not let us punish her if you don't care to marry her?" Bishop Faraday asked in a gentle tone.

Gideon stood taller. "Because sir, Lorelei has always been a good girl. I know our traditions should be held sacred, but I can't fault her for not loving me as a wife should love a husband, and I care for her too much to let her suffer for it."

"A noble answer," commented Lord Drusely, "but we believe she fled to help a friend in trouble."

"Well, perhaps that's true," replied Gideon, "but to me, the mark of a loyal friend who would sacrifice her own safety to protect a loved one demonstrates good character."

"Can you be serious?" asked Bishop Monnegan, with a sneer. "You think it was honorable for her to run off, away from your wedding, to protect a known whore?"

Lore looked around for Sawyer's father in the crowd, but Lord Hillbury had not made an appearance. She learned why once the bishop continued.

"A whore whose actions drove her father to take his own life? You think that's a mark of good character?"

Gideon swallowed hard. "Sir, with all due respect, I think maybe she didn't know the extent of Miss Hillbury's indiscretions."

Bishop Monnegan now turned his pursed face to her. "Is this true, Miss Fetherston?"

As she looked into his dulled eyes, his sour stare, Ursula's story began to echo inside her.

"Most people don't know where I came from. They think they know, but they don't. I circulated that I'd been disappointed with the lack of opportunities at home and moved to Landraven as a young woman to work in the houses of Parliament as a secretary. Then I moved up to communications officer. That last bit is true. Eventually, I caught the eye of Archibald, then a young widower.

"But I didn't grow up in a poor little town outside of Hopespoke like I've allowed everyone to believe. I grew up in Lucien's Basilica, right in the heart of the Seat and extremely close to the Imperial Family.

"The Dubonnet line of women they've always taken to be their empresses is said to be a barren line. You may know this is why the current emperor never had a blood child. Yet they still upheld the agreement to wed those girls that had been made between Lord Henley and Lord Dubonnet all those years before. It's believed, though, that there is something wrong with the virility of the emperor's

male line as well, since producing an heir with any woman proved to be difficult. When their empresses failed to create offspring, they turned to a bevy of designated servants – servants who were kept fertile explicitly for that reason, and my mother among them. On the rare occasion a servant became pregnant, they were put on bed rest and waited on hand and foot. But most miscarried and were severely punished if they did, especially if the child inside was male.

"My true name is Lavinia Emmanuelle Berclay, the daughter of Emperor Julian Shale Berclay, father of the late emperor, Percival. Had I been born a male, my mother would have been rewarded with a comfortable life in the countryside while I'd have attended the best schools and been groomed to someday rule. Instead, they hid us in a separate wing along with another pregnant servant.

"But before the second servant even had her baby, which turned out to be another girl child, a miracle happened. The empress gave birth to Percival. We were kept close growing up. The emperor wasn't completely unfeeling to his own blood. Sometimes he visited and brought us treats. Governesses taught us in the domestic arts and we even had a taste of the schooling aristocratic males received – Vitruvian history, English, a bit of political theory, languages. I appreciated this learning because I had a sharp and curious mind and so did my younger half-sister.

"We were Percival's playmates growing up, there at his every beck and call. As we became teenagers, he requested my presence more often. He never realized we were blood, though we clearly had similar facial features. When it was time for him to marry Imogen Dubonnet, I came to understand our place in the Imperial Family even before our mothers explained it to us. We would be to our own half-brother what they were to the emperor – concubines, used to breed an heir.

"Well, I had other ideas, but before I could properly plan our escape, Percy came to each of us one evening. I fought him off and he stopped trying to force me. He looked so despairing when he said, 'If I don't produce an heir, I'm not sure what father will do. You and I could both be dead.' I felt so sorry for him, but I still could not oblige him. 'Fool,' I said without mercy, 'haven't you figured out that you're our half-brother?' He looked shocked. He was so naïve, but those words took his innocence as if I had let him have me. 'Is that why the thought of this is making

me so ill? Is that why I felt so wrong when I did this with Augustine?' he said, sobbing into my shoulder.

"My half-sister had just turned seventeen. I was nearly twenty and I knew I had to save us both. We used our wiles to seduce two of the guards and escaped. The emperor didn't know we'd gone missing until we had reached New York. There, we blended so far into the nit that he would have had to employ every bit of yocto-technology in existence to find us. He would have, too, if he had known what became apparent on our journey. Augustine was with child.

"We had no problem getting by in the nit since we were a lot smarter than the dregs. I immediately sought out a doctor who could help rid Augustine of her burden. After some inquiries to the working women in the area, I found an old man called Dr. Godwit, who operated out of his wife's herbalist boutique in the wealthy shopping district. But the harsh ways of this new world held some terrible surprises for us. Yet, we were more terrified of the incestuous monster growing inside of her than we were by the risk of removing it. By the time Dr. Godwit had finished the procedure, Augustine had almost completely bled out. There seemed to be nothing left of her insides at all. She had no more menstrual cycles after that, and I'm sure she blamed me for it most. I certainly blamed myself. And I think whatever higher power exists blamed me, too, since I've never been able to carry a child to term. Eight times during my life I've been pregnant and all of them died in my womb.

"After Augustine recovered, we conned our way around, hustled fools out of money, and seduced rich merchants into supporting us. We struggled with the everyday muck of life, though. It made me angry how most of the population lived in such conditions only to be forgotten by the Seat. Even though the upper echelons of society followed the standards of Victorian propriety and high morals, these were lost to the poverty-stricken areas. Either that or they were enforced only when it suited those policing it. Otherwise, the dregs were left to rot, to be little more than slaves to the merchants and constant victims of the Vitruvics.

"An entire people had been systematically siloed and disenfranchised. But it had started hundreds of years before, and it continued only because those in slightly more privileged positions refused to sacrifice what small power they had to lift up others in the name of what was right. And the people in charge — the ones making all the money – understood this well, and they wanted to keep society divided. They wanted us engaged in a perpetual fight over our differences so we'd stay blinded to our true enemy: them. And this is what we've come to.

"Augustine and I both grew bitter at the hypocrisies around us since we knew the other side of life. The region's bishop used to visit and make blessings in the nit's many dilapidating churches. He preached morality in the streets at assemblies and condemned lustful behavior, gluttony, and sloth. And yet, we found out from close friends that he secretly frequented the brothels and accepted luxury gifts from merchants whom he then pardoned from the religious tax.

"The lords were no better. They indulged in illicit goods smuggled in from Orsia and took bribes from the merchants to keep quiet. They came with their entourages and roughed things up around the nit because they could. One lord even had a hobby of brutally murdering the prostitutes he slept with. And yet, more and more, there were laws being enacted against women. Harsher punishments for those caught selling sex and new restrictions put up for female shop owners like higher taxes.

"Augustine and I decided that we needed to put our brains to use for the good of the commoners, many of whom we now considered dear friends. Together with some members of our craftier inner circle, we formed a group called Les Chattes Rebelles. We planned a few protests to coincide with visits from the Seat and, once we had a plan, we slowly involved other women. They had no idea what we were about to unleash on them. Protests had never been allowed, and it could have meant our lives. It could have meant life in prison or worse, a women's asylum where they practiced tortuous experiments, yocto-shock, and lobotomies.

"We all wore black dresses with cat masks and veils. As the bishop stood in the center square of the nit, pontificating about the dangers of the rapid descent of feminine virtue and how it needed to be kept in line with boundaries and firmness, hundreds of us started squalling and hissing like angry cats. He faltered and didn't know what to do. The few Vitruvics in the crowd began to beat us with their clubs, and yocto-creatures came out of nowhere to attack us as if propelled forward by the bishop's command. But we were also armed.

"What the Seat failed to understand was that the forgotten nit was the greatest threat to peace because most of the people there had nothing left to lose. And they also had to grow sneaky about getting the few things they did have. A proper woman of the aristocracy could never imagine being able to obtain a weapon, but in the nit, you could get whatever you needed if you knew the right people. We did.

"But we hadn't expected others in the crowd not associated with our group to join in. They did, though – men, women, young, and old. It seemed that everyone was properly fed up with the ruling class. They were tired, hungry, broken down, and sick of being preached to by those who were known liars.

"You've learned of the Great Rebellion back in 2252 and the brief mention of the small group of women who started it. Well, that was me. And I was fighting for a purpose, fighting for the Vitruvian throne, fighting for bloody everyone. As the firstborn, I didn't believe my rightful place should be ripped from me simply because of my gender, especially since I had a vision of a country reimagined and equitable – better than anything that idiot Percy would ever accomplish. They couldn't contain us in New York, and we made it down to the Seat, to the front of Lucien's Basilica. Word had spread to the other regions, and scores of people abandoned their posts in the factories and on the farms to join us. We were nearly successful in waging a coup, but in the end, the Seat squashed us. They got scared, expanded their army, recruited like mad, and empowered more and more dregs by turning them into Vitruvics.

"And then the mess with Ollie and the Starter happened. He was a known cyber pirate, the son of the woman who ran the herbal boutique where Augustine nearly died. He hacked into the Starter and reprogrammed the galateans in the Seat to turn on their owners and join us that day. They did, and unleashed widespread death among the aristocracy and the Council. It allowed us to break into the Basilica itself. But the engineers in the Seat were able to regain control of the Starter and programmed the galateans to turn on the crowd, to turn on us.

"So many innocents were killed, mostly women. Those rebels who survived faced imprisonment and madhouses; others still, were probably tortured for information. Though I was a leader in this movement, I'd kept my identity secret and escaped the Seat a second time. But I had failed, and the guilt I felt on behalf of those now suffering because I wanted to change things, and to change things *mostly for my own personal gain, affected me too much to remain in Vitruvia. Some of my closest friends had perished – and my sweet Augustine...*

"*I made it to Hopespoke with little trouble. Citizens across the country knew of me, and I just had to find the right places, flash my signature cat mask, and I received the help I needed. Once or twice I feared I might be caught, but I made it over the border and then into the mythical city of Landraven where women were free. I made myself a life here. A beautiful life. But all the while, my early failure marked me and I strove to be better, to be perfect. And I began this school with the tiniest grain of an idea that, someday, I could seek revenge – that I could reenter that backward country with more of a lethal force and right all those past wrongs that have continued to be committed since. I hoped against hope that, with the combined power of a multitalented female intelligentsia, I could change the course of Vitruvia from oppression to liberation.*

"*And now is my chance. My only chance.*"

Lore shook at this remembrance. How could everything be so unjust? Anger coursed through her now as she met the bishop's hateful glare with one that matched it. She seized what could be her one moment to speak, trusting that she'd be protected.

"No, Your Excellency. Lieutenant Danaher is mistaken, but through no fault of his own."

Bishop Monnegan's sneer turned into a malicious grin. "You are admitting, then, to associating with a fallen woman, a woman who had illicit relations with a member of the Vitruvian Brotherhood?"

"If that's what you wish to accuse me of, then I admit it. But my own estimation of what I did is far different than the crime of which you're accusing me."

Gideon turned to her with eyes that warned her to stop, but Lore no longer cared.

"Do enlighten us," the bishop prompted.

"I don't deny that my friend's actions were sinful. But yes, I felt compelled to protect her, because even though she did wrong, what would have served as her punishment felt even more wrong – and brutal, and frankly, uncivilized. I couldn't allow it."

"That was not for you to decide," said Bishop Faraday.

"No, it wasn't. But I did it, anyway."

"And where is your friend now? Still in Landraven?"

"The Sawyer Hillbury who left Vitruvia is no longer."

"Speak plainly, girl. You mean she's dead?"

"To this world, yes. Perhaps she's joined her father."

"In hellfire and damnation."

"I don't think those who are victims in life are made to suffer in death. That would supersede logic, don't you think?"

"Your defiant nature is most shocking, young lady," he continued. "We can only assume this is the corrupt influence of life in Landraven."

"No, Your Excellency. This is the influence of the truths I've learned in place of your lies."

The audience buzzed at these words.

"Silence!" a voice bellowed.

Fallon stood, leaning over the balcony. For a moment, she mistook him for Avery and her heart flipped over on itself. But it wasn't her other love. It was this one – her first.

"I want silence."

He stared hard at her and drew his brows together, not in anger but in firm concentration. The crowd obeyed and, in the tomblike stillness, he made a decision.

"Miss Fetherston, despite the panel's inability to sentence you to a punishment given Master Danaher's pardon, as acting emperor, I have the right to overturn his pardon and sentence you according to my will. Thus, you will remain with me under strict guard until I formally release you from bondage."

Next to him, Bishop Gerathy appeared, wearing a look of righteous approval. Lore looked into Fallon's eyes, trying to decipher whether he meant any of this or if he just wanted to get her alone in his private chambers. The spark behind his stern gaze indicated the latter.

"Yes, my lord," she said, casting her eyes down and then slowly back up at him like she had been taught in her lessons. "As you wish."

Chapter XIII

The girls blended into the bustling nit of the Seat all too easily. Apparently, Madame Ermengarde's Boarding House for Young Misses functioned more like her own version of the Escadrille. Her charges kept small jobs in shops with milliners and seamstresses – and they ran side cons as well. Some of the younger earned their keep as master pickpockets. And most of them also slept with men for money in addition to secrets.

Madame Ermengarde, a respected seamstress herself, proved to be very useful with her information. Since her girls were always so well-dressed in her creations, they attracted very elite clientele, the kind of aristocratic scum who like to sample the other half. And much of this scum happened to be lords on the Council, and even a bishop or two.

"Madame Ermengarde is quite the lady," Artemis whispered in her head shortly after her trial ended and she'd been locked back into her chambers with Jesseny.

She nervously awaited a final visitation with her parents before her formal sentence began.

"Really? How so?"

"Well, some of the girls say she reminds them of Ursula in her mannerisms. She has a type of magnetism that makes you want to confide in her. But she's coarse, too. In any case, she's given us quite the arsenal of intelligence on your precious Council, and they've been very bad boys, indeed. We also know the venues they haunt looking for company, so the girls plan to infiltrate soon."

"How is Sawyer?"

"She's thriving in her new appearance. It's made her rougher, I think. Sometimes she seems troubled, though, and she's taken up with some of the older girls here – some of the more entrepreneurial types. I wouldn't worry, though. Clementine seems to keep a sharp eye on her."

"Clemmie," Lore breathed out, ashamed to just be considering how her friend was adjusting to this unknown world – a world that certainly wasn't set up to welcome her with open arms. "How is Clemmie doing? And the others who didn't come from Vitruvia? Are they all right?"

Artemis let a bitter sigh escape. "It's a culture shock, to be sure. There are a few who won't venture out at all, and Madame Ermengarde has been sympathetic. She's so respected here that I think Clemmie feels safer in her presence than she otherwise might, but I'll make a point to check with her later."

"Thank you, please do – with all the girls."

"And how is everything there?"

"We've heard Hawfinch has men searching for you."

"Ha, good luck to him."

"I can't imagine why you would say such a thing."

"Let's just say, I'm innocuously concealed most of the time. And I'm keeping very busy building a few tools for you from scratch. Sawyer has been getting me the proper materials. I don't know how she's finding everything I request, but she does –"

A knock at her chamber door cut him off.

"My parents are here to see me, so I have to go, my friend. Goodbye for now."

Jesseny opened the door and then excused herself to another room. To Lore's surprise, just her mother stood there, wearing another enormous mourning gown like the one she had worn to Mathilde's funeral. Dozens of dyed roses, glistening in inky greens and violets trimmed her tall silk hat like oil stains in the sun, and a veil of black lace made the eyes behind it stand out even more like two bright sapphires. She had Lore's old orbis caputs with her. Tobias and Wilfred sat drooping on each of her shoulders, both donning little, black capes. Lord Izzy orbited her enormous hat, his air balloon decked out in its own black ribbons, tears staining his monocle as he moaned.

"Hello, Mother. Is Father unwell? Did he not feel up to paying me a visit?"

Miranda shook her head. "Your father is too sad to look on you, too sad and too ashamed. In fact, he's gone to see Fallon and Bishop Gerathy about resigning his title." At these last words, her hand trembled and she raised a handkerchief to her mouth as though to stifle sickness. She looked again at Lore with even sadder eyes. "It's been humiliating for him – for both of us – to be publicly mocked, even by people we thought were our friends. Do you know what they're calling you in the gazettes?"

She reached into her purse and pulled out a crude cartoon of Lore and Sawyer, each with kitty ears, whiskers and tails, sneaking over a drawn border between the two countries as a rowdy bar scene with men, drink, and loose women awaited them on the other side. The half of cartoon-Lore still in Vitruvia donned proper Victorian attire, but the half that had crossed over the border in Hopespoke wore the clothes of a harlot. The cartoon read: *NAUGHTY ARISTOKITTENS HIGHTAIL IT INTO HARLOTRY.* Underneath that, another rendering showed a completely altered, rebellious kitten-Lore being dragged back across the border by a triumphant Gideon in his fighter plane. This one read: *LOOK WHO DRAGGED IN THE CAT! BAD ARISTOKITTEN NABBED BY JILTED FIANCÉ. LET'S HOPE IT'S NOT HER 9TH LIFE!*

Lore laughed aloud and caught herself. Miranda squinted at her.

"You think the pain that your carelessness and depravity has inflicted upon those who gave you life is funny? Do you know what they're calling me?"

She blew her nose and it honked like a discordant trumpet as she handed Lore another issue. This one had a cartoon of Miranda and Clarence, both dressed like proper aristocrats but with cat features and sitting in a litter box atop a mountain of dung. It read: *HUMILIATED SIRE AND DAM FETHERSTON CAN'T BURY THEIR SHAME.*

"'Dam Fetherston,' they call me, or 'The Cat's Mother.'"

"I'm sure you hate the attention," Lore muttered and immediately felt sorry. She realized this may, in fact, be one of her last conversations with Miranda. She wished she could explain why her father leaving the Council actually guaranteed his safety, considering what their fates would likely be.

"I blame myself for this," Miranda whispered into her handkerchief.

"Yourself? Why?"

The sapphires blinked and wetted a little before looking back at her.

"Oh, I don't know. I smothered you, perhaps, but without also giving you the proper attention. Maybe I made too much of your growing up about myself instead of about you. Maybe because I – I never really wanted a child."

Lore felt a stinging in her breast. Miranda's lack of maternal instinct had been frightfully obvious throughout her childhood in the absence of any genuine affection or nurturing, but to hear her verbalize it felt worse.

"I know you didn't."

"I'm so sorry. You were a good little girl, you know. You never required much, and yet I always felt so put upon." She wiped her eyes and Lore foolishly peeked to see if any of the incandescent blue had leaked onto her kerchief.

"It's all right, Mother. You had no choice but to have a child, so it's not your fault. I forgive you."

"Your grandmother, she didn't want me, either. She didn't want any of us. I know she can't bear the fault, but it was hard being her child, craving attention. Most days, she'd stare at a wall as though she were watching a film play out on the blank white that only she could see, and it was the same story over and over: what her life would have been without us. I never intended to do the same thing to you. Please, believe me."

Lore grasped her mother's hand. Miranda recoiled at first, but then relented and entwined her fingers with her daughter's.

"I wish you had told me all of this sooner. We could have fixed it."

Miranda sniffled once more as she got up to leave. "They said you might be able to have visitors again someday, but not just yet."

"Well, when I do, I hope you'll come. And Father, too."

"Someone else came with me today, intent on speaking with you."

Miranda opened the door to reveal Alastair, his pale face set off by dark hair and an even darker suit. If she didn't know him as her own beloved cousin, Lore may have taken him for something more sinister, like Dracula himself. His normally dour expression cracked into a joyous smile at the sight of her.

"Darling Lore."

"Alastair!"

"Well, I'll let you two speak."

"Goodbye," Lore said, holding open her arms for a hug. Miranda responded with a stiff pantomime of the act, but it felt hopeful.

"Goodbye, Lorelei. Please take care of yourself."

"Don't worry, Mother. I will. And you as well."

Once the door closed behind Miranda, Alastair spoke freely.

"It's happening," he started. "I'll be assuming your father's lordship now that he's resigning. Do I dare try to invoke change? I must say, part of me is a little bit hopeful about it, albeit a very small part."

"No, you can't!" she cried. She hadn't remembered this succession until now.

He frowned. "Aren't you happy for me, sweet cousin? Perhaps my enthusiasm is a bit insensitive given your predicament, but of course, my first action would be to appeal to His Imperial Majesty on your behalf."

"No, no. It's not that, Alastair. It's something else."

His face fell again. "What is it? Tell me."

"I can't tell you this, dearest. But will you trust me if I do tell you something?"

"You're scaring me."

"I don't mean to scare you. It's just – there's danger if you assume the lordship now."

"Danger? How do you mean?"

"You must believe me. There will be a time and a place for you to make change. In fact, the opportunity will arise sooner than you think. Before that's clear though, I beg of you, do not assume any duties relating to the Seat just yet."

"How can I refuse?"

"It's very simple. Stay away. Stay away until after Fallon's coronation. You must."

"What? That's absurd?" His brows came together.

She took his hand. "Alastair please, we've always been frank with each other. I know your mere presence here is a marvel considering the shame I've brought upon our families. So please, I beg you – you must, for your life, stay away. Trust me, I would never put you in harm's way but only shield you from it. Nor would I reveal too much to burden you with knowledge that could be used against you. Someday soon, you and I will be able to work together to heal the deep wounds of this nation. But until then, will you promise to stay safe?"

The weight and reality of her words seemed to settle in his expression. He gripped her hand with even more fierceness and brought it to his lips.

"I promise, darling. I promise."

She tried to suppress the loud swallow in her throat, but Gideon heard it. It echoed off the marble halls as they entered the Imperial Hall.

"Don't be nervous. I think seeing you again may help him – at least part of me hopes it will." He swung open the opulent carved doors and ushered her in.

"Jesseny will be sent up with your things in a bit. He wanted to speak with you alone first," he said with a last reassuring nod before making a swift exit.

Beyond the deep foyer, there were scores of other apartments. Lore poked around through the rooms, wondering how long Fallon planned to tease her with anticipation until he chose to appear. Sunlight flooded in through massive arched windows and illuminated the white marble floor, countering the darkness of the heavy draperies and jewel-toned fabrics. One room seemed dedicated to important discussions with its coteries of deep leather chairs and small conversation tables. A library area for research and rumination took up the grandest space, and a bar nook full of fancy decanters and imported whiskey filled another corner. Some servants moved about, tidying. Some were so busy they didn't discern her presence, but single-mindedly focused on their task with impenetrable concentration.

Further down a hallway were two adjoining private apartments. One that had most likely belonged to the empress before she left for her mourning confinement, exuded a simple femininity. The hard cream of the floor complemented the gleaming white of the sheer canopy bed. Fleurs-de-lis adorned the striking violet fabric of the walls. Dried mums and hydrangeas of different purple hues stood silent in vases on the mantle above the fireplace and on the delicate bedside stands. A dressing table made of mirrored glass brought a modern finish to the otherwise old-fashioned space. Two other doors led to a sitting room and a private bath. Lore noted that the door to this apartment locked from the outside.

"Well, how are you finding your accommodations?" said a voice from behind her, its familiar low notes swelling inside her head.

She turned and met his face, now a year older but just as she left it, as though he'd not moved until this very moment.

"Everything satisfactory?" He moved closer and grasped both her shoulders, peering down into her face. "Come on, then. Vitruvia's bad little kitty is all over the press. The country is quite obsessed with you, you know. And now, silence. What's the matter, cat got your tongue?" he finished with a devilish grin.

"Hello," she mustered.

He laughed. "Oh please, you can do better than that." He let her shoulders go and looked her over once more, carefully scrutinizing every last detail of her.

Now that her trial had ended, no one told her she couldn't wear the clothes she had brought. Deviating from the traditional Victorian costume in favor of the demurer look of Landraven's elegant set, she dressed quite properly so that nothing foul would be suspected of her training at Vandeleur's Preparatory School for Young Ladies. She decided on an A-line skirt of robin's egg blue with a tiny print of deep red cherries on it and a cardigan of the same rich crimson over a cream-colored blouse with a rounded collar and little eyelets at its edges. On her feet were mustard colored t-straps. She kept her hair down, spilling over her shoulders, but pinned the sides back loosely with pearl-ended bobby pins. She wore no makeup save for some light color about her cheeks and a hint of rosy glow on her lips.

He stood back and a smile curled at the edges of his mouth. He looked amused and disappointed all at once. "Humph," he grunted to himself.

"What?"

"You, something is different about you and I think I know what it is," he said under his breath, moving closer again.

"What's that?"

"You've known a man, haven't you?"

"How can you possibly think that's an appropriate question?"

He snickered now, still close. "Let's see, if it weren't true, you would simply say, 'That's not true at all.' But since you've decided to point out my impropriety instead of dignifying me with an answer, that only proves me correct in my assumptions, be they inappropriate or not."

"You didn't give me a chance to answer, did you? You just decided to stand there and make disgusting conclusions, based on what, anyway? The fact that I'm not wearing a high collar and a corset?"

"There's my little friend," he said, before roughly grabbing her arm and pushing her into the empress's room.

"What in Lucien do you think you're doing?!"

"Excuse me, sir." Jesseny stood behind him.

"What is it?" he demanded. Jesseny squirmed her way past him and into the room with Lore's large trunk. "And you will address me as 'Your Imperial Majesty' unless you want your tongue removed, maid," he spat.

Jesseny looked up to meet his glare and nearly dropped the trunk on his foot. He also stopped at the sight of her and his face changed, paled a little, and then softened.

"I–I'm sorry, Your Imperial Majesty," she mustered.

"As you were, then."

He turned his attention back to Lore, but he'd been bothered. "You, Lore, have been arrested for crimes against Vitruvia. You've been a very naughty girl, see. And in this country, naughty girls must pay for their crimes."

With one last condescending smirk, he slammed the door shut and Lore listened as someone locked her into yet another room. But at least she had company. She turned to Jesseny, who occupied herself pulling the clothes out of her trunk at lightning speed.

"What is it? What's wrong?"

Jesseny paused and looked at her. "Because, Lore, it's him."

"Who?"

"Remember my story about the little boy in the factory? Well, if there's any face that's ever been etched into my mind, it's his."

Lore thought for a moment and chastised herself inwardly for not realizing that earlier on. Of course, it made complete sense. A little boy in the factory who loses his mother and then has an accident, is rescued by someone...maybe even the rich man who pined for her – the lord in Jesseny's story, whom everyone believed to be his father.

This truth came to Lore in the same way she had realized R.J. was Eva and Avery's son. Lord Berclay hadn't just plucked Fallon out of a gutter. He had rescued his son and the rightful heir.

"I have a task for you, while you are under my supervision," Fallon said without looking at her as she entered the sunroom to join him for breakfast the following day.

He didn't seem to belong in such a bright and cozy space. Four large windows made of smaller, diamond-cut glass reflected the sun and dappled the other walls with dancing light. He had just returned from his morning ride and still wore his high-collared white shirt, black velveteen jacket, riding pants, and boots. He smelled like the outdoors, of freshly cut grass and cherry blossoms.

"What might that be?" she asked.

He looked up at her now and made a face like he had just tasted horrible food. "These clothes you've brought will have to go. I'm summoning a dressmaker here today."

She wore a blush-colored blouse that tied in a large bow at the neck with a creamy cardigan and brown, high-waisted pants.

"I see. You wish to bind me up in corsets, then."

He paused over his eggs. "I wish to turn you back into the Lore I knew."

"What if I told you she no longer exists?"

"Nonsense. A person doesn't completely change in a year."

"You have, haven't you?"

"And how would you know? You haven't been here."

"That's irrelevant. I don't have to have been here to see that you've been radicalized."

"Maybe I became this way because the one person I loved chose to abandon me."

"That's not fair."

His fork made a loud clunk on the side of his plate as he dropped it. He stood and threw down his napkin. "It's perfectly fair. Do you even know the pain you've caused me? Can you even imagine the anguish and worry I've gone through on your behalf?"

He moved around to her side of the table to sit next to her and bent his head close to her ear, cupping her face to pull it closer to his lips. "It was so easy for you to leave me, wasn't it? Do you know how it feels to be forgotten?"

Lore struggled out from his grip and forced herself to look at him. "I never forgot you. How could I? You were my best friend."

A tear lingered in his dark eye, matching the one that had formed in her own. His eyes had always made him seem so honest and warm, where now they were harsh and appraising. But no, he still existed there behind them, didn't he? She could almost see a glimmer of her old playmate behind that stare if she looked hard enough. She still contemplated this when he leaned forward and kissed her. Instantly, she thought of Avery. This kiss wasn't like his that had awakened something in her spirit, but it wasn't unwelcome, either. Full and soft, Fallon's lips felt electric when they touched hers. But they were also familiar, like kissing herself.

He pulled away. "I wish you had stayed, for my sake."

"What for? To be your mistress after I married? And what about after you married?"

"At least we could have been together. The Dubonnet line of sisters ended when Fannie died in childhood, so I was no longer betrothed. I could have taken my time finding a suitable match."

"And you would have done that to me? To Gideon?"

"He wouldn't have minded. He never loved you like I did and we both knew it."

"And what now? Now that I'm released?"

He smiled and tried to kiss her again, but she pushed him from her.

"Answer me. What's my purpose here in these chambers?"

"Your purpose is to help me write my coronation speech since you're so very talented with words."

"And then what?"

He laughed to himself a bit.

"Tell me."

"Well, you're not going to like the process, but I think you'll be pleased with the outcome." He tried to kiss her again, but she dodged him.

"I wish you'd stop resisting me."

"I suppose you think you're irresistible."

"To you, anyway. Unless someone else has your heart now, as I suspect," he wheedled.

"I won't kiss you again until you tell me about this plan you seem to have."

"You have to do as I say, so if I want you to kiss me, you will," he snapped.

She glared at him.

"Unless you want some harsher punishment. Instead of passing the days with your alleged best friend, you could be spending some quality time in one of the women's asylums. Would you like that?" He traced a finger around her lips.

"No."

"No, Your Imperial Majesty," he corrected.

"Technically, you're not emperor yet."

"No, Your Imperial Majesty," he repeated.

"No, Your Imperial Majesty."

"Kiss me, then. Right now."

Lore obeyed and leaned forward to meet his lips. This time, he pulled her closer, pressing against her, his muscles still tight from riding. She felt herself falling into it more easily than she wished, and her words to Avery in the manifest she had sent him alleviated her profound guilt in this moment.

My dearest Avery,

This parting of our hearts could not come at a worse time, and I can't begin to properly describe my feelings whenever I think of it. The closest I can come is to liken it to a death – my own, an utter crumbling and decomposition of my soul. But there's nothing to be done, and we must both remain strong to endure this time without one another.

If anything comes of this, perhaps it will make our love stronger and our reunion even sweeter. For I won't allow myself to imagine a scenario where I may never see your face again.

You are the best man I have ever known, and I love you. Whatever happens to me on my mission, whatever acts I may be forced to commit, or words I may be forced to utter, please know that nothing will ever usurp your place in my heart. You have it. You have me. All of me. And someday I hope to be able to fully share myself with you.

And even though neither you nor Eva ever told me outright, I know that little R.J. belongs to you. If we are able to grasp that idyllic future in the countryside that you so long for, I want him to be part of it, too.

Think of me. I'll be thinking of you, always.

Your Lore

Lore pulled out of the kiss.

"Now, that wasn't so bad, was it?"

"No, Your Imperial Majesty."

"Good. Since you're suddenly being so obliging, I'll share my plan with you. I want a stricter moral code enforced. I especially want this since it was so easy for you and Sawyer to escape. It's setting an awful bad example, and we don't want another generation of females causing a second Great Rebellion. Your leaving only made me realize that perhaps my father and Bishop Gerathy's ideals aren't so wrong. We need a purer society, and I want reform, not just in the aristocracy and the merchant class, but among the poor. Because that's where our problem lies. They have too much freedom in the nits."

"And what would you do to remedy this that could possibly involve me?" asked Lore.

The change Gideon had described in Fallon didn't seem that far off, but now she had a reason for it: her. Her leaving had done this to him.

"How could you not be involved?" He grinned. "In the coming month, I'm going to properly reform you and then parade you through the streets again on the day of my coronation to show that through the obedience of women, we can reclaim a pristine culture for our children and our traditions. You see, Lore? I'm going to make an example of you."

Chapter XIV

The sea of faces blurred past her and the noise of hundreds of thousands of voices rang in her ears. Her gown of champagne satin embroidered with gardenias around the neckline, waist, and hem, billowed out around her. Flowers made of pearl and diamond nestled in the sides of her hair; the rest had been pinned up in a cascade of curls. Her hands, in delicate gloves, held a bouquet of gardenias, freesia, and baby's breath.

"You have all the makings of a glowing bride," Madame Ermengarde had said during her final fitting just days before.

Of course, after Fallon had demanded new clothes for Lore, Jesseny knew which seamstress to bring in for the business. When Madame Ermengarde first alighted on the Imperial Hall with Clementine in tow, Lore believed the breeze had carried in a fairy godmother. She nearly thought Ursula had shown up in disguise, but it couldn't be. This woman had her same sharp features – her slim shape, her keen black eyes, but perhaps with a few years shaved off.

"Now, let's get you fitted for some proper Vitruvian garments. Young Master Berclay has said that we should spare no expense."

She happily moved about Lore, herself wearing a velveteen lime green day dress and matching hat. Clementine stood next to her, attired like a seamstress's apprentice, handing her measuring instruments and making important eyes at Lore like she had something to say. Hopefully, they would be able to steal a moment alone. Lore watched as Madame Ermengarde took her inseam, and then the name fell out of her mouth as it came into her head.

"Augustine."

The black eyes swept up to meet hers. "Clementine darling, could you go fetch me a glass of water?"

"Come with me," Jesseny offered, steering Clementine away.

Madame Ermengarde stood slowly. "What did you say?"

"Augustine?"

A sadness spread over her face. "How do you know that name?"

"Ursula told me about her past, only she said you'd died in the Great Rebellion. But you must be her half-sister."

"Someone reported to her that I had died. A good friend rescued me, and I've been hiding in the nit ever since. Lavinia...Ursula, as she now calls herself, she didn't know. And I don't blame her for fleeing when she had the chance."

"Does Sawyer know who you really are?"

Madame Ermengarde clucked to herself. "Your little friend, Sawyer, has a knack for charming the truth out of people. I suppose that's why some of my girls like her so much. They quickly see that she's indispensable. But no, as endearing as she is, I've never shared that secret."

"Will you reveal yourself to Ursula, then?"

"I haven't decided yet. I feel like some things are better left untouched. But I know why you girls are here. That's what she always wanted, to be empress. Well, she deserves it. She is the rightful heir, after all. Although, well, things might have been different had we stayed here."

"She told me what happened when you escaped to the nit in New York."

"Did she?" Ermengarde let out a bitter laugh. "Did she tell you it was against my will?"

"No, but she's never been able to carry a child herself."

"Now then, isn't that a karmic debt? Look at us, we've both managed to surround ourselves with more daughters than any one woman could be lucky enough to have," she said with forced merriment. "Did she tell you about Arnold?"

"Arnold?"

"Yes, you must have heard the tale of Arnold, my father's nephew."

"You mean the story of how Emperor Julian used his parts to make a galatean?"

"Well, not just that." She lowered her voice even more. "You see, Lavinia and Arnold were in love, but he was promised to another aristocrat, a real debutante. On the day of his wedding, they discovered him dead in his room, killed by his own hand. My sister was inconsolable. And when the galatean, Arnaud, emerged, she grew furious. She thought it heinous for our father to have such a gross disrespect for the dead."

"She never told me this." Lore remembered Ursula mentioning that she'd been in love once and the melancholy that had crept into her face.

After Madame Ermengarde left that first time, Jesseny filled her in on what Clementine hadn't had the chance to communicate to her. Working closely with Gideon, the girls had discovered that nearly half the military had joined the Resistance, including about one-third of the Imperial Guard but none of the small Religious Guard that protected the bishop. They'd planned the coup on the day of Fallon's coronation. After the parade and ceremony, when he adjourned to his private chambers to prepare for his first formal meeting with the Council in the Great Hall, he'd be lightly drugged and tied up by Gideon.

Lore then needed to sneak in through Fallon's chambers from the outside, make sure he remained unconscious, and enter the Great Hall where the Council waited, signaling the official start of their ambush. Members of the Escadrille and Madame Ermengarde's crew would already be strategically hidden throughout the room, and Gideon and his men were to lay low in the second balcony and charge down at Lore's entrance. Once they annihilated the Council, they'd force Fallon to publicly renounce his title and agree to become a civilian president, forming a Parliament similar to Hopespoke's.

"Just so you know, Avery is here," said Jesseny when she finished describing the strategy.

"Avery...here?"

Part of her had felt relief at his nearness, but part of her feared it – feared something horrible might occur if he and Fallon crossed paths.

"But that's not all."

"What else could there be?"

"Clemmie tells me that Sawyer is going to find herself in trouble at the rate she's going. She's taken up with the worst of Madame Ermengarde's girls. She's playing good girl during the day and working at a florist's shop, and she's also gotten us some crucial information about the other members of Council, their weaknesses, and the security in the Great Hall. But at night, she's running amuck. Clemmie thinks it's good that this will all be over soon, but she thinks we'll have a hard time winning her back permanently. She might stay here if we succeed."

Then, during that final fitting for her Coronation day gown when Madame Ermengarde paid her the glowing bride compliment, Clemmie had pulled her aside to say that Sawyer had been missing for two days. She and some of Madame Ermengarde's more headstrong girls had now formed a sort of gang.

Now, as she found herself once again paraded through the streets of the Seat as a reformed criminal – a paragon of innocence and virtue – she noticed that people were making noise, but they weren't necessarily cheering. In fact, as her eyes selected certain faces in the crowd to land on, some looked perfectly somber; others looked angry and frightened. And these eyes, these eyes coming up looked so familiar. Under a homburg hat, stood Avery with some of his men around him.

All of his features seemed to turn down at the sight of her, his eyes, his mouth. But before she passed completely, he winked. Lore remembered the time Mathilde had winked at her seven years ago, and how she somehow knew it meant she would never see her again. She hoped that wasn't the case with Avery, but a pit in the bottom of her stomach argued the contrary.

A few days after Fallon had ordered her to kiss him, something altogether strange had happened. They had been working on his coronation speech, pages and pages of extreme dogma that ultimately called for a retraction of women's rights – the right to move about freely, enforcing stricter dress codes in all regions, including New York, and more rigid moral regulations among the poor and merchant classes inhabiting the nits. It meant that young girls could no longer travel alone in their own carriages, and it called for all women, even dregs, to receive a mandatory Vitruvian religious education. This required a surge of new blood among the Vitruvian Brother-and-Sisterhoods and demanded that the current bishops and brothers embark on a major recruitment initiative.

"Take this to Bishop Gerathy in his chambers," Fallon ordered. "Make sure he approves the language here."

"Must I?"

He looked at her bemused. "If I command it, then you must. Don't be afraid of the bishop. He would never harm you while you're under my care."

"Must I go alone?"

"Yes, I need to sort through some of my father's personal effects in his office. You can find me there afterwards."

Lore carried the speech down the long corridor connecting the Imperial Hall to the bishop's quarters. As this hallway turned down another, the windows became smaller and narrow. The vaulted wooden ceiling mimicked the inside of a church and, from their stations on the walls, carved angels held lanterns that bathed the entire stretch in an eerie light.

The hallway ended in a massive door painted deep blue, the color of the Vitruvian Brotherhood. Lore lifted the brass knocker in the shape of the bishop's emblem, a wreath of sage with a scepter through it. She knocked and waited, but no one answered. She nudged it open into a foyer. In the corners of the small space stood life-sized statues of the preceding four bishops, each marking the entrance of another hallway.

Lore traced the square, examining the stern faces. In life, Bishop Heonan Head had been assigned to the Granary. The plaque over the hallway his imposing figure now guarded said Meeting Rooms. The immortalized likeness of Bishop Wilford Spillaine, who had lorded over the Turbine in one of the most brutal eras for factory workers, according to Jesseny, now presided over the hallway marked Private Quarters. Bishop David Zeffert Oxenforde III had been the Tree Vale's religious leader and now made a regal display on the way to the Dining Hall. Finally, the direst statue, Bishop Barnabus Deverall, mentor to old Gerathy and former head bishop to Emperor Henley, had been carved a bit larger than the others. He loomed in front of a hallway called Libraries & Parlors.

She chose this way because she heard raised voices behind a door halfway down. Lore eased her way towards the slight opening, just enough to clearly make out the words spoken inside. Gerathy seemed to be admonishing someone.

"...fortunate you are that it burned to the ground. And do you know what a loss it is to have him missing? We don't know who has him. What if he's in the hands of the Hopespoke government? What if the prime minister is just playing nice with us for appearance's sake but he really knows what we've been doing? This kind of careless mismanagement on your part could implicate us, not just in SOGATROW, but in the emperor's death. If anyone in his close circle, which I took painstaking measures to limit to very few, including his ward, were to connect the serum subiecta with his recent demeanor, then our part in all of this would be most obvious. Don't you think, Hawfinch?"

"Yes, of course, Your Excellency, but we were innocent in that. The serum was never intended to kill him, only to make him submissive like the women. His fool galatean kept putting too high of a dose in his food."

"But it did, didn't it? Because you are apparently a blundering moron!"

"I do apologize, but the dregs that you've been recruiting over there have proven most unreliable. They left that test site completely neglected and failed to follow my careful instructions."

"Can you possibly be blaming common ignoramuses for your failures? I suppose it's also their fault that old Craft escaped? Another threat to our operation. You should have killed him when you had the chance. He was never going to share his secrets with you no matter how much you starved or tortured him because unlike you, he's a man of principles!"

"Miss?" a hushed voice startled her from her eavesdropping.

She turned to see a young man carrying a tray full of tea and biscuits. He had smooth, olive skin, solemn eyes, and a stiff elegance about him.

"Hello there, I'm here to see Bishop Gerathy. His Imperial Majesty ordered me to show him this."

He cocked his head at her in an unnatural way, as though there were mechanisms involved in his movement. She felt a chill move through her. This galatean looked so extraordinarily lifelike that Lore wondered about the other servants she had observed in passing, so singularly focused on their tasks.

"What are you?"

"I'm a servant of the bishop."

Lore could tell he purposely evaded her question, making his existence even more perplexing.

"You aren't human, are you?"

"Please don't ask me such questions, miss. I would not want to refuse you answers because I've been created to serve your kind. But the answers I have to offer will only cause you despair."

"I'll risk that. Please, tell me. You aren't human, then why do you look human? Do you know?"

He looked around and whispered in an even lower tone.

"Parts of me are. Parts of all of us are."

"Who were you, then?" Lore felt sick asking this because she knew she was speaking with the dead. What Artemis said about Arnaud had been true. This must be Hawfinch's great work alongside his biochemical innovations – putting souls into machines.

"My name was Henri. I lived in a place called Orsia. It's hard to recall the details of my former life, but I know I had one. And I know that others here had them. We can all communicate without speaking because our spirits are connected inside the machine that gives us commands."

"The Starter. It's called the Starter. Our country is at war with your country. Orsia attacked us."

"No," he squinted. "No, that isn't true. I remember. Your country attacked us. They sent scores of missionaries who held a campaign to convert Orsians to your national religion, but the people rebelled. They ended up killing missionaries in a public display and then Vitruvia declared war. It's a war that continues today with random attacks from your end. They captured me as a soldier. They brought me here where a man tortured me. He's the one who did this. He was teaching a young apprentice when he worked on me and he kept referring to it as 'animus latro.' It means 'soul stealer.'" Henri's perfectly engineered mouth frowned. "We are all here against our will."

"Maybe you could rebel."

"No miss, there aren't enough of us to rebel, and we're afraid. Unlike regular galateans that are mere machines, we can feel pain, and we are disciplined like human servants. Still though, our numbers are growing. Each time they have a soul at their disposal, they take a shell from the vault downstairs and use it to create a new one of us. Please, I'm late now with his tea."

At the sound of their entrance, the bishop clamped his mouth shut. "What in Lucien did I tell you about knocking before you enter?" he demanded.

"I'm sorry, Your Excellency. My hands were full." Henri quivered so much that the tray shook, the teacups clinking and inching precariously close to the edges.

"Never mind that, set it down here. And you've brought a visitor, I see." He looked meanly at her. "You also neglected to formally announce her. Have you so soon forgotten your training?"

Henri shook his head.

"That's all right. We all need a little refresher now and then. I will be sure to remind you later of the way we conduct ourselves around here. You may go. Hawfinch, you're dismissed as well."

But Lafayette Hawfinch paid no attention to the bishop's command. His hawk eyes rested on Lore's face as though she were a rabbit in an open field. Concurrently, she wondered when it would be the right time to inform Fallon of his father's murder, thus ensuring the execution or, at the very least, the life imprisonment of both Hawfinch and Bishop Gerathy.

"Hawfinch?! Have you gone deaf as well as incompetent?"

"My apologies, Your Excellency," Hawfinch said, his hard mouth flickering in a semblance of a smile. "I just never expected to see the Aristokitten up close and in person."

"Well, have a good look because at the rate you're going it might be your last. I won't have you in here acting like a starstruck commoner in the face of her amoral lowness. Get back to your lab where you belong, in the bowels of this place with the other rats."

Hawfinch's face turned the same hue of red as the hair that hung messily in his sharp eyes. "Yes, Your Excellency," he mumbled, making his exit as hastily as the poor galatean.

Bishop Gerathy now turned his leer, which seemed to be his resting face, towards Lore. He stood, fluidly moved his robes aside, and approached her. "Well, to what do I owe this unexpected pleasure?"

Lore ignored his lewdness and began to state her errand, but he shushed her by putting one of his shriveled fingers to her lips. Liver spots covered his gnarled hands, and his fingernails looked hard and yellow like dried kernels of corn.

"No, no. Before we do any business here, I must give you a blessing. Not that you deserve one, but perhaps you need one most of all," he said, gripping her right arm and making the sign of Lucien, nothing more than drawing an elaborate "L" in the air. He stood with his wicked face entirely too close to hers. "May Lucien and the saints guide and protect you, from impurity, vice, and sin."

He hissed the last word and Lore caught the stench of his breath. It smelled like a potent mixture of strong moonshine and festering meat.

"His Imperial Majesty asked me to have you approve the text of his coronation speech," she stated, handing him the papers and stepping as far away as possible.

"Very well, let's see what he's come up with."

"Particularly, he wanted your approval of the doctrinal language."

The bishop sat down in a fat leather chair, muttering the words as he read through the document and tapping his pen. Every now and then, he raised his brows and uttered a "humph," but he made it through all eight pages without so much as one correction.

"This writing is quite good," he said, handing it back to her. "I didn't know he had it in him to be so eloquent. This gives me new confidence in his abilities. You can tell him that."

Inwardly, Lore gloated that her words, as fanatic and divergent to her own beliefs as they were, had garnered such high praise from an elevated official. But the bishop's hand on her bodice cut her rejoicing short.

"Hey! What do you mean by that?"

He chuckled under his breath, a malevolent coo. "Oh please, Miss Fetherston. Let's not pretend to be innocent when we aren't. You didn't think he sent you to my quarters alone just so I could read this speech, did you?"

She nodded, backing away as he continued to advance.

"Of course not. We have a little arrangement when it comes to you."

"What kind of arrangement?" Lore found herself up against his desk where the tea set rested, the pot's steam hitting her back like a low fog cloud.

"Let's see, how can I describe it in terms simple enough for your feeble, female brain to comprehend? How about this: joint property. Do you know what that means? It's like when two farmers share the same cow. They both benefit from what she has to offer."

He pressed himself against her and she felt a hardness poking into her dress. Without thinking, she reached behind her for the teapot and threw it in his face. He screamed, clutching his scalded skin.

"Satan's whore!" he screamed and lunged at her, though he still couldn't see through the burning liquid in his eyes.

Lore managed to push him out of her way. He tumbled to the floor, tripping over his robes. Determined to reach Fallon before the bishop recovered, she ran back to his quarters as fast as she could. She found him in his father's office where he said he'd be, his back to her. A letter hung limp in his hand as he watched the sun set over the skyline in yellows and violets.

"Fallon!"

"Leave me alone!"

"I need to talk to you. Something just happened, and it wasn't my fault."

He turned to look at her, his face twisted in grief. "Did you hear what I said? Get out!"

At the sight of him, Lore forgot about Gerathy's certain wrath. "What is it?"

"God, Lore, please go away."

"Did you have an arrangement with the bishop to share me like a cow?" she blurted.

"What are you talking about?"

"Gerathy, he just tried to–" she stammered. "He said you told him he could."

"Could what?" His concern for her instantly jolted him from his own sadness. "Did he touch you?"

"He tried to, but I defended myself."

"How?"

"With some tea."

"Some tea?" He couldn't help but crack a smile at this. "How does that work?"

"He had me backed up against his desk and tea had just been served, so I threw it in his ugly face. Then he screamed and called me 'Satan's whore,' and tried to come at me again, but I pushed him to the ground."

"Really? Little you, pushing a grown man to the ground?"

"Well, he had burning liquid in his eyes and he's very elderly. I think those two facts worked in my favor."

He laughed softly again. "I'm glad you did it."

"Don't you think he's on his way here now?"

"Course not. He fears my wrath, not the other way around. I warned him never to lay a hand on you, the bastard." He looked down again at the letter in his hand and sighed.

"Please, tell me what's upset you, and I'll try to make it go away."

He swallowed hard, searching her face as if to uncover any trace of insincerity.

"I found this in the locked middle drawer of his desk with my name on it." He folded the letter and tucked it into his breast pocket. "It–it made me sad is all."

"I'm sorry. I know grieving doesn't always happen right away, especially in cases like yours where you're under such pressure. It's only natural for these kinds of feelings to sneak up on you and that's all right. You should let yourself feel them."

She used her handkerchief to wipe his remaining tears while he watched her.

"Why am I playing this game with you?" he asked.

"What game?"

Another wave of tears looked as though it might overcome him, but instead he suppressed it and pulled her close in a kiss that soon turned frenzied. He pushed her onto his desk and his hands found their way up her dress.

"Fallon, you can't order me to do this. It wouldn't be right."

"I'm not ordering you to do anything anymore," he whispered, finding her neck with his lips. "This is real. This is supposed to happen, and I should have been the first it happened with. I should have been the only."

"You are the only," she whispered back as his hands feverishly undid her corset. "I'm still untouched."

"You are?"

"Yes."

His eyes met hers with a mixture of intense melancholy and joyous relief. "So am I," he whispered, kissing her gently. "I need you right now, but only if you feel the same, my darling love."

"I do." Her heart beat wildly in her chest.

"Tell me you love me as much as I love you."

"I love you. I've always loved you, even when I tried so hard not to." She felt the hot tears streaming down her face – feverish tears, tears of guilt, tears of an unconditional, aching love.

He scooped her up into his arms and carried her over to a sanguine velvet chaise. Lore's spirit felt suspended during what passion unfolded. It was as if they had both lost control of their own bodies, but instead met each other in that purplish in-between world while divine strings pulled at their forms below, pulsing together in a union much anticipated by each, and more so, by the Universe.

The bishop never showed up to interrupt their tryst. Instead, he blamed Henri and had him whipped for it. He walked around wearing a hooded cloak to hide the blisters on his face that had faded to scars. Lore decided not to share what she'd overheard with Fallon for the time being, although she did share the conversation between the bishop and Hawfinch with Gideon and Artemis. If Fallon didn't already suspect it himself, having the information now would only cause him more pain, and Lore wanted to minimize his discomfort until after his coronation.

The parade ended back at Lucien's Basilica. The crowd gathered across the expansive lawn, picnicking and setting up camp to witness the ceremony and Fallon's speech. Lore stood in the background as Bishop Gerathy, now in his full blue regalia and sporting light make-up to hide his scars, pronounced him Lord Fallon Johnarres Parlon Berclay, Emperor of Vitruvia. Fallon recited his speech and mostly the men in the crowd cheered and applauded. He noticed this and addressed it.

"I see that I haven't yet convinced the female population to support my plan. I understand your doubts. But please, consider the transformation of Lorelei Fetherston and know that a better and more rewarding life awaits you if you submit yourselves to living up to the moral standards we're putting into place. For too long now – nay, since the Great Rebellion – there has been a film of your discontent lying upon our country like a persistent fog. These laws are for your spiritual benefit and for the benefit of our society. They are for our children, who are the future of Vitruvia. To prove to you how strongly I feel about this movement, today, right here, I will take the reformed criminal, Lorelei Fetherston, as my empress."

A collective gasp filled the air as Fallon turned back to Lore, grinning, and held out his hand. Bishop Gerathy, Gideon, and the members of Council who stood on the balcony with them all gaped at him.

"Lorelei, darling, come here. Bishop, can you perform the marriage?"

Bishop Gerathy nodded. "Emperor, are you certain of this?"

"I'm as certain about this as I am that I've just been crowned Emperor of Vitruvia."

"Very well, then."

Lore looked at Gideon throughout the entire ceremony, wondering what her life might have been had she simply stayed and consented to be his wife. None of this would be happening now. She would never have met Ursula, Eva, Jesseny, and Avery. She would not now be marrying Fallon while Avery watched from somewhere in the crowd. And what would become of all this in a few hours – after Fallon retired to his chambers on the other side of the building and they waged this elaborate coup? Gideon gave her a reassuring look as if to say, "Go along with this now. What will it matter in a few minutes?"

"I pronounce you husband and wife, Emperor and Empress of Vitruvia. You may kiss." Bishop Gerathy finished his mirthless officiating.

Fallon cupped Lore's face gently and kissed her to the elation of the crowd.

"And now, we will retire," Fallon once more addressed the crowd. "I will have a rest and then conduct my official first meeting with my Council. This evening, I will go to bed your happily married emperor, and tomorrow, I will rise with the purpose and resolve to make this country strong and safe for those who live within these hallowed borders. I hope you will all help me in this endeavor. May Lucien be with you."

He took her hand and led her back into the Basilica.

"Emperor, Empress," Gideon stopped them. "Congratulations to you both."

"Gideon, I hope this is okay by you. It was a bit spontaneous, but I thought you might not be bothered."

"Not at all, Your Imperial Majesty. I'm very happy for you. If you will excuse me, we must begin preparing for the grand ball later on this evening and there's much to do. The boys in the Air Force are working on something special for you." He smiled.

"Of course."

"What was that?" Lore demanded as they entered his chambers.

"Are you upset to be empress and married to the man you've always loved?" He looked incredulous.

"You didn't even ask me about this...or warn me. Do you know how it felt to have it happen like that?" she cried, on the verge of tears. "It was humiliating. Like I'm some charity case you fixed into a suitable enough bride."

"Lore, don't be like that. You saw what was happening. I had to do something."

"So, marrying me against my will is your cure-all for society?"

"Against your will? I didn't hear you say 'no.'"

"How could I? You probably would have had me gunned down for it. Or thrown in an asylum for being insane enough to refuse you, the crown jewel among men."

He took her hands. "Don't fight with me, love. What if I told you that it wasn't so spontaneous, hmm? What if I told you that I'd been planning it all along, ever since I discovered you were coming home? Would you believe me?"

"Is that true?"

"Yes."

"Then I'm even more irritated with you."

"How can you be?"

"You should have pardoned me, then, in my hearing. Because I didn't do anything wrong and you know that. Instead, you treated me like some lowlife to be made an example of and used my situation to suit your own agenda. You took the cowardly way, and now you think you'll have your cake and eat it, too?"

"Well," he said with a sigh, "I didn't intend our first moments as a married couple to be full of such hostility. I'm going to go have a rest before I hold my meeting. Why don't you do the same, and then I'll see you at the ball. Maybe, by then, you'll feel differently." He forced a smile.

She calmed herself as Ursula would in a moment like this and returned his smile. "You're right, Your Imperial Majesty. Maybe I will."

Chapter XV

Lore found that Jesseny had left her everything she needed in the corner of her room. She ignored her ball gown of coral organza hanging on the door and donned the black jumpsuit made of impervia. She set her hair high in a tight knot, the only movement in the fringe of bangs that fell into her eyes, so innocent in their deception. Silent as the soft breeze from the west that blew through the windows, even the steel-toed boots that fit like gloves on her slender calves made no noise, although if she wanted them to, they could crush a human skull. That was the beauty of their design, the beauty of her design – a delicate angel built to destroy, light as a petal and as lethal as a Black Widow that creeps in corners, waiting for the right moment to strike. Now was that moment. Her weapons were also there, deftly hidden, disguised as a box of siphons.

"Show your true form," she whispered.

Lore examined the double-barrel Fairbolt Rogue and the atomic blaster belt, checking them to make sure they would properly work. Just like the daggers in their sheaths strapped below her breasts, both of these machines seemed ancient with their copper cogs and wheels, dependent on the perfect ballet of gadgetry to set them off, but she knew better. They were as multidimensional as the intricately layered psyche of their creator. In her mind, she thanked old Artemis for his skillful craftsmanship.

"As you were," she whispered again, and they changed back into a box of smokes.

She climbed onto the balcony to enter the chambers from the other side. Skirting the length of the arched windows, she found the one left slightly ajar, its long train of curtain fluttering out in the breeze and beckoning to her of her grim task. She moved in behind it, squinting into the fading sunset. He was in there; the sound of his breathing as familiar as her own. Inside, her heart gave a flutter like it always did in his presence, only this time she reconciled herself to the fact that it may be the last. A deep irony gripped her. Wasn't this the same game they'd always played in childhood?

She swept back the curtain and wondered if this time would be any different? How do you kill the one person you love most – obliterate them – for the good of so many others? But no one knew about this part of the plan save for herself and Ursula. She could let this all go, remain empress, and hope that love might change his heart and make him see reason. As much as she wanted to, the stories of some forty girls and a woman who led them rang out in her head, striking her so deeply to the core that she stood paralyzed, debating with herself.

Slowly, she crept up behind him. He sat in his throne, unmoving. Gideon should have drugged him, but part of her wondered if he was only pretending to sleep like he had during their rebellion game all those years ago. Only this time, would he wake up and overtake her? But no, a strangeness permeated the space. There were figures there, his army of yocto-creatures strewn on the ground around him like broken toys, even Lazarus.

"My sweet Lore," he whispered. "I know you're in here…and I know why."

She froze.

"It's all right. Come around."

She moved cautiously to the front of his throne only to start at the sight before her. He looked shriveled and shaking, as though struck with some kind of fever, like something had drained his life force from the inside out. He half-laughed at her expression.

"See? I'm already dead."

"What happened to you?" She approached him, grasping his quivering hand.

"This is my fault."

"What is?"

"All of this, Lore. It's all my own doing." He sighed. "I should have told you the truth, but...I wanted this to be a surprise." He looked up at her, his eyes glassed over, desperate.

"I don't understand."

"The Resistance was my idea. I began staging a revolt against this regime since before father died. It was the only way around Gerathy's power."

"What? And Gideon?"

"He's in on it with me, of course."

"Why didn't you tell me?!"

"Because I'm a sentimental idiot. I wanted it to be like when we were children and you'd sneak up on me. I would grab you in my arms and tell you the truth about this revolution. And then we would go into the Great Hall and fight side by side for your freedom. Foolish, I know."

"Who did this?"

"The person who did is still in this room. He released it into the air, but it backfired and affected him as well. He's over behind the curtains."

Lore looked over to the drapes on the other side of the room and, sure enough, she could make out a form quietly heaving on the other side.

"An air toxin. It's Gerathy. His man, Hawfinch, is behind several heinous creations. They're the ones who killed your father."

"Lore..." he said.

As she looked at him now, Lore felt her life falling beneath her. He was dying. His convulsing grew worse by the second, but he pulled her into his lap and held her.

"There's not much time...It hurts."

Now his eyes implored her in another way. His shaking hands that held her own, guided them to the sheath where her largest dagger lived.

"No, Fallon."

"You have to, my love…This was always the end, wasn't it? The tragic glory of you and I – never to be together but for one fleeting, beautiful moment." Tears spilled out of his eyes that soon turned to blood. He coughed, and red stained the back of his hand. "I would have cherished you, but the world got in the way of us, didn't it? And now, you need to end me. As Emperor of Vitruvia, I order you."

She hovered above this scene of the two of them, watching herself try to make the moment last longer, hoping someone might rush in with an antidote.

"Maybe we'll be children again somewhere, somewhere with no obstacles," he whispered. "In dreams, I'll find you."

Lore tried not to succumb to the sobs beating their way out of her chest. She would be brave for him in this last moment, she thought, as she freed the dagger and poised it atop his breast. She kissed him goodbye, not caring about the bitter taste of his blood on her lips nor fearing poisoning herself. She would have gladly died right there in his arms. He kissed her tenderly, his fingers stroking her cheek. She turned and whispered something to him, just three small words.

He smiled up at her. "You can take this empire back, Lore. I always knew you would." He reached inside his breast pocket and handed her the envelope from his father, marked in wax with the royal emblem.

He still smiled when she plunged the blade in, and he held her eyes until the light dimmed complete in his own. She sat there, knowing what she had to do. But first, she read the letter.

My dearest son,

If you have found this letter, it means I am gone, and you will soon be emperor. You may have doubts about your right to inherit this title, but let me put them to rest. You aren't just my son because I saved you from outside that factory and raised you as my own. You are my own. My own son, my blood.

I loved your mother. I met her during my assignment in the Turbine and immediately fell in love with her. She was a rare beauty, but more than that, pure goodness radiated from her. As an aristocrat and as the emperor's son, I could always have whatever I wanted. And I wanted her. But as a lady, your mother resisted. Other women knew they could get expensive presents and other types of support from lords; they angled for it. Not her. I sent her all manner of gifts and she still refused to part from her virtue. Finally, I asked if she might at least spend an hour with me during each of my visits. She consented to that.

We got to know each other. We read together, for someone had taught her in childhood. We discussed matters of state. I often asked for her advice because of her goodness and wisdom. Eventually, she warmed up to me. She let down her guard and reciprocated my love. I coveted those hours I spent in her presence until my death, remembering her every day of my wretched life.

Of course, I begged my father to allow me to wed her. I told him all about her upstanding character and how she didn't belong in the filth of the Turbine, but he would have none of it. He ordered me to forget her. And then, you were born. I saw you when I could, but she knew it had grown increasingly difficult for me to visit her. My father had yoctos watching me and spies in the Turbine. I had to be careful. She said she took comfort in the fact that she could see me through you, and I couldn't risk my father learning of your existence and taking you away from her. I'd been looking for a place for her, a new situation where the two of you could be safe, but I waited too long.

When she died, so did I. But I was determined to claim you. And thank God I arrived when I did. My father knew you were mine. How could he not? You were the spitting image of me. He approved of you because he, himself, had used concubines to produce an heir. It had been an inexplicable miracle that the empress bore me. So, to him, it was the same difference. You were blood and that's all that mattered.

My views grew to be extreme after that because I had lost the only woman I had ever truly loved. Why should I bother about the happiness and care of others?

I grew complacent in my authority. I let others advise me where I should have made decisions. I gave the bishops and the Council far too much power. As of late, I feel strange. I hear myself saying yes to all of Gerathy's absurd and brutal ideas, but I seem to have no power to stop myself.

I don't want you to fall into the same patterns as I did, but I fear that you will. I see how you've changed since your Lore ran away, and I believe that perhaps your feelings for her go beyond platonic. If that is so, I wish you had told me. I want nothing more than for you to know the happiness I could never hold onto, and if it meant flouting a bishop's decree then so be it. I would have done it for you, my son.

I only hope that you may have a chance at reclaiming this love. If she should come back into your life, keep her, for Lucien's sake, and never let go.

Your father,

Lord Percival Allenum Berclay, Emperor of Vitruvia

I see you've found my little wedding present," a snide voice hissed from behind her.

Lore tucked the letter into her breast and turned to face Bishop Gerathy. He had the emperor's former galatean, Chauncy, with him and a young girl at his feet. Her short hair hung in her eyes and he held her from a chain around her neck.

"I have another present for you. Stand up!" he ordered the girl, kicking her to her feet.

Lore looked at this young woman, not knowing her at first. Her raggedy clothes resembled those of the newspaper boys who hung around the nits. Her black hair emitted a purple glow when the light hit it, but as she brushed it aside to show her bruised and bloodied face, Lore recognized her.

"Sawyer?"

"Yes, that's her name, although now she goes by the alias, Anemone. But I knew her straight away. I never forget a face like this. In case you're wondering, I haven't doled out the punishment you helped her to avoid a year ago. I waited to do that in your presence."

Sawyer fell limp again at his feet.

"And you can't even do your own dirty work," Lore said, moving to where his emissary lay dying. She drew back the curtain and Father Hollengarde grabbed her ankle with a green hand.

"Kill me," he begged through labored breaths. "Please, kill me."

"Samuel?" Sawyer seemed to come to life at the sight of him. She tried to run to him, forgetting the collar around her throat, and snapped back down to the ground.

"Let her go to him while I deal with you," Lore demanded.

"Deal with me? You're going to deal with me? How? Are you going to throw one of those siphons at me?"

Before Lore could unmask her weapons, she felt Chauncy's hands like marble locking around her arms. Gerathy pulled a blade out.

"Pull your pants down, harlot," he ordered Sawyer.

Lore thrashed around to no avail while her friend obeyed the order. He knelt next to where she lay on the cold floor.

"Now, this might sting a little," he chuckled, holding the blade like a scalpel. "I jest, of course. It's going to sting a lot. You see," he said to Lore, "in the end, you cannot escape justice."

As he lowered the blade, Lore felt a change. Chauncy's grip on her had loosened. She craned her neck and watched as a vacant look came over his eyes, like he'd been shut off – or reprogrammed. She wasted no time uttering the words. Bishop Gerathy didn't have time to realize what had happened. Lore slung the Fairbolt Rogue over her shoulder as soon as it manifested and blew a hole straight through his middle without making a sound.

"For once, we're in agreement," she said, watching his agony.

He looked from her to his stomach, while his guts spilled all over the white marble. He fell backwards on his side. Sawyer ran to Samuel and knelt beside him, cradling his head.

"How did you get caught? Were you out with your gang?" Lore asked her.

"You know about that?" Her cracked lips formed a smile. "We're called the Afterlife, and we dole out justice. We only victimize bad people – bad men, mostly."

"Is that what you were doing?"

"No, I was trying to sneak in here to warn you before you did something stupid," she said, looking over Lore's shoulder at Fallon's form. "Ursula knew."

"Knew what?"

"She knew he was staging this coup against himself."

"How could she have known that?"

"Because I told her."

"You? How?"

"Alaric Kitt, he's the only one who knew besides Gideon. I took him out last week on his day off and got him drunk. I slipped him an herbal tonic, poor guy. He didn't know what he was saying."

"But how did you know what my role was in this?"

"I followed you both that night when she took you in the airship. I heard what she asked you to do. She's on her way here right now in that same vessel. I also know something else, Lore. I know what's behind the golden door. After I heard her forbid you to ask about it, I went to her office and picked the lock. What I saw – he was beautiful, just like the story. He had the dark curls, the green eyes, the human teeth: Arnaud. He even had hands with wrinkles on the knuckles. I touched his skin to see what it felt like and he woke up and spoke to me.

"'You are not Lavinia,' he said.

"'Are you – can you be, Arnaud?'

"'Yes,' he said. 'Lavinia loves me. She asks me for advice, and I counsel her like I would have my former master, the emperor. But though I make her happy, I am unhappy.'

"'Why are you unhappy?' I asked him.

"'Because, I am a monster.'

"'No, you aren't. You're an artwork.'

"He looked angry when I said this, as angry as one of them can look. He has brows that can move and everything.

"'No, I'm not. I am a dead man trapped in a machine. People think Arnold killed himself, but he didn't. Ursula did. When she couldn't convince him to shun his royal duties and run away with her, she flew into a heated rage and murdered him. Shortly after, he found himself trapped within me. Then, she came to claim me. I am her prisoner, you see.'" Sawyer finished. "I wanted so much to be like her, Lore. I envied her power, but now I don't want to be like her. I want to be better. I want to be like you...He's dead."

She gently set down Samuel's head and stood with some struggle. Lore helped her unfasten the chain from around her neck, taking extra care in the areas where the metal had dug into her skin. The only thing about Sawyer that hadn't changed were her brilliant hazel eyes, eyes that now filled with tears. Lore gently put a hand to her face, and she winced.

"Lore, I went to see Drass last week."

"What? You went to New York alone?"

"No, one of the girls came with me. His shop is still there, you know."

"And?"

Sawyer looked proud for a moment, but then could no longer meet Lore's gaze.

"You killed him, didn't you?

"I did." She looked up this time. "And he deserved it."

"I'm sure he did."

"The things he said to me..."

"What did he say?"

The Death of Drassilis Rinn Mara

"It was almost a replay of the day I first met him. Almost. The shop door creaked open and I walked in. He sat there the same way I'd found him before, ready to dive into a dirty mag. I could feel his eyes while I pretended to browse the designs. Finally, he spoke.

"'You lookin' to get inked, lovely?'

"'In a way.'

"'In a way. What's that supposed to mean?' The gravel in his voice hit me like silk.

"Here I turned really slowly to look him in the face. He stared for a few seconds, befuddled, until he recognized me.

"'Soy? Is that you, girl?'

"'In a way.'

"He grinned menacingly, but sensual. 'You're about to be in a way soon, if I catch hold of ya.'

"He moved towards me, but I wanted to be caught. He grabbed hold of my arms and looked down into my face.

"'What are you doing here?' he asked, rubbing his front against me. 'Never mind, I know what you came for. And you'll get it, too. Step into my parlor so I can finally mar that perfect, porcelain skin.'

"He brought me over to his inking chair, strapped the leather bindings around my wrists, and started charging up his needle with a terrifying smile. Bending his head, he forced his tongue into my mouth and tugged at my shirt until it ripped open.

"'What could be better than my name on your flawless skin and right over that fickle, little heart?' he whispered and then began his design, moving the laser as slowly as possible to draw out the pain.

"I hadn't entirely planned for this scenario, so I had to be clever in the moment.

"'Wait!' I shouted.

He paused. "What is it?'

"Drass, before you do this…will you?' I bit my lip.

"Will I what?' he started grinning again. 'Go ahead, I wanna hear you say it.'

"I want you to take me right here.'

"He set down his needle and roughly pushed up my skirt. He ripped a hole in my tights and began without mercy.

"I knew getting out of there without his full name across my chest like a brand required me to pretend I liked this. I let him kiss me again. Once he stopped biting my neck, I whispered for him to untie me. Like a fool, he complied. And, after a few minutes, right as he reached his most vulnerable moment, I grabbed his needle from the counter and shoved it deep in his eye. He fell backwards, screaming bloody murder.

"That's for our child you kept from being born.'

"He struggled with the needle, too scared to pull it out. His one eye seared through me. 'You heartless bitch. I did that kid a favor. I did you a favor, or your father and the other aristocrats would have sent you to an asylum – might have even killed both you and the baby. Besides, what kind of a mother would you even have made? A dumb slag like you.'

"It doesn't matter. You should have let me decide for myself. But I was young, and you manipulated me. How many other girls have you treated this way since? Like all those women snaking up your body. Did you add me to the lot?'

"Maybe so. Maybe you're right here, crawling up from the lowest part.' He pointed to his groin.

"But I silenced him soon enough – with his own part. He passed out after I cut it off, and then I stuck it in his mouth. I left before he bled out entirely, but his blood felt alive and snaked across the floor, like he couldn't help but keep making sinister art, even as his sordid life came to an end."

"Soy, thank you for trying to warn me. But now, I need you to get out of here."

"No way, I came to fight."

"Don't argue with me in this. I've just lost the love of my life and then had to watch you nearly be taken from me, too. Go now and take care of yourself. Better someone on the outside to gauge the crowds. I've got this."

"Fine. You win this one time."

"Just promise me something."

"Anything."

"Promise me I'll see you again."

Sawyer hugged Lore close, then turned and made her way to the window. Before she ducked out, she looked back. "I'll be around, especially when you need me." And she was gone.

Lore could hear nothing from the other room, but she knew they awaited her cue. She secured the atomic blaster belt onto her waist. And then she ran. She ran straight towards the bishop's body where it had fallen in front of the doors to the Great Hall. She took a leap and, when she landed, her steel toe met Gerathy's head with an impact so forceful that both of his eyes popped out in a milky sludge.

With another mighty sweep, she kicked open the massive double doors to the sight of a shocked Council. At this, a symphony of movement began like the first act of a ballet. From their hidden points in the room, the girls surfaced and came to the main floor. A commotion in the top balcony signaled that Gideon and his men had sprung into action. Half of them charged down and joined the others in facing Vitruvia's chief oppressors. The bishops and lords sat in their regular seats and now found themselves surrounded by the rebel arm of the Vitruvian Army and the Winged Escadrille. And as wicked as these men had been, something in Lore felt a twinge of empathy for them as Clementine stepped forward and began describing to each how he would die. A quick scan of the dais and their confused expressions confirmed that Alastair had thankfully taken heed.

"Gentlemen, gentlemen," Clementine began with a particularly mocking lilt, shaking her head as she read over a list of their crimes. "Actually, I shouldn't say gentlemen, should I?" She looked up at them. "Because you're not. In fact, I'd say you're all very much the opposite. You've been quite bad."

She began pacing back and forth in front of the dais, and their heads turned to watch her like a litter of curious kittens.

"Quite bad." She nodded to the girls. They approached the men in pairs. "So, just in case you're confused as to where this is headed, let me set you right. You're about to die for the crimes you've committed against the people of Vitruvia. And just in case you've forgotten what they are, Miss Jesseny, Miss Lore, and I are here to remind you."

At this, Bishop Pawnsworthy tried to stand, but the girl next to him forced him down and kept her hand on his shoulder.

Clementine smiled. "I see we have a volunteer to go first. Bishop Michael Pawnsworthy of the Turbine. You have been accused of money laundering, intimidation, and accepting bribes from certain merchants for favoritism; but the worst thing you've done is turn a blind eye to the brutal conditions of child labor in your region. And more explicitly, it had been brought to your attention on multiple occasions that many people in the Turbine, especially children, were falling ill and dying due to the chemical poisoning of the water system. You accepted bribes in the form of money, drugs, and prostitutes from the offending factories responsible for the chemical dump, and you worked tirelessly to cover up their fatal handiwork. Twelve children and seventeen seniors have died because of your willful negligence. So…"

Clementine looked up and smiled again, meaner. Bishop Pawnsworthy cowered in his seat, his narrow eyes filling with frightened tears. She finished, "…you'll no longer be able to turn a blind eye. Because you'll have none, see?"

At this, the two girls wasted no time. One forcefully held the bishop's head while the other gouged out his eyeballs. His screams shook Lore, and even Clementine faltered as she handed the list to Jesseny.

"Stop this, right now!!" yelled Bishop Faraday. "What is the meaning of this violence? Lieutenant Danaher," he said, his crisp, grandfatherly eyes finding Gideon among the officers, "how can you betray your own father by siding with these venomous Liliths?"

But Jesseny had already begun reading. "Next up – oh look, Bishop Faraday. You've made millions of Edison notes extorting suspected gay members of the aristocracy, threatening them with death if they didn't pay you what you wanted and then at the same time forcing them to attend exceedingly painful conversion yocto-shock therapy. Not just this, but in parallel to your secret crusade against this group, you yourself have had a succession of young male servants over the years, all of whom confirmed that you forced them to have sex with you against their will using blackmail and threats against their families if they didn't obey you. Your call, Gideon. What shall we do?"

Gideon didn't hesitate. "Cut the bastard's tongue out and make him eat it."

"Girls, you heard the man."

Pure gore followed. Now, with two bishops moaning in agony, Lore held the list. She scanned the names and the crimes, looking for the absolute worst next to Gerathy. He wasn't hard to find.

"Lord Dudley Dunst. What a ridiculous name."

The Seat lord didn't even bother sitting up in his chair. Instead, his lumbering, rounded shoulders hunched over even more and his thin lips clamped shut like a rotten clam. Small piggy eyes turned up at the edges and darted about the room. They were the only part of him that moved. A cakey makeup covered his porous, pock-marked skin – the brute was vain.

"Let's see. You're a founding member of SOGATROW. You've said publicly that women who disobey their husbands should be regularly beaten to be kept in line. You and your family have been the force behind several violent shakedowns of merchants for a share of their profits. You pushed your elderly mother down a flight of marble stairs, killing her, and then threatened servant witnesses that you'd have their families killed if they spoke of it. You're responsible for the heinous deaths of hundreds of dregs, especially underage orphans, lured with the promise of fortune to a dungeon in your basement where your favorite thing to do to them is…" She couldn't finish reading this last sinister detail.

Lord Dunst snickered. "Some people don't have the stomach for this kind of power, sweetheart."

Lore cringed as she scanned the recommended punishment, but she decided to change it given his last words. "Perhaps not, but now neither will you…sweetheart."

His mad piggy eyes looked up from their dull, watery recesses to meet hers. Likely for the first time in his privileged, marauding life, Lord Dunst felt afraid.

She nodded to the girls. "Go on, gut him like a fish."

Beside her, Jesseny had begun to breathe as fast as a cat, her eyes locked on Lord Dunst's now petrified face.

"No!" she shouted at the executioners and turned imploring eyes to Lore. "Let me do it."

The latter understood – *underage orphans*. Her friend was once that vulnerable innocent.

"As you wish," she granted, watching Jesseny unsheathe the very blade that had annihilated her previous abuser.

"For Lucien's sake, Gideon, stop this! Stop this!" Lord Carlton yelled. "This is brutal madness what these girls are doing."

Lord Dunst's screams were by far the worst. But after a few more deaths, Lore began to feel uneasy. It was true that, in general, these were bad men, but some of their crimes were much less severe. When there were four men left – Lords Foxcomb and Previtt from the Tree Vale and Lords Hucksville and Romilly from the Granary – Lore stopped it.

"I can vouch for Lords Foxcomb and Previtt. They were dear friends to my and Sawyer's fathers. And Lords Hucksville and Romilly haven't committed egregious or offensive crimes enough to warrant death. We must be fair."

"Yes, cher," began Clementine, "but they knew about the crimes of these other men. That means they're complicit. In my estimation, that's just as bad – maybe even worse."

Before they came to a decision, a door at the other end of the room burst open and, just like that, the rest of the Vitruvian Guard fell upon them. In the chaos, the members of Council, already artfully butchered, sat in two rows on their dais as macabre spectators; the remaining lords ran for their lives. The rebels in the balcony, Avery among them, began shooting down on the Imperial and Religious Guards in a hail of gunfire while, on the main level, the Escadrille wielded their different brands of lethal talents. Clementine, skilled in both the martial arts and knives, didn't just throw knives – she had an arsenal of poison darts and other types of blades that she could use to slice up any opponent. The other girls had similar skills – some were street fighters, some knew the ancient fighting styles, and others had crossbows, nunchucks, brass knuckles, bo staffs. A girl from the Turbine named Ellie fought with two cordless welding torches.

Suddenly, Chauncy flew past Lore from the chamber behind her and jumped into the action, saving Jesseny, who'd been battling two guards at once. As she looked around, Lore realized they'd been joined by scores of galateans, lethal and indestructible, all fighting on their side. Someone must have hacked into the Starter and reprogrammed those that were part of the guard – that silent army in the deep recesses of this place.

"Resistance down!" Lore yelled, as she ran to the center of the room. Her party ducked while she swiveled the atomic blaster belt, taking out several of the guard in one go.

"Lore! Watch out!"

She looked up to see Avery watching her through his goggles. He frowned and screamed for her to duck. His bullet missed Lafayette Hawfinch, who now grabbed her by the throat so hard that she dropped her Fairbolt. He lifted her off the ground.

"You think you can get away with this?"

The remnants of the Religious Guard now fired at the balcony, and Avery couldn't save her. The crowd outside shouted in protest of the apparent mayhem inside. Leagues of galateans continued to reanimate in their underground prison and came stomping in ranks up the basement steps, shaking the building like an earthquake. Hawfinch held a vial of hissing purple liquid in his shaking hand and he forced it to her lips.

"This is the concentrate form of what we gave your darling husband."

Lore tightened her mouth shut even though his grip on her throat made her want to gasp for air. In an instant, his face turned strange and he dropped the poison. It shattered on the marble, its contents boring a frighteningly deep hole. Hawfinch fell to his knees, and there behind him stood another grinning version of himself, which soon morphed back into old Artemis.

"You think you're the only one around here with metal in your boots?"

"Artemis! Innocuous concealment, eh?"

"Who better than the one person with spies out looking for me?" He pointed a slim pistol at the back of Hawfinch's head, but Lore stopped him.

"No, no. Don't kill him, just incapacitate. We'll want answers out of him."

"Clever girl."

The other side stood no chance once the galateans appeared. In a final wave of gunfire, they defeated what Imperial and Religious Guard still stood. "Cease!" someone ordered.

Gideon appeared first, grabbing her shoulders. "Where's Fallon?"

She shook her head and allowed the sobs to finally come. He embraced her, but a new presence in the room distracted the crowd of allies gathered around them. Lore lifted her head from Gideon's chest to see a vision, certain she must be hallucinating. Ursula stood, in a flowing gown of golden shimmer, with the prime minister on her right and Oliver Woodlock on her left. He shrugged at Lore, embarrassed.

"Well done, Lore," she said. "Mission accomplished."

"What does she mean?" Gideon stepped back.

"I didn't know you and Fallon were staging this takeover together."

"Of course not. Nobody knew that except Alaric." Gideon looked for his lover in the crowd. Alaric stepped forward with a guilty look on his face.

Lore continued, "Gideon, I'm an assassin. I was sent here to kill Fallon."

"What? Kill your best friend? How could you agree to something like that? Did this woman put you up to it?"

Lore began to cry. "Because I believed he'd turned radical. I thought I was doing the right thing. And I thought she was the rightful heiress."

Everyone turned their eyes back to Ursula, who stood her ground. "I am the rightful heiress. And my birth name is Lavinia Emmanuelle Berclay."

"Then you killed him? You actually went through with it?" Gideon turned on Lore again.

"No, it's not what you think. I went there, not fully knowing if I could do it. But he'd been poisoned by Gerathy and he was already dying. He forced me to – he ordered me."

"Oh, Lore…"

"Well, have we put all this to rest? If so, I would like to begin my reign," said Ursula.

"You knew," Lore said to her. "You knew, and you were still going to let me go through with it."

"That's impossible, your friend just said that no one knew except for him and one other."

Lore looked at Alaric, his eyes wide and sorrowful. "Alaric told Sawyer. She got him drunk one night and slipped him one of her herbal tonics. He probably doesn't even remember what happened."

Gideon's face clenched in anger and he began to charge at his lover, but Avery held him back.

"I'm so sorry," Alaric cried as two of the other men removed him. "I'm so sorry, Gid."

Ursula looked through her now with no semblance of remorse on her face, just gross entitlement. Lore didn't want to feel this way about the woman who had given her freedom, a place to stay, an education. That made her feel as though Ursula had at least cared something for her, but those gestures benefited her just as much. Like Avery had said, she never acted without purpose, and you meant nothing to her unless you could play a role in her grand scheme to reclaim the Vitruvian throne. They were all her pawns. All of them. Even her pitiable love affair with a dead man was a sham. But Lore had one move left in this game, and even her patron's blood lineage couldn't trump it.

"Lore, this has all been a misunderstanding. And regardless of what transpired today, you still need to honor the fact that I am now empress. I'm empress, and I'm very grateful to you for all your work."

"You're wrong, Lavinia," Lore said flatly, using her birth name. "You're not empress. In fact, the only thing you are is under arrest for plotting the murder of Emperor Fallon Johnarres Parlon Berclay, the blood son of the previous emperor, as this letter states."

She brandished the note from Lord Berclay. Gideon came forward and took it.

"What were your plans as empress, Lavinia? Who would be your emperor, hmm? Your husband? Oliver even, the poor man you've let waste half of his life pining after you?"

Oliver bristled at this and stepped a bit away from his love with an appraising grimace.

"As I understand it, Oliver saved you lot by hacking back into the Starter," Ursula defended. "This Resistance was poorly planned. You can't just set people free without structure, or there will be anarchy. There needs to be an empress." She pointed to herself. "Me. And I need to be supported by the leagues of galateans we've just reanimated while I establish a new order. Your idea of creating a democratic system is much too premature."

"I know whom your emperor would be," Lore continued. "It would be Arnaud, wouldn't it?"

Ursula stiffened.

"That's right. Arnaud, the legendary galatean you keep hidden behind that door, created from the parts of a dead man you couldn't have! Is that why you staged the Great Rebellion? So you could break in here and steal him from your father?"

"Shut up," Ursula spat, and liquid flew out of her mouth. "You do not speak of him! No one speaks of him!"

"Sawyer spoke to him. And do you know what he told her?"

"Stop it!" Ursula screeched, her face distorted and manic. She lunged for Lore, but guards held her back.

"He told her he's unhappy because he's a monster. He said you murdered him. And then, you've kept him in your office behind that gilded door, acting as if you make all your major decisions yourself when you still just rely on a man. You're nothing but a sham, Ursula, and we all fell for it. Well, no more."

"Galateans, seize all members of the Resistance! I order you!" Ursula yelled into the room. "Now! You are under my command!"

But the galateans, especially the ones harboring human souls, didn't move. They stood in a semi-circle regarding each other, and Henri held his hand up and shook his head. The others nodded in agreement with him. Those that were just programmed automata didn't act upon her request, either. Oliver stood further apart from her now, closing his eyes to focus as he muttered code into the air and waved his hands around under his chin. When he finished, he zeroed in on the culprit.

"You, then, you wasted your life loving a dead man. And me? I might as well have been dead, throwing away these years on you. You weren't worth it in the end, were you? Not one bit," he said.

Ursula breathed and somehow managed to gather herself together even though she clearly had no more allies. "Very well. But those are the words of a machine," she said in a calm voice. The guards relaxed their hold and now she stood straighter. "They can't be taken as evidence of a crime. And how am I not empress? Percival and Fallon are still both dead, are they not?"

"Because I'm empress," Lore said with as much certainty as she had ever felt. And then, she repeated the three small words she'd whispered into Fallon's ear moments before, only here they took on new meaning. "I'm with child."

She caught Avery's eye as she said this. He frowned and looked away at first, but then met her eyes with a milder expression – maybe the start to an acceptance of actions she'd had to take, which now seemed truly fateful. She hoped that, in this bittersweet moment, he would realize their life together had once more become a viable possibility. She looked around the Great Hall at the faces of her subjects, and visions of a new world came to life in her mind, a world as she would have it. When she said these last words, she imagined herself handing Fallon's child to Constance to be put down to bed and listening to the maid sing sweet lullabies.

"I want a nation where people are once again free and where everyone is equal, and not just in theory but in practice. I want a nation where no one is oppressed because of race, religion, gender, or sexuality. I want a nation that cares about the individual safety, health, education, and security of its citizens. I want a nation where the people are united, not segregated – a nation where there's trust in lawmakers and authorities, and where lawmakers and authorities deserve that trust. And I am hell-bent on making this that nation. It's what I want, it's what my husband wanted. I'm carrying the Vitruvian heir...and changes must be made."

Epilogue

Many say my story is one of violence, but I disagree. It may seem that way, but you need to consider it from all angles. Violence is only the surface, the superficial. It's what's below that outer layer that speaks of the real truth. Yet, of all the stories I've recorded, mine will be the shortest.

I fought a fight, and many will say that it was against men. But it wasn't. Others still will say that ironically, it was against a woman. That's not entirely true, either. Still some will argue that I fought against a repressive dictatorship. But no. Nor was it against any institution. My fight was against ego.

I did what I did to overcome those who would continue to put themselves before others. And ultimately, I didn't win this battle by my activities with the Escadrille or the Resistance, by shooting people, or by killing the emperor. I didn't even win it by sacrificing myself in any way. I won it by doing the one thing that only a woman can do. I bore a child, Evangeline.

And that was a meeting of two conflicting forces in one brief and beautiful moment that proves how even good can come from a world bent on chaos if we put others before ourselves. And that is called unconditional love.

My daughter will grow to be a strong leader, like her mother. She will hear my story. Maybe she'll even record it. But those others that I captured, those other women, even the worst one – those are the stories she'll inherit. Those are the stories she'll read and know and remember, so that she can play her part in making sure they remain simple words on a page and are never again repeated.

The End

Book Club Discussion Questions

Hi Reader,

If you enjoyed this novel, please consider leaving a review on Amazon and Goodreads. It helps, and I appreciate it more than I can ever say. Also, check out my other novels at lskilroy.com and stay tuned for two more volumes in *The Vitruvian Heir Trilogy* – there's even a sneak peek a few pages away!

Happy reading,

1. This book contains strong sociopolitical commentary about issues within our own society. How do you feel about that? And how are these issues still (or not) relevant and represented in today's world?

2. Kilroy has said that she chose the steampunk, Neo-Victorian backdrop once she began writing because she thought it made the most sense for a setting. What are your thoughts about this setting? How did it enhance or take away from the story? What could an alternative setting have been?

3. What themes are emphasized throughout the book? What do you think Kilroy is trying to convey to readers?

4. What's the overall message of the book?

5. Many other works of literature are referenced throughout. What did you think about this? Do you think they are all relevant to the story or simply reflective of Kilroy's own personal tastes?

6. Who is your favorite character and why? Whom do you relate to/ empathize with most?

7. Are the characters three-dimensional and believable?

8. Is Lore a likeable protagonist? Why or why not? What do you think of her evolution?

9. Who is your least favorite character and why?

10. Much of this story is told by skipping large chunks of time and then flashing back to events that transpired in between. What do you think of this narrative pacing? Did it enhance or take away from your understanding of what was happening?

11. There are some very disturbing scenes and depictions of sexual violence throughout the book, especially towards female characters. Did these parts make you uncomfortable? Did they lead you to a new understanding or awareness? Did they make you consider sexual violence or our reactions to it in a different way?

12. Do you have a favorite line, passage, or scene? If so, what is it?

13. The story is told in third-person limited omniscient meaning Kilroy sticks closely to Lore's character, but the narration remains in third-person. What did you think of this narrative voice?

14. Did you like the book? Have you read any of Kilroy's other works and, if so, how does this compare?

15. What did you think of the ending? Was it predictable or were you surprised?

16. Did you figure out what was behind the golden door before it was revealed? If not, what did you think it was and how did you feel once it became clear?

17. Someone once pointed out the irony of Ursula's leadership. How do you feel about that?

18. Who is the worst villain in this book and why?

19. If there were to be a movie adaptation of this book, whom would you cast?

20. This is the first book in a trilogy. What do you think will happen in the other two books?

An Excerpt from

The Vitruvian Heir, Book II: The Awakening

The woman sat in a darkened room within her holding chambers, evoking a patience she'd never had until this moment. Part of her felt proud of the girl, a clever protégé, for besting her in this battle. And part of her grew embittered that she'd come so close to assuming her rightful place as heir and empress of Vitruvia only to have it dashed because the same silly girl went and got herself in a family way – something she herself could never do. What a fine, ironic joke for the Universe to pull on such a villain as she. And then, another part of her, a part buried deep inside where her ego lived – weakened now, yes, but sure to rise again like the indubitable phoenix it was – took comfort in the fact that from every obstacle comes an opportunity. Perhaps she would never hold the title she'd always dreamed of, but now, a far more delicious challenge presented itself, and her will rose to the occasion like a flower turns its face to the sun. She knew the girl would eventually need her sage counsel. She smiled in the dimness of burgeoning twilight. As if on cue, a knock at the door confirmed that the Universe did not disappoint.

"Come in."

A young sentry entered, clearly scared out of his wits. He tried to put on a brave face for whomever stood outside the door.

"Mrs. Vandeleur, you have a visitor."

"A visitor, you say? I wonder, who would visit such a person?"

She switched on the single lamp next to her, illuminating her striking features. The same sharp black eyes, determined chin, and pert mouth animated her heart-shaped face, framed by shining chestnut hair that stopped where it complemented her long neck. She stood to face her guest, her green silk dressing gown brushing the floor, and the jeweled lavalier her husband had sent ending just above her narrow waist.

"I present Her Imperial Majesty, Mrs. Lorelei Henriette Fetherston Berclay," he announced, then exited as hastily as he'd come in.

"It's you, then. Something told me you'd want to see me sooner or later."

The young woman stepped farther into the room, the grimace on her face in stark contrast to her delicate features and porcelain skin.

"Be clear, Ursula, this isn't a visit, and it holds no pleasure for me."

"Really? Then why bother? You're certainly not doing me any favors. As I recall, your company was always quite dull."

"Silence!" Lore commanded. "Regardless of your lineage and your perceived entitlement to the Imperial Seat, I am your empress, and you will pay me the respect that comes with it."

"You hold a stolen title. I believe Vitruvian law states that once an emperor dies, the position must be assumed by a member of the bloodline and not a spouse. And I'm sure the surviving members of your Council don't approve of your claims."

"Funny you should say that. They're the very ones who agreed to rewrite the law so I could keep this title. They were feeling quite generous after I spared their lives, and they understood as well as I did the danger that an upstart intruder from Hopespoke presented to the fabric of our society and the welfare of our people."

She had underestimated this girl. Her innocent looks hid a sharp cunning that Ursula almost, in this moment, admired. But her inner rage soon squelched that sentiment, though she didn't betray any of these feelings to Lore. The girl continued.

"But I can certainly be less accommodating. The last time I checked, regular prisoners can't receive jewels and clothes to make their lives more comfortable, let alone those being charged with the kind of heinous crimes you've committed."

Ursula nodded. "Very well, then, Your Imperial Majesty. I stand down. What brings you to my chambers then, may I ask?"

At this, Lore's face changed from authority to defeat. "I come with an offer."

"An offer? I'm intrigued."

"Things aren't going as...smoothly as I would like. I'm facing much more opposition than I expected and from angles I hadn't even anticipated."

"Yes, well, total upheaval doesn't always go according to plan, does it? What are you proposing, then?"

"What you did is unforgivable, know that. But your abilities to lead and to persuade others to follow you are undeniable, and I want you to teach me."

"Really? And what are you offering in return?"

"Freedom."

"What?" Ursula froze. It couldn't be this easy, could it?

"Freedom. I'll let you go. But only if your guidance proves useful. It might take a while, you see. It might even take years. However, at the end of it, there will be no trial. I'll simply pardon you. If I do this, you must leave Vitruvia and never return. Is it a deal, then?" Lore put out her hand.

"How do I know you'll keep your word?"

Lore gave her a wry look. "Come now, Ursula, you know I don't lie. Have we got a deal?"

Ursula took her hand. "Yes, indeed."

Other Works by L.S. Kilroy

THE VITRUVIAN HEIR, BOOK II: THE AWAKENING

LSKILROY.COM

ABOUT L.S. KILROY

"The first thing I do in the morning is brush my teeth
and sharpen my tongue." – Dorothy Parker

L.S. Kilroy is an irreverent sort of person who likes to write about things. Growing up an asthmatic only child in a neighborhood of geriatrics, she made friends with books at a young age because she had to – luckily, she also really liked them. Early exposure to the classics fueled her own writing. At fifteen, a man in a bookstore asked her what she wanted to be when she grew up and she replied, "Writer," without hesitation.

Writer is a title that has driven her both personally and professionally. She holds a Bachelor's degree in English from Merrimack College and a Master's degree in Writing, Literature & Publishing from Emerson College. By day, she's a communications professional; by night, she's an award-winning indie author.

Kilroy lives in a rural community in Massachusetts with her family and fur babies. Aside from writing, she loves being creative in the kitchen, belting out show tunes, traveling, throwing epic dinner parties, reading, and scouting out vintage finds at consignment shops.

Made in the USA
Middletown, DE
27 July 2023

35818038R00156